BELONGING

"Did it feel like this when he kissed you?" He set his mouth on hers and she tried to turn her head, but he held her chin easily, kissing her relentlessly until she stopped struggling and desire mixed sharply with her anger.

He sensed it and eased her back, using her towel to protect her from the earth, and now his mouth found her breasts. The wet heat, the soft tickling of his mustache against her naked skin inflamed her against her will, and her nipples hardened under the onslaught of his tongue.

"My name, Hannah. Say my name."

She turned her head away from his kisses, but his skin pressed against hers, rough where she was soft, and the ache between her legs intensified, making her gasp with desire.

He reached for the finger that wore the engagement ring and slowly, gently, pulled it off.

"This is a lie, Hannah. You belong to me. You've always belonged to me."

Other *Love Spell* books by Bobby Hutchinson:
NOW & THEN
A DISTANT ECHO

BOBBY HUTCHINSON

YESTERDAY'S GOLD

LEISURE BOOKS NEW YORK CITY

A LEISURE BOOK®

October 1997

Published by

Dorchester Publishing Co., Inc.
276 Fifth Avenue
New York, NY 10001

ISBN 0-8439-4311-4

Printed in the United States of America.

YESTERDAY'S GOLD

Chapter One

Hannah Gilmore was hot and tired, and her patience was wearing thin.

It was early July, and the city of Victoria was experiencing a heat wave. This discussion she was having with her fiancé wasn't exactly cooling her down, either. In spite of a sense of growing irritation, she did her best to make her voice quiet and reasonable, mindful of the other people also strolling in the waterfront park where she'd suggested they meet after work.

She'd thought a walk would be relaxing for both of them, but she'd been wrong. Brad was holding her hand, and she could feel the tension in his grasp.

"I'll only be gone for the weekend, Brad. Well, four days, actually. I've taken off Friday and

Monday at the hospital. I had some time banked."

"*Four* days?" Brad Langston's attractively bony face tightened with displeasure, and his light blue eyes narrowed behind his fashionable glasses. "So you're leaving tomorrow?"

"Yes." Hannah nodded. It had been wrong of her not to let him know earlier, but she'd kept putting it off.

"That's pretty short notice. And it just seems irresponsible to me, Hannah, going traipsing off to some ghost town in northern B.C. two weeks before our wedding. What're you going to do up there, anyway?"

Hannah shrugged. "Walk around. Visit the cemetery. Mom wants to find her great-grandfather's grave." She felt defensive. She hated feeling that way, and her stomach clenched the way it always did when she and Brad had a difference of opinion. They seemed to be having a lot of them lately, in spite of the fact that they were well suited in temperament, if not in background.

Well, at least they never actually *fought* about anything, she consoled herself. They could usually settle whatever minor differences they had with a quiet, rational discussion. In this instance, the trouble was that she knew going to Barkerville at this particular time wasn't really rational, and for some reason that made her feel impatient and annoyed with Brad. Now why the heck should that be?

Maybe she was just having premarital jitters. Her friends at the hospital had warned her about them.

This is the man you love, Hannah, she reminded herself sternly. *Explain this properly, and he'll understand.*

She drew in a calming breath and deliberately wove her fingers through his, palm to palm. "I promised Mom years ago I'd take her on this trip someday, and for some reason she's suddenly got it in her head she wants to go right now. Her great-grandfather was a prospector up there during the Cariboo gold rush and she thinks he's buried in the old cemetery in Barkerville."

Brad let go of her hand and gestured in a way that reminded Hannah he was a lawyer. "He's not going anywhere, is he? So why does this have to happen now? Or, if Daisy absolutely has to go this minute, why can't she just take the bus up there herself? Barkerville's only a couple of hours drive from Prince George; there must be bus tours. I'll tell you what, I'll pay for the plane ticket, the bus—I'll even spring for a motel for the weekend for her, how's that?"

Why did he always have to make her feel that money was the major issue, even when it wasn't? Hannah tried for a smile and failed. "That's very sweet, Brad, but you know Mother wouldn't consider flying because of Klaus. She wants me to drive her, and I've agreed."

Not that driving for long hours with her mother and that neurotic dog was exactly Hannah's idea of a pleasant way to spend a weekend. Klaus had bad breath and an unpredictable temper, but he was her mother's closest companion. "They won't take dogs on the bus, and she wouldn't put him in the baggage compartment of a plane. He's getting old."

"Well, in my opinion," Brad began, and Hannah could tell that he was about to make a pronouncement on Daisy and Klaus that she really didn't want to hear. Hannah might criticize Daisy herself, but she didn't appreciate having Brad do so.

She dodged a girl on a skateboard and interrupted him, which she knew he hated.

"This is the first time since my father died that Daisy's shown any interest in going farther than the supermarket," she said rapidly. "You know I've been worried about her, so if it'll make her feel better to spend a couple of days tramping around a ghost town, I don't see any harm in taking her."

She knew she was annoying him, doing what he called filling the air with unnecessary words, but she couldn't stop herself, and she didn't want to anyhow. She'd had a long, distressing day at work. A young boy she cared about had almost succeeded at a suicide try. She was hot and tired and discouraged, and now she was losing her temper.

"Brad, please. It's over two years since my mother's ventured off this island, and even then it was just to take my father to that specialist in Vancouver. For all the good *that* did. When somebody's liver's shot, it's shot. Maybe going on this trip is something I should do for her. Maybe it'll get her out of the rut she's in, give her a new lease on life."

Brad snorted. "You'd think our wedding would get her out of a rut if anything was going to. But"—his voice assumed a self-righteous tone that raised hackles on Hannah's neck—"You've got to admit Daisy doesn't seem very interested in our wedding. It's *my* mother who's putting in twelve-hour days planning this whole thing. And you know how often she's asked for Daisy's input, with absolutely no response."

Hannah bit her lip and told herself not to remind him that it was his mother, not hers, who'd wanted a wedding where the guest list included a sizable portion of the city.

Lydia Langston made it plain that she wanted her youngest son married in the same elaborate fashion her two other sons had been wed, and all of Hannah's desperate assurances and not-so-quiet insistence that she preferred a modest little ceremony with just family present had gone unheard and unnoticed.

After all, Lydia was paying for the wedding,

as she reminded Hannah at frequent intervals, and so she felt she had the right to have the whole thing her way. Hannah had even overheard Lydia say that the wedding was a perfect opportunity to pay back social obligations to certain people without having to invite them to the house for dinner.

And maybe Lydia did have the right to have it her own way, Hannah told herself wearily, trying not to feel bitter about the fiasco her wedding had become.

Lord knew Hannah and her mother had precious little money to spend on anything since her father's death eleven months ago. They'd had to borrow to pay for the funeral, never mind finance a wedding. She supposed she ought to be grateful that Lydia was being generous and footing the bill.

The trouble was, Hannah couldn't help but suspect the lavish preparations were more a control issue on Lydia's part than a show of generosity, and she had black moments when she visualized what it was really going to be like to be Lydia's daughter-in-law, living a short ten-minute walk from the huge stone house and landscaped lawns where Brad had grown up. He'd insisted on renting a house for them in the same neighborhood his parents lived in, even though it meant spending more on rent than Hannah thought wise.

There were further inklings that weren't reassuring about her future mother-in-law.

Hannah's thoughts went unwillingly to last Tuesday and the *Emily Post Book of Etiquette* that Lydia had given her as a shower gift. Hannah had opened the box in full view of twenty-three women, of whom only half were her friends. The rest had been strangers, invited by Lydia, and when Hannah lifted the thick, heavy book out of its gift-wrapped box, she felt a wave of hot embarrassment. Anger and humiliation followed as the implications of this so-called gift sank in, and she was painfully aware of the telling glances that several of the guests exchanged, and the sympathetic ones her friends sent her way as she stammered her way through thanking Lydia. She had felt more like smashing the heavy, gold-embossed book on her future mother-in-law's perfectly coiffed head.

She knew Lydia thought her lacking in what the Langstons considered social graces, but giving Hannah the book at a bridal shower seemed an outright insult.

Daisy thought so too. She'd claimed to have one of her migraines the night of the shower, so she wasn't present, but when she saw the book among the other gifts, she'd been outraged.

"So that—that *despicable woman* thinks that I didn't teach you any manners," she'd fumed. "Just because we don't have money doesn't mean we're ignorant. Doesn't she realize that?" Daisy's wide, dark-brown eyes, identical to

Hannah's own, filled with tears. "You come from good, sturdy stock, Hannah, and don't you forget it. My ancestors were respectable tradespeople, and your father's people were once lords in Scotland. Your father was a gentleman."

Daisy's defense of him always made Hannah furious. *A gentleman, all right, who died penniless,* she wanted to scream. A gentleman who one way and another gambled his way through her mother's inheritance, a tidy fortune by anyone's standards. A gentleman who relied on his silver tongue and movie-star good looks to ensure that he'd be forgiven, no matter how many foolish risks he took with money, how many promises he broke.

But of course Hannah didn't say any of those things to her mother. In spite of everything, and in Hannah's opinion there'd been more than enough of everything as far as her father was concerned, Daisy had adored Michael Gilmore, and since his death she'd mourned him so deeply and so passionately that Hannah had begun to have serious concerns for her mother's health.

"I really wish you'd change your mind about this, sweetheart," Brad was saying to her now in a cajoling way calculated to melt Hannah's heart: "I'll miss you. I've got that tax evasion trial coming up next week so I won't get to see you much. I thought we'd go out for dinner Friday, maybe catch a movie. We could spend the night at your place." He looped an arm around her shoulders and drew her close, and for a moment Hannah seriously considered telling her mother she couldn't make the trip after all.

"I've got the stag on Saturday night, but you know Mom's counting on us being there for Sunday dinner," Brad said.

Hannah's resolve to go to Barkerville firmed up again in an instant.

"I'll have to miss out this time, Brad," she declared without a shred of regret.

The dinners always followed the same pattern. Brad's father, Chuck, and the boys, as Lydia called her grown sons, disappeared all afternoon for endless games of golf while the women rode herd on eight grandchildren.

In between chasing kids, the women were expected to help Lydia cook the enormous, heavy dinner. Hannah hated cooking, and the women's conversation drove her nuts. It was limited to hairstyles and fashion and who was divorcing whom on the television soap operas they all adored.

Most of the time, Hannah didn't have the slightest idea what they were talking about. She preferred real people and their problems to television drama. Of course, she liked clothes, but her wardrobe was purchased more for comfort than the whims of fashion, suitable for her job as a social worker at the hospital. She'd tried countless times to discuss things she was interested in, like the astonishing rate of pregnancy among very young teens, or the closing of one of Victoria's shelters for battered women, but the others weren't interested. They quickly changed the subject back to skirt lengths and *People* magazine.

"I think you're being really unreasonable, Hannah," Brad declared, releasing her abruptly. "Your van isn't even up to a long trip. You could run into trouble on the road."

"Barkerville's only a day's drive from Vancouver," she said defensively, admitting to herself that Brad did have a point about the van. It had belonged to her father, and it was the only thing of any material value that she had from him. For some perverse reason, she had a soft spot for the old thing.

"I'm a very careful driver, and I have a membership to the Automobile Association," she reminded him, holding on to her patience with difficulty. "It's July, so it's not as if I'll get caught in a snowstorm or anything."

"You're heading for northern B.C., and the weather up there's unpredictable," he said in an ominous tone, making it sound like the furthest reaches of Alaska.

Hannah straightened her shoulders, aware of the pain in her neck that had bothered her all day. She adored her job, but today had been tough. And getting married was proving to be stressful.

It might be sort of relaxing, being alone with just her mother and the blessed dog for a while. Maybe it would give her and Daisy a chance to really connect.

She rubbed at her neck and reminded herself how ridiculous that idea was. She and Daisy had never connected over anything in her entire life, and if it hadn't happened in twenty-eight years, the chances weren't great it would start now.

Hannah grinned, a sad grin, amused at her own stubborn naiveté. She should have learned by now, in all her dealings with people, that relationships very seldom changed in any significant way once their basic pattern was established.

And the pattern set so long ago between herself and her mother wasn't one that included emotional intimacy. They were as different, Daisy was fond of saying, as night and day.

So why, Hannah wondered, did she go on naively hoping things would change?

She stopped and turned to face Brad. "I have to go now. I promised Mom I'd drop by and finalize the plans for the trip."

"I've got that meeting tonight, so I guess I won't be seeing you until you get back, then," he said in a sulky voice.

"You know what they say about absence." She

dredged up a smile and looped her arms around his shoulders, lifting her face for a kiss, but when it came, it was more dutiful than passionate.

Chapter Two

An hour later, at her mother's house, Hannah wished fervently that she'd given in to Brad and canceled the trip.

"You invited Elvira to come with us? Mother, how could you do a thing like that without even asking me?" She was staring at her mother, aghast. Hadn't the day been difficult enough without this? The beginnings of a headache thrummed just behind her ears, and she had to struggle hard to control the urge to out-and-out holler at Daisy.

The only thing that really stopped her was knowing that if she raised her voice to her mother, Klaus would leap up from his pillow near the fireplace barking hysterically. He'd growl and nip at Hannah's ankles with his sharp teeth, wrecking her panty hose, and these were the last pair she had without runs.

Damn, she hated that dog.

"I don't think I really came out and invited Elvira, Hannah. I think actually it was she who suggested coming along when I mentioned the trip yesterday, and what could I say?" Daisy lifted her hands in a helpless little gesture. "She's my best and oldest friend, after all. I've known her since you were nine. I know she's got her funny little ways, but she promised to share the gas and motel expenses, and there's plenty of room in the van. I really didn't think you'd mind."

Not mind? Hannah was enraged, but if she told Daisy how she really felt, her mother would tremble and then start to cry, and Hannah would feel like a bully.

Unlike Hannah, Daisy was a woman who cried easily and effectively, never getting red-faced and swollen and stuffy-nosed the way Hannah did on those rare occasions when she broke down. It was just one more example of the enormous gap between them.

Why was it so easy, Hannah wondered, for her to suggest what her patients should do in similar situations? *Just say no, quietly and firmly,* she'd advise them. *Get in touch with your own feelings and stick with them.*

Why was it impossible for her to apply her

good, strong, sensible advice to situations in her own life?

Hannah's shoulders slumped in defeat, and her anger subsided abruptly. She felt as inept as she always felt around her mother. Part of it had to do with her size. At five-ten, she'd inherited her father's height and his strong bone structure. She'd towered over her tiny mother since she was twelve.

The only genetic advantages she'd gotten from Daisy were her thick, wavy flaxen hair and her leaf-shaped, brownish-black eyes. Daisy said the eyes came from a bedouin forefather, although how a bedouin ever got tangled up with Daisy's family was never explained.

Actually, when she wasn't around her mother, being tall didn't really bother Hannah. In fact, she found her height gave her a distinct advantage at times, when she faced down some patient's bullying husband, for instance, or when she had to stand up to a doctor who wasn't paying enough attention to a patient's emotional needs. But around her mother, she just felt big and clumsy.

"Mom?" Hannah knew she sounded stern. "Why did you invite her without talking it over with me first?"

Daisy didn't quite meet Hannah's eyes. She fiddled with the top buttons on her frilly blouse, her thin fingers flitting here and there like the small birds hopping around in the poplar tree outside her kitchen window.

"Elvira's almost like part of the family, and you know how she and Gordon get on one another's nerves. It'll be good for her to have a couple of days away from him. I thought you liked her, Hannah."

There was a defensive quaver in Daisy's voice, and Hannah noted with alarm how much her mother seemed to have shrunk in the past months. She looked as if she was wearing a much larger woman's clothing.

"I do like her; she's been like an aunt to me. That isn't the point." Heaving a sigh, Hannah flopped down into a nearby chair, trying to figure out what the point really was. "I just get tired of hearing her complain about Gordon all the time. He's a really nice guy. And she still treats me like some stupid little kid who needs to be told what to do."

"Well, she doesn't mean anything by it, Hannah. Elvira's a nurse, and it's made her bossy."

"You ask me, she was born that way." Elvira Taylor believed she had the solution to every one of the world's problems, which irked Hannah because it seemed to her that Elvira should begin solving her own first, at home.

"It's not only that she's bossy, either. She's a terrible backseat driver. Don't you remember the day I took you both to that tea in Ladysmith?" The memory still made Hannah shudder. "And does she still have that problem with her bladder?"

Daisy hesitated. "She's been to the doctor. He gave her exercises to do."

Hannah groaned and shut her eyes. "Lordie. We'll be stopping every five miles so she can pee. It'll take all four days just to get halfway there, never mind up and back again. I'll probably be late for my own wedding just because of Elvira's leaky bladder."

"Oh, don't be silly." Daisy waved a hand in the air, airily dismissing Hannah's concern. "Klaus has to go quite often, too, so it won't make any real difference, will it? Stopping for one, you might as well stop for two."

Hannah rolled her eyes. A trip with Daisy, Elvira, and her mother's dog would be nothing short of a nightmare.

She couldn't do it. She wouldn't do it.

A wave of absolute rebellion rose in her, along with a mental vision of all the things in her life that didn't seem to be working out as well as she'd hoped. For an intoxicating moment, Hannah seriously considered telling her mother she'd changed her mind about making the trip.

And she wouldn't tell Brad either, she plotted. She could go somewhere all by herself for the weekend, sort of a last private holiday before marriage. The idea was so appealing that Hannah opened her mouth to tell her mother Barkerville was off and that was that, but Daisy spoke before she could say a word.

"I've made us a huge lunch for the trip, those vegetable samosas you like so much, Hannah, and oatmeal cookies and some date squares to take along. And I thought maybe that pasta salad, the one with olives and feta cheese. It would travel well, don't you think?"

For the first time in months, Daisy had been cooking. Cooking had always been her passion, but since Michael's death, she'd seemed to live on toast and tea and canned soup.

It was the food and that touch of animation in her mother's voice that made Hannah cave in.

What the heck. It was only four days out of her life. How bad could it be?

"Sounds wonderful, Mom." She got to her feet. "I'll pick you up at seven tomorrow morning."

"I'll call Elvira right now. We'll try to be ready on time, dear."

But Hannah already knew it would be closer to nine before they got away. Elvira was prompt, but Daisy was chronically late, unable ever to meet a deadline of any sort.

Damn. It was going to be a memorable weekend, all right, in the very worst sense of the word.

* * *

By six the next evening, Hannah fully understood and sympathized with Lizzie Borden and the forty whacks she'd purportedly given her mother. If there'd been an ax handy, the temptation to use it on all three of her traveling companions might have been overwhelming.

"Hannah, I hate to say it again, but the draft from that window is going to bring on one of my sinus attacks. It's blowing my hair all over, too, and it's chilly back here. I swear that rain is turning to sleet," Elvira complained for the twentieth time in the same number of minutes.

"Can't help it. I can't stand the smell in here," Hannah growled, crouching over the wheel and scowling through the windshield at the steady downpour. She'd turned off onto this narrow two-lane highway a short time ago; it represented the final lap on a journey that felt as if it had lasted years instead of a single day.

The interior of the van stank because Klaus had been sick repeatedly, and even worse than the pungent odor of dog vomit was the sickly sweet smell of the air freshener Daisy sprayed around each time Klaus heaved.

"Poor wee doggie, this long drive is too much for him, isn't it, Klausie?" Daisy crooned and patted the animal sprawled across her lap. "I still think we should have stopped at a motel in that last town, Hannah," she said in a plaintive voice. "We could have made the rest of the trip in the morning and arrived feeling refreshed.

This way, we're all going to be exhausted by the time we get there."

"My sentiments exactly," Elvira immediately chimed in. "The man back at that gas station told me there were plenty of nice motels in Quesnel."

"He also said the drive to Barkerville would only take us one more hour. One . . . measly . . . hour," Hannah pointed out through gritted teeth. "I want to get where we're going and settle in without having to get up and drive again in the morning. We're booked into the Wells Hotel tonight, and that's where we're going."

Barkerville was a ghost town without accommodation. The small community of Wells, eight kilometers this side of Barkerville, apparently had several restaurants as well as the hotel.

"No need to be snappish, Hannah. Your mother and I were only making a suggestion," Elvira said in an aggrieved tone. "You're certainly not in the best of moods, are you?" She sniffed several times and blew her nose noisily before she lapsed into injured silence.

Hannah prayed that it would last for the remainder of this damnable drive. Just as she'd feared, the day had been a nightmare from beginning to end.

She'd been prepared for Elvira's constant backseat driving, her litany of complaints about Gordon, and her bladder problems, but she hadn't anticipated Klaus's newfound and voracious appetite for samosas. The piggish little animal had devoured four of the spicy concoctions, and then vomited up what seemed like seven. Then he'd whined incessantly, feeling sorry for himself.

Even the weather had conspired against her. It had been drizzling when they left Victoria at eight-thirty that morning, and the rain had turned to a downpour as the day progressed. In spite of it, Daisy and Elvira had insisted on stopping at every single tourist attraction their guide books mentioned, and, of course, every rest stop.

Fast food outlets also became a point of contention as the hours passed. In spite of the huge basket of food Daisy had packed, the women insisted they needed fresh coffee or more juice at regular intervals, which of course meant even more frequent stops at bathrooms.

Hannah's temper had shortened as the miles crawled by, and now she was near exploding. Her head ached in earnest, and it seemed it was growing more difficult by the moment to see where she was going.

The road had been quite decent until now, winding up and down the mountainous terrain, but in the past two kilometers it had narrowed into a tortuous path snaking its way along the bottom of a rocky canyon. A fast-flowing river bordered the highway.

"Look, Daisy. I'm sure this gorge we're going

through is the place my guidebook calls Robber's Roost," Elvira trumpeted from the backseat.

Hannah glanced at her in the rearview mirror. Elvira's thin blond hair barely covered her pink scalp, and her sharp features were dwarfed by the large glasses she wore. Undaunted by the growing darkness, she was using a small flashlight to illuminate her guidebook.

"It says here this was a popular place for holdups back in the 1860s," she continued. "The stagecoaches had to slow down to get through here because the road was twisty, and there was a bridge over this river to our right. That's where the ambush usually took place, it says. Of course the bridge is gone now. They put a culvert in when the road was improved . . ."

But the guidebook was wrong. Hannah rounded a corner at that moment, and the headlights illuminated a narrow, flat wooden bridge, peculiarly unsuited to the paved highway they'd been driving along.

It had grown darker these last few moments, and the rain had turned to hail, pelting the van with huge, frozen globs of white that the headlights couldn't seem to penetrate.

Hannah squinted through the windshield. The hail and what looked like a thick mist obscured the other end of the bridge, and it suddenly felt as if she were driving into oblivion.

She stepped hard on the brakes, slowing the van.

A chill crept up her spine, and she quickly rolled up the window beside her. Her heart began to beat a little faster, and she gripped the steering wheel with both hands as the front wheels bumped hard onto the wooden surface.

Something didn't feel right about this bridge. The double row of planks that formed a track for the wheels of vehicles looked strangely rickety and extraordinarily narrow. And why on earth had the road crew used only logs as a surface, with no side railings?

Daisy sat up straight and peered out, giving a little squeak of fear. "Oh, be careful, Hannah, it's so narrow—"

"Steady on, steady on." Elvira leaned forward, her head almost on Hannah's shoulder, her stale coffee breath wafting to Hannah's nostrils. "This doesn't look very sturdy, does it?" Her loud voice was higher than usual. "The rain must have washed out the culvert and they've put up this temporary crossing. Just look at the fog up there. Be sure your wheels are straight on, now. . . ."

The warning trailed off as Hannah braked again, concentrating on keeping the wheels of the van on the planks. When it seemed the rickety structure was able to support them, she stepped a little harder on the gas, wanting desperately to get safely across this barrier.

But the wheels spun on the slick surface and the van skidded. Daisy squealed, a series of short, sharp bursts of sound which sent Klaus into a barking fit.

Elvira babbled directly into her ear, "Easy, Hannah, take it easy, there's no guard rails, we could—"

Hannah, fighting to get the van back under control, heard the chaotic, frightened noises that her companions made, but they seemed to come from far away.

The bridge, which she'd thought to be short, barely more than two van lengths, had inexplicably extended until it seemed as if it had no end.

The van shuddered and steadied, and she pressed harder on the gas, and still harder.

This simply couldn't be. The van was rocketing ahead, and still they were on this confounded bridge. Hannah had the uncanny feeling that she'd become trapped in a nightmare, that whatever was happening couldn't be real.

In a panic now, she depressed the gas pedal even further and with white-knuckled hands gripped the wheel, willing the van ahead.

If only she could see. . . .

Obligingly, the enveloping white cloud parted for just an instant, and Hannah's mouth opened wide in a soundless scream.

There was a horse on the bridge, trotting

straight towards her. She was about to hit it full-on.

The animal's terrified eyes flashed in the headlights' gleam, and as Hannah applied every ounce of her strength to the brake pedal, she saw the horse rear. Only then did she realize it was hitched to an open wagon.

In the chaotic instant before she turned the wheel and steered off the side of the bridge, she saw the man sitting on the wagon. He wore a brimmed hat and a dark coat. His mouth was open wide in a scream, and on his whiskered face was an expression of abject terror.

The van went over the edge with a thunk, and then there was an endless, silent instant when they were airborne.

They landed, right side up, with a thud that jarred every bone in Hannah's body.

The jolt sent her lurching forward, and her head connected hard with the steering wheel.

There was a magnificent explosion of unbelievable color inside her brain, and she lost consciousness.

Chapter Three

Somewhere far away a dog was yapping, and the sound annoyed Hannah. It interfered with this lovely darkness and the perfect sense of peace.

Something cold and wet and horrid flopped across her face, and she gasped. She had to wake up to get rid of it. With great reluctance and a sense of outrage, she opened her eyes.

Darkness and light swam in dizzy circles and cold water trickled miserably down her cheeks and into her ears and the neckline of her T-shirt. Hannah raised an arm and tried to remove the sopping cloth clamped to her forehead, but Elvira had wrists of steel.

"There, she's coming around now. Hannah, can you hear me? Do you know who I am?"

Hannah realized the car door was open and Elvira was standing there, shining her flashlight right into Hannah's eyes. Her head ached with a force that made her nauseated.

"Please turn out that light," she begged.

But Elvira was pitiless. She went on shining it into Hannah's eyes and repeating, "Do you know who I am? Do you remember what happened?"

Hannah swatted at the flashlight as disturbing images came back to her—a horse and a man and a bridge.

"I drove off the bridge. Oh, my God." She tried to sit up straight. "Mother? Oh my God, where's my mom?"

"Fine. She's just fine. She's over there on the bank of this river. Klaus is fine too; he fell in the water and went for a little swim, but Daisy managed to grab him."

Elvira snorted. "Darn good thing it's not flood season. We could all've drowned if this water was even two feet deeper."

As it was, Elvira was standing in water that reached almost to the knees of her white polyester pants. "This isn't doing my bladder one bit of good, I'll tell you that. Now, are you going to be able to climb out of here by yourself so we can both get somewhere where it's at least dry?"

"I think so. Ouch." Hannah put a hand up to her forehead, encountering an impressive lump that made her wince when she touched it. Memories suddenly flooded back.

"The horse, Elvira. There was a man in a wagon, and a horse."

"Up there." Elvira jutted her chin towards the bridge that loomed above them. "We'll go see about them the moment you feel able to move. First things first." A trace of concern tinged Elvira's matter-of-fact voice. "You *are* able to move, Hannah? Nothing's broken? You don't feel as though there might be internal injuries?"

"Nope." Hannah shook her head and swore under her breath at the pain the movement caused. She swung her legs gingerly out the door. Apart from the discomfort in her skull, she figured she was intact.

"Owww, that water's like ice." She shuddered when her feet hit the stream.

"The bottom's slippery, too—be careful," Elvira warned, and Hannah gingerly took one step and then another. Her good summer sandals would be ruined, and the bottoms of her jeans were getting soaked.

"Take it slow." With one hand Elvira took a firm grip on Hannah's upper arm; with the other she used the flashlight to indicate where the shore was.

"Is Hannah all right? Are you all right, Hannah?" Daisy's voice was panicky, coming from out of the darkness somewhere ahead.

"She's fine, just a little bump on the head like I said," Elvira assured her friend.

Hannah was doing her best to overcome the dizzying waves of nausea that washed over her each time she took a step. None too soon for her, they were out of the water and Daisy had wrapped her arms around Hannah, the top of her head resting on Hannah's breasts, her arms clenched around her daughter's waist.

Daisy was soaked, her cotton pants and shirt clinging to her thin frame. Hannah could feel the tremors that rippled through her mother's body, and Daisy's voice also trembled when she said, "Oh, my dearest, I was so scared. Your head hit on that wheel, and then Klaus fell out the door and almost drowned, and I fell trying to get to him. And now what are we going to do?"

Hannah held her mother close for a long moment, peering over her head at the dark outline of the van and wondering exactly what they *were* going to do.

At least the weather had cleared. It wasn't raining or hailing any longer, and all of a sudden a gigantic full moon popped out from behind a cloud, making it much easier to see.

The van had somehow, miraculously, landed upright, on all four wheels, Hannah noted. Maybe it wouldn't be too hard for a tow truck to pull it out. Maybe it would even run. And it was likely there'd be a car along any minute.

This road to Barkerville must carry a fair amount of traffic.

She sagged with relief. Maybe this wouldn't be a total catastrophe after all. At least none of them had been seriously hurt.

"Come up here, you two." Elvira's voice came from above them, up on the bridge. "I need help. This man's unconscious."

Hannah grabbed her mother's hand, feeling sick with guilt for forgetting about him. What if he were dead? A new wave of dread spilled through her. It had been an accident, but maybe she'd been driving too fast. There'd been that moment of panic, when she'd imagined the bridge was endless and stepped on the gas.

"C'mon, Mom." Tugging Daisy along, Hannah scrambled up the steep bank, slipping and sliding on the wet grass, more or less dragging her mother behind her. Puffing, they reached the road and hurried towards Elvira's flashlight beam.

The wagon was on the bridge. It had overturned, but fortunately it hadn't slipped over the edge of the narrow logs. An assortment of what looked like camping gear lay scattered across the bridge, and it was obvious that part of the wagon's load had probably fallen into the creek.

The poor horse was still attached to the overturned wagon and he was making terrified noises. The whites of his eyes showed silver in the moonlight. He was down on his hind end, caught in the harness, trying repeatedly to struggle to his feet. Daisy whimpered fearfully as Hannah edged past the animal to where Elvira crouched some distance away, still on the wooden logs of the bridge, beside the crumpled figure of a man lying face-down.

"Hold this light, Daisy, so I can see if he's got any broken bones." Elvira handed the flashlight over and made a swift and efficient survey of the man's arms and legs.

"Nothing broken from what I can tell. He might have internal injuries, but there's no real way of knowing. Breathing seems okay; face is lacerated from this wood; he's got a contusion on his scalp; heartbeat seems steady." Elvira muttered away as she conducted her examination.

"Hannah, help me get him turned over so I can check his ribs. If all he's got is a simple concussion, he oughta be waking up before long. If not, there's nothing I can do anyway except keep him warm and make sure his airway's clear. Daisy, go see if there was a blanket on that wagon. Darn it all, I should've brought the one from the van. I wasn't thinking straight."

"I'm not going near that horse," Daisy objected, clutching Klaus to her bosom. "I don't want to get any closer to it. It's liable to kick."

Elvira shook her head, exasperated. "Honestly, Daisy, you're no help at all. Hannah, help me here and then you go see."

Fortunately, the man was small and thin, so turning him wasn't difficult at all. He had long, straggly hair, and when they got him rolled over, they could see he was middle-aged, unshaven, with an unkempt salt-and-pepper beard and a bushy mustache.

Hannah got to her feet and hurried over to the wagon. On the ground there were several blankets tied into a clumsy bedroll, and she brought them over to Elvira, undoing the cord that held them and shaking them out.

"Phew, those blankets absolutely stink. And I swear this guy hasn't bathed in a month of Sundays either," Elvira said in disgust. "Judging by the state of his clothing and these blankets, the nurses are going to have a fine time when he gets to hospital," Elvira pronounced. "What we're going to do, Hannah, is roll one blanket like this and use it like a stretcher if we have to move him. We'll cover him up with the other one."

Hannah followed Elvira's instructions, and the man was soon on the blanket. With a grimace of distaste, Elvira undid his coat and slid her hand across his chest. His shirt was gray flannel.

"Might have broken ribs—" Elvira stopped abruptly. "Shine that light lower down, Daisy. Oh my goodness." Horror was evident in her tone. "I don't believe this. Look, he's wearing a gun and a holster. And a knife."

The three women stared at the leather gunbelt. The single handgun was large, and there were bullets all along the length of the belt; a sheath held a sizable knife.

"It's against the law to carry a gun in B.C. He's either some kind of criminal or an undercover policeman," Daisy said, her voice shaking. "And I don't think a policeman would ever be as dirty as this man, do you? Which means he's a criminal." She gave a little scream and hopped several steps back. "He could wake up and kill us all at any moment." Her voice squeaked into the upper registers, and she backed up still farther, clutching Klaus to her breast.

"Whatever he is, we can't just leave him here and run," Elvira pointed out. "We were at least partially responsible for the accident, and he doesn't seem to be waking up. And even when he does, there are three of us and only one of him, so calm down, Daisy. We'll get rid of this gun right now." She fumbled it out of the holster and handed it to Hannah, who held it gingerly by the end of the barrel.

"I'll just undo this . . ." Elvira unfastened the gunbelt, extracted the knife, and slid the belt from under him. Hannah took the knife and belt in one hand and the gun in the other and walked to the edge of the embankment.

"I'm throwing the whole works in the river,"

she announced and heaved first the gun, then the knife, and finally the belt and bullets as hard as she could. They splashed into the water.

Hannah put her hands on her hips and looked up and down the road, hoping again for the lights of an approaching vehicle. "What we need is an ambulance and a tow truck and the R.C.M.P. You'd think *somebody* would come along so we could get help," she complained. "And in the meantime, what I'm gonna do is find a good-sized rock and keep it handy just in case this guy wakes up with any ideas." She said it to reassure her mother, but Hannah doubted whether she was capable of deliberately hitting someone on the head with a rock.

"Smart thinking. God helps those who help themselves," Elvira pronounced. "And now that we've done what we can for this sorry excuse of a man, we've got to do something for that poor horse. He's liable to break a leg struggling like that. Daisy, you stay here and keep an eye on this fellow and holler the moment he wakes up. Hannah, find her a rock, too."

"You stay here yourself, Elvira, if you're so worried about him," Daisy said. "Why should I be the one to be raped and held hostage and then murdered by some maniac?"

"Oh, come along, then. He's not going anywhere anyhow."

Elvira marched purposefully over to the

wagon with them, and the three of them studied the overturned contraption.

"It's not that big or heavy. Maybe we can hoist it back on its wheels," Hannah suggested, taking a grip on one side. "You two go to the other side and pull down when I pull up."

Elvira and Daisy did as she instructed, and together they heaved and pulled. The wagon was heavier than Hannah had guessed, but on their fourth try they managed to get enough momentum going to right it. The moment it was back on its wheels, the frantic horse scrambled to his feet, but as soon as he was up he began to trot away, dragging the wagon along behind him.

"Whoa. Whoa, boy, whoa there." Elvira raced after him and quickly found the reins. She tugged on them, and the horse obediently stopped.

Hannah was impressed. "Good going, Elvira. How d'you know what to do?"

"I grew up on a farm. It was all work and no play, but I learned a lot of things."

A breeze ruffled the air and Daisy shivered. "I'm freezing in these wet clothes. I've got another pair of slacks and a sweater in my suitcase. Do you think our bags got wet in the back of the van?"

"I'll go down and see," Hannah volunteered. "I've been wondering if the van might just start and then I could drive it out of the water." It was a faint hope, but worth a try. "If it won't, I'll bring up all our stuff," she decided. "Mom, you can change into something dry, and at least we'll have our bags with us when a ride finally comes along."

"Be sure and bring the food, too," Daisy instructed as Hannah made her way cautiously down the embankment again.

Not surprisingly, the van wouldn't start, and it took several trips to transfer all their belongings to dry land. By the time she'd emptied the van, Hannah was sweating from exertion, but her headache had eased and the trips up and down had cleared her mind.

Daisy changed her clothes and they all put on sweaters. Then they waited for help to arrive, but after twenty minutes there still was no sign of another vehicle from either direction.

Elvira checked the unconscious man again. "He's been out for a long time," she pointed out. "That could mean his injuries are more serious than I can detect. Whoever he is, we should try to get help for him. I don't want him to die while I'm taking care of him," she declared. "We've got the horse and wagon—what about loading him and all our stuff in it and trying to find a farmhouse or something?"

"Oh, that's crazy! No, I couldn't ride on a wagon with a horse pulling it," Daisy objected, but Hannah and Elvira ignored her and agreed it was the logical thing to do.

"Should we head back towards Quesnel, or continue on the way we were going, Hannah?"

Hannah had been wondering the same thing. "We're over half way to Barkerville, and there weren't any houses that I noticed for quite a long stretch. I think we ought to keep on going. With any luck somebody'll come along, or we'll come to a house with a telephone."

Using the blankets as a stretcher and with Elvira directing the procedure, the three of them managed to hoist the unconscious man in a relatively smooth maneuver into the box of the wagon. He groaned several times and thrashed around a bit. Once his eyes opened, but he lapsed back into unconsciousness almost right away, which everyone agreed was a relief.

Hannah quickly loaded their various bags in beside him, and they gathered up what they could find of the man's belongings as well. These consisted of a small duffel bag of clothing, several battered pots, some dried peas and rice in a burlap bag, and three extremely heavy canvas sacks whose tops were tied tightly and intricately knotted.

"These could be more ammunition," Hannah said, heaving them into the wagon. "But that won't do him much good without a gun, so we might as well take them."

The wagon was a crude affair, with a plank across the front for a seat. There was only room for two of them on it, so Hannah crouched in the crowded box beside the injured man as Elvira confidently clucked to the horse and shook the reins. They had to turn around in order to head towards Barkerville, which caused a bit of confusion.

Elvira urged the horse to the end of the bridge and turned him, accomplishing the three-hundred-and-sixty degree maneuver without too much difficulty. But then the horse balked when Elvira tried to get him to cross the bridge again, whinnying and shaking his head about and shying when he approached the bridge. Klaus, held firmly on Daisy's lap, didn't help matters at all. He yelped frantically and even howled in a high, eerie way, which further agitated the poor horse.

Eventually, with much urging from Elvira, the animal gave in and trotted nervously across the planks, flicking his tail, throwing his head from side to side and blowing heavily through his nose.

Hannah, doing her best to steady the injured man as the wagon jolted around, thought about how calm and capable Elvira had been all through this crisis. She was actually admirable when she was like this, Hannah thought in amazement. And she hadn't complained about Gordon once in the past hour, which had to be some kind of record.

As the wagon bumped its way off of the rough planks of the bridge and onto the road again,

Hannah looked back at the scene of their accident, but to her surprise she couldn't see either the bridge or the van in the river below.

The mysterious thick fog had suddenly obliterated both bridge and river, giving the uncanny impression that nothing existed behind the wagon. Hannah turned and looked over the other women's shoulders. Ahead of them, the night was clear and absolutely free of any mist. She squinted back at the fog again, and an alarming sensation made the hairs on her arms and the back of her neck stand up.

For an instant, she felt as if her entire existence had been broken into two parts, that everything that had occurred before this moment in time lay abandoned behind that ominous, solid wall of mist.

Just then, she also realized with a sense of alarm that the injured man was waking up. He opened his eyes and stared silently at her for a long, unnerving time, and then he reached a hand out and grasped her arm with surprisingly strong fingers. His voice was thin and reedy, and he had to clear his throat several times to get the words out.

"Please, ma'am, what's happened ta me?"

Well, if he was a murderer, at least he was a polite one, Hannah thought, making sure the large rock she'd brought along was in her right hand.

"You were thrown out of the wagon and hit

your head," she explained, worrying over how he'd react when he found out she was the one driving the van that had hit him.

"We met in the middle of the bridge. It was hard to see. Your horse reared, and I tried my best not to hit you. I drove off the bridge."

"Lights," he muttered. "I recollect bright lights and some big bejesus contraption—" he clapped a hand over his mouth. "Beggin' yer pardon, ma'am. I ain't used to talkin' much ta ladies. Owww, son of a—" He struggled to a sitting position and rubbed his head. "Ahhgggg, me head feels like it's gonna crack open." He looked around, suddenly agitated. "Where's all me gear, ya didn't leave—ahhh, there's me bags, right as rain." He reached out and grasped the canvas bags, patting them as if they were pets.

Then quite suddenly, he dropped his hands to his midriff. "Damnation, where's me gunbelt?" He sounded panicky. "Where's me sidearm gone? And me knife?"

Hannah didn't answer. Instead she moved away from him, as far to the front of the wagon as she could, taking her rock with her and keeping her eyes steadily on him.

Elvira and Daisy had both turned around when they heard him wake up. The horse plodded on, and the wagon bounced and rattled.

"We threw them away. What were you doing with a gun in the first place?" Elvira demanded with alacrity. "It's against the law to carry a gun, everyone knows that."

"Threw . . . ya threw me gun . . . ?" His voice cracked, and the whites of his eyes flashed in the moonlight. He looked from one of them to the other, his bearded countenance twisting into an outraged grimace.

"You threw away Billy's gun?" He rolled his body to the side and struggled to get to his knees, cursing a steady stream.

Hannah half rose, her heart hammering, fear making her breath come quick and short. "Stay where you are." She steadied herself by grabbing the wagon seat with one hand. Her other arm was raised, and in her hand she clutched the rock.

In that instant, she knew that if he lunged at her, she'd be quite capable of smashing his head in with the rock.

Chapter Four

Hannah didn't have to hit him.

As his knees came into contact with the wagon bed, an unearthly shriek was torn from the man and he collapsed, half sobbing, both arms clutching his right leg.

"Maybe there's a fracture after all, one I couldn't detect," Elvira remarked in a calm voice. "Lie down and keep still," she warned him. "Otherwise you'll do yourself even more damage, you silly damned fool."

He didn't seem inclined to argue. Alternately moaning and cursing, he stayed where he'd fallen, and after a moment he clumsily pulled the dirty blankets over himself, cowering underneath them.

Hannah lowered the rock and used her nylon

travel bag to sit down on. She was trembling violently, and for a moment, hysterical tears threatened as the traumatic events of the past few hours caught up with her. For the first time she thought of Brad.

She'd have to call him, of course, and tell him what had happened. She felt reluctant to do so, because he'd most likely think, just as Elvira and Daisy had, that Hannah should have stopped overnight in Quesnel. He would see that as the logical, reasonable thing to have done, and all of a sudden Hannah was furious with him.

She already felt horribly guilty and responsible about the accident. She didn't need him reminding her of her shortcomings. She needed unconditional support, not logic and reason and should have's.

After a moment, it dawned on her that she didn't really know how Brad would react. She was anticipating something that might never occur. With an effort, she dragged her thoughts away from Brad and the accident and paid attention to where she was.

The wagon was bouncing slowly along, jolting and rocking, and for the first time, Hannah wondered why this ride should be so rough. She twisted around and peered over the women's heads at the roadway in front of them.

"This road isn't paved," she exclaimed,

shocked at the discovery. "It isn't even graveled. It's just a dirt track."

"Yes, Hannah. Daisy and I already noticed that," Elvira said with more than a tinge of irony. "I can't remember what the map indicated, whether there was a paved road all the way to Barkerville. Do you recall?" Elvira snapped the reins and clicked her tongue to make the horse go a little faster. He seemed to have a tendency to go slower and slower if she allowed it.

"I'm certain it was supposed to be paved all the way." Hannah frowned and a new concern made her uneasy. "Do you think I could have made a wrong turn somewhere? I mean, the bridge wasn't supposed to even exist, and then suddenly there it was, and now this terrible road." She frowned, going over the route she'd followed in her mind. "But I couldn't have taken a wrong turn," she insisted. "There wasn't even a sign indicating a detour. This has to be right."

She turned back to the man huddled under the blankets, reluctant to have any further contact with him but concerned over this road business.

"Hey, mister . . . ummm, what's your name, anyway?"

There was a moment of silence, and then he pulled the blanket down a little and turned his head towards her.

"Name's Billy. Billy Renton, ma'am." He

sounded weary and subdued, and he seemed to have forgotten his rage about the gun. Hannah was certain he couldn't move; the pain he'd experienced had been obvious. It wouldn't hurt to be polite to him.

"My name's Hannah, and that's Daisy. She's my mother. Elvira's driving the horse." Hannah sucked in a breath of the cool night air. Under the circumstances, she wasn't about to bother with formalities like last names. "Billy, are you familiar with this road?"

"Ya might say I bin up and down it."

"So we are on the right road to Barkerville, then?"

"Barkerville." Instead of answering her question, he let out a groan and another muted stream of curses.

Hannah wasn't about to let him get away with that.

"Look, I'm asking a civil question, and I expect an answer. Is this or is it not the road to Barkerville?"

"A'course it's the road. Cariboo Road. Damn good road, too, compared ta what it used ta be. Only good road inta the gold fields, ain't it?"

"That's what I'm asking you, whether I could have taken some . . . some side road or something. This sure doesn't seem like any main road to me."

"Ya don't like it, why'nt'cha turn around and head on back down ta Quesnellemouth?" His voice took on a wheedling note. "Yessir, that's what you oughta do, alrighty. Ladies like youse don't belong in Barkerville nohow, nothin' up there but wild, fightin' miners and drink and precious little gold. No place for ladies, you take it from Billy. Best turn this wagon round and get back where ya come from, don'tcha think? Barkerville's a wild and sinful place," he ranted.

Quesnellemouth? And Barkerville, a ghost town, wild and sinful? His tirade convinced Hannah that Billy was probably mentally unstable, living in the past or something. That would account for his being on the road with a horse and wagon in the first place, and also for the gun and the knife he'd worn. He was probably harmless, just some old local crazy hermit. She felt a stab of sympathy for him.

"Don't get upset, Billy. We'll see that you get medical treatment, don't worry. Just lie quiet until we find a telephone or something."

Billy gave her a wild-eyed look and groaned hopelessly.

"Me leg's broken. I'll wager I ain't never gonna walk again. Seen broken bones afore, in the gold fields. Man's as good as dead with a broken leg like this 'un." He sounded quite pitiable.

"Nonsense," Elvira declared with spirit. "Broken bones heal wonderfully well. All you'll need is a bit of therapy. Hannah, there's a vial of painkillers in my purse back there. I take them for migraine. Give him two with some apple juice."

Hannah found the pills and a tetrapac of juice.

Billy acted as though he'd never seen a box of juice. His rheumy eyes grew panicky, and it took all of Hannah's patience to convince him it was apple juice, but once he'd mastered the straw, which took some doing on Hannah's part, he swallowed the juice and the medication.

"What's the horse's name? He'd probably respond a lot better if I knew his name," Elvira called back.

Billy had collapsed again on the wagon floor. "Name's Jupiter," he mumbled, drawing the blanket up over his head. Within a very few moments, he was asleep.

It was an enormous relief to hear him snoring. Hannah realized how tense she was. She stretched and peered over Elvira's shoulder, hoping for lights that would indicate a house, but the only light was the eerie brightness of the moon.

"We must've been riding in this wagon for over an hour already," Daisy complained. "Wouldn't you think there'd be houses along the way, or that a car would come along?"

Elvira didn't answer her, and neither did Hannah.

Daisy was absolutely right. It didn't seem possible to travel this far on what should be a well-used route without a single sign of human habitation or a vehicle from either direction.

A terrible foreboding was beginning to frighten Hannah, a sense that something was very wrong. The road hadn't improved; in fact, it was now so narrow and rutted that Hannah couldn't see how a car could manage to drive along it. Branches from trees overhung it, and several times she'd had to duck to keep from being scratched.

They'd come so far now that there was no sense in turning around and going back, but she felt they'd made a serious mistake in not heeding Billy's suggestion that they go back to Quesnel.

Quesnellemouth, he'd called it. It hadn't been called that on the map, so maybe he meant another town.

Slowly, the night deepened. The moon reached its zenith and dipped towards the mountains. Elvira stopped the wagon beside a stream and Hannah filled Billy's tin bucket with water for Jupiter. When they were moving again, the women shared some of the remaining lunch, bagels stuffed with tuna and sprouts, and apples. They talked in quiet voices, discussing the accident.

Billy was now heavily asleep, his snoring punctuating the silence, and Hannah set aside a bagel and an apple for him.

Elvira and Daisy were quiet now, too, as if the ominous fear that Hannah experienced had transmitted itself to them.

Slowly, the terrain changed, and for a while the narrow trail again bordered a stream that glimmered like pewter in the silver moonlight. Then once again trees overhung the trail, and it became tortuously narrow, one side bordering a steep hillside and the other dropping straight down into a dark and terrifying ravine. There were no guardrails, no highway signs, nothing to indicate that the path they were on even led anywhere. The women were silent, and Hannah put her hand on her mother's shoulder and gently squeezed, giving and getting a measure of reassurance from the contact.

There was a long, gradual hill that led down to the bottom of a narrow valley, and gradually the thick forest they'd been passing through disappeared. The wagon rounded a corner, and all three women gasped in unison.

Ahead of them, bathed eerily in white moonlight, was a town, its single main street narrow and lined with wall-to-wall buildings with steeply peaked roofs. It lay in a barren landscape, as if some gigantic hurricane had come along, shearing off trees on either side of the mountains and leaving only stumps, miles and miles of them.

The smell of wood smoke hung in the cool night air, and as they drew closer, Hannah could hear noise, shouts, laughter, the tinny sound of a piano.

"Oh, thank goodness," Daisy exclaimed. "This must be Wells. Didn't the guidebook say we'd come to Wells before we got to Barkerville, Hannah?" She didn't wait for a reply. "I'm so glad we're finally here. I'm getting really tired. But why do you think they cut down all these trees? And there aren't any streetlights."

Hannah's heart was pounding, and her throat was so dry, she could hardly talk. Elvira turned and looked at her, and Hannah saw a reflection of her own ominous foreboding in the other woman's anxious glance.

"I'm sure this isn't Wells, Mom," Hannah finally managed. "The town of Wells is set up on a hill, not down in a valley. There was a picture of it in the guidebook, and I paid particular attention because I wanted to find the hotel easily."

"There aren't any electric lights at all," Elvira commented, puzzlement in her voice. "All these buildings seem to be up on stilts. And look at the horses tied along the street. You'd think they'd never heard of cars. Is that a waterwheel off to the side, making that noise?" She sounded perplexed. "I wonder if this is some little native village, Hannah? It's certainly not Wells, and of course it can't be Barkerville."

"There's something wrong," Hannah said in a

faint voice. "I knew that road wasn't the one we should have been on. We're lost."

Behind her, Billy had stopped snoring. He cleared his throat and raised himself enough to spit over the side of the wagon. He looked around at the crude, one-room cabins they were passing as the horse pulled the wagon farther along the single main street of the town.

"Damn it all ta hell," he moaned. "Here I be, back in Barkerville. I'm a dead man. Ya just had ta bring me back to Barkerville, didn't ya?" With a groan, he slumped back down on the floor of the wagon, and Hannah stared around again and then gripped the plank seat with all her strength to keep herself from collapsing.

Barkerville was a ghost town, and the guide book had warned that there were gates which locked the public out from seven in the evening until nine in the morning.

She hadn't checked her watch, but it had to be near midnight. And whatever this strange place was, it was certainly no ghost town. It was noisy. There was the sound of rushing water from some nearby stream, and off to the right the waterwheel Elvira had remarked on thumped and squeaked. Several dogs had appeared out of nowhere, running alongside the wagon and barking hysterically, which of course sent Klaus into a frenzy. There seemed to be horses tied up on either side of the street, and she had the impression that every second building they were passing was a pub. Voices and laughter spilled out, along with murky light that seemed to come from lanterns. A crooked wooden boardwalk ran along in front of the buildings, raised about three feet above the dusty street.

A horse neighed, and their own patient animal answered, his gait picking up as he made his way along. He seemed to know where he was going.

Crudely lettered wooden signs overhung the buildings. Hannah could make out the lettering on some as the wagon passed beneath them.

BREWERY. BREWERY SALOON. DRUG STORE. NEW ENGLAND BAKERY. BENDIXON SALOON AND BOARDING HOUSE. TIN SHOP. ST. GEORGE SALOON. LIVERY FEED AND STABLE. NUGGET SALOON AND ROOMS.

Music, male voices, raucous laughter. Midnight, and yet there was a sense of incredible energy and aliveness in this strange place. Hannah could feel it.

A tall, thin man came staggering out of the Nugget Saloon as they passed. He braced himself on the wall to peer curiously at the wagon and its cargo.

"Women, as I live and breathe." He stuck his head back inside the saloon and bellowed, "A wagonload of women has arrived, boys. There's a wagonload of women out here."

He turned towards them again and swept his brimmed hat off and bowed low.

"Evening, ladies. Welcome to Barkerville. Zachary Willings, barrister, at your service." He bowed again and almost tumbled down from the boardwalk, staggering along beside them, detouring now and then to stick his head into several other saloons and excitedly holler, "Women! An entire wagonload of women just rolled in."

The next few moments were confusing and terrifying.

Men came pouring out of doorways, jumping down from the raised boardwalk to the street, talking and laughing and calling boisterous greetings to the women. In what seemed to Hannah only an instant, the wagon was surrounded with tightly packed male bodies.

Several of them took hold of Jupiter's harness, and the horse stopped. The cacophony of voices was deafening. Questions and comments were directed at them in such a confused babble, it was impossible for the women to make sense of any of them at first.

Hannah felt trapped, threatened, terribly at risk. She stood up and put her arms protectively around Elvira and Daisy's shoulders. They huddled together on the wagon seat, as completely overwhelmed by what was happening as Hannah was.

She looked down into the sea of rough male faces, desperately trying to make some sense of what was occurring, but for the life of her, she couldn't. She'd never been the center of such a frenzy, and she couldn't begin to figure out why their arrival would create such a stir.

Why were there so many men? And where was the R.C.M.P? A town this rowdy had to have some sort of police presence, her mind insisted.

A heavily muscled man with a full red beard had now elbowed his way through the crowd and was standing directly below Hannah, but he wasn't smiling or calling greetings the way most of the other men were. Instead, he scowled up at her, his bearded face ugly, his tone threatening.

"Ain't that horse Jupiter? Ain't that Billy Renton's horse?" His voice was gruff and angry, and he bellowed up at Hannah. "And this's Billy's wagon, too, ain't it? So where the hell is Billy Renton, lady?"

Hannah turned to confront him, glad that standing on the wagon bed put her much higher than he was. She was aware that the men's voices had quieted completely. "This *is* Billy's wagon and horse, and we need a doctor. We had a collision on a bridge, and Billy was injured." She gestured down at the strangely still figure huddled under the blanket. "He's right there, under those blankets, and we could use some help getting him to the hospital—"

With a curse, the big man grasped the edge of the wagon and threw his body up and over the side, making it tilt precariously and bringing screams from Elvira and Daisy.

He bent and hauled the blanket off Billy and yanked the cowering little man upright in one smooth movement.

Billy shrieked and batted at the much larger man with his fists, but he was no match for him. The other man held Billy like a ragdoll, his booted feet not even touching the planks.

"Billy Renton," he roared through clenched teeth, "you miserable, thievin' little bastard, where's my gold? Where's the gold you stole offa me? Tell me or I'll blow your brains out."

"There," Billy shrieked, pointing at the canvas bags beneath the blanket. "It's all there, Dutch, I swear it is. Take a looksee, it's all there. I ain't even armed. Ya can't shoot an unarmed man . . . these women threw my guns away."

"Like hell I can't."

The crowd guffawed and whistled in approval as Dutch unceremoniously lifted Billy even higher and dropped him over the side of the wagon and into the dust of the street.

Billy screamed in agony as his injured leg hit the earth, but Dutch paid no attention at all. He bent over and hefted the canvas bags.

Elvira and Daisy cried out in horror at the terrible sound Billy made when he hit the ground, and Hannah's terror gave way to outrage.

"You . . . you miserable coward! You, you . . .

you bully," she hollered at the man called Dutch, drawing herself upright from where she'd been cowering along with Elvira and Daisy. Hands on her hips, she confronted the big man who crouched over the bags, fumbling with the knots in the rope that held them shut.

"How dare you treat another human being that way? You ought to be ashamed of yourself. Billy's probably broken his knee, and you've made it worse. What are you, some kind of psychopath? How dare you treat him like that? I'm reporting you to the police for brutality."

She then turned her wrath on the men now gaping up at her as if she was speaking in tongues.

"And what's the matter with the rest of you people? Can't you see that poor man needs an ambulance? Isn't there a hospital here, a doctor? Why don't you do something for him instead of standing there like—like a bunch of lamebrained idiots?"

There was almost total silence for a moment, and then an amused male voice sounded. "You heard the lady, gents. Somebody go get Doc Carroll, he's playin' poker in the back room. Jacob, why don't you go and roust him out? And a couple of you can carry Billy into the Nugget and lay him out on the floor so Doc can figure out what's wrong with him."

Hannah squinted through the half darkness towards the authoritative voice. The speaker stood silhouetted against the lamplit interior of the Nugget Saloon. She couldn't make out anything more than a tall, broad-shouldered outline, but the tone of his deep voice and his air of quiet assurance told her that here, at least, was someone civilized, someone who could make order of this bizarre event.

A sense of profound relief spilled through her as he ducked his head to clear the doorway, jumped down from the boardwalk, and came strolling towards the wagon.

"How do you do, ladies? I'm Logan McGraw."

Chapter Five

Logan was intrigued by the tall, spunky woman, and as he drew close enough to see more of her in the moonlight, he was also shocked and startled at her immodest attire.

She had a black knitted garment on top, but below it, at hip level, she was wearing close-fitting pants that outlined her shape in a fashion that left little to the imagination. Undoubtedly she'd come to Barkerville to make her fortune in one of the sporting houses.

She didn't sound like any of the soiled doves he'd ever met, however. She was well-spoken, obviously educated. He had some education himself, but some of her words weren't familiar.

He studied her closely, wondering where she was from. She was a big woman, not blatantly fetching, but attractive all the same. Her fair hair was pulled back into a single long braid.

She was no shrinking violet, that was evident. Even in the shadows, her dark eyes flashed indignation. Her face was striking in the silvery moonglow, its strong features and clean jawline arresting and unusual, her mode of dress and hairstyle strange. Someone held up a lantern, and he noticed a lump on her forehead, as if she'd bumped it hard.

She was in a temper. "Are you all playing some sort of joke on us with this Barkerville thing?" She glared down at him, and there was accusation in her tone. "Because it's late, we've had an accident, we're really tired, and I don't find any of this funny in the slightest." She looked around at the other men. "You're all actors, aren't you? You've having some sort of celebration, Barkerville Days or something, and you're having a huge, elaborate joke at our expense."

Logan frowned up at her, unable to understand what she meant. Several miners were carefully lifting Billy, and he gestured at the little scoundrel.

"Does this look to you like a joking matter, miss? Billy here stole Dutch's gold, and in a mining town, I assure you, such a thing is taken very seriously indeed. I'm sure Dutch will express his gratitude to you for apprehending Billy and bringing him back to Barkerville, along with all the missing gold." His voice became steely.

"Isn't that a fact, Dutch? It seems to me you owe these ladies both an apology and a token of your gratitude. You've obviously frightened them with your behavior, and they've done you a great service."

The miners cheered and nodded, and Dutch Charlie, who'd now climbed out of the wagon and taken the canvas bags with him, ducked his head in embarrassment.

"Sorry, ladies. Didn't mean ta scare ya. I was just some put out with that little bastard . . . uhhh, with Billy." He reached a hand into the canvas sack he'd unfastened and shoved a closed fist towards Hannah. "Here—here's a little somethin' fer ya, darlin,' and many thanks."

The tall woman didn't immediately reach out to accept what Dutch was offering.

"Take it," Logan advised in a firm tone. "You've earned it honestly." He hadn't intended any crude innuendo in the remark, and he was relieved when she took no offense. Instead, she reached out hesitantly and allowed Dutch to spill the handful of nuggets into her palm.

Logan had paid scant attention to the two older women, still seated on the front of the wagon. Now, the one handling the reins turned to the tall young woman and said in an impatient voice, "Hannah, I don't know any more than you do what this crazy scene is all about, but I'm too tired to care. Billy seems to have been taken care of, so just find out where we can leave this horse and wagon and get a motel room. We can sort the whole mess out in the morning."

So her name was Hannah. Logan supposed the older woman was a madam, come to set up a gaming establishment in the town.

Hannah gave him an inquiring look. "Well, Mr. McGraw? Is there somewhere to leave the horse? He must need water and feed. He's pulled us for hours. And where's a motel?"

"The livery stable's just down the street," Logan said. He'd never heard the other word, but he assumed it was the same as hotel. Unfortunately, housing horses in Barkerville was much easier than finding lodging for people.

After all, it was 1868, and the Cariboo gold rush was at its peak. The steady influx of men from all corners of the globe, eager to make their fortunes overnight, meant that there wasn't a vacant bed in the entire town. In fact, it was commonplace for several men to rent one bed and then sleep in shifts. There were some doing so right now in Logan's upstairs rooms, and in most of the other hotels as well.

But women were far more precious than gold in this town. Logan estimated there were probably ten thousand men in the vicinity of Barkerville, and perhaps a hundred and fifty women, many of them whores.

Certainly these three would have the offer of any number of beds as soon as word spread that they'd arrived. Hopeful suitors would pour into town, unmindful of the women's profession.

"Lodging's at a premium here, miss," Logan began. "I doubt you'll find anything available." He was amazed to hear himself add, "However, I have a room at my establishment which you and your companions are welcome to use for the night."

Now what in tarnation had possessed him to say that? The Nugget had five bedrooms in all, and four of them were rented at a fair rate by miners. The fifth was his own.

"Only one room? For three of us?"

"Yes, ma'am." Logan grinned and wondered if this young woman had ever heard the old saw about looking a gift horse in the mouth. "There's a double bed, and I'll arrange for a pallet."

He'd bunk out in the workshop with Angus. There was an extra iron cot out there.

It was the older woman who said, "And just how much are you going to charge us for this room?"

He'd guessed her occupation correctly, Logan concluded with a feeling of scorn. Madams and pimps were always conscious of money. Her words rankled, and he was sorry for the impetuous offer of his room. He had no use for these carrion who profited from the selling of human flesh.

He was about to name an exorbitant sum, but something made him decide to go the opposite route. "No charge, ma'am."

"Why, that's very generous of you, Mister . . . McGraw, was it?"

Logan nodded.

"Thank you very much, Mr. McGraw. My name's Elvira Taylor, and this is Daisy Gilmore, and that's Hannah Gilmore, Daisy's daughter. The dog's name is Klaus. We're tourists from Victoria."

Tourists? Here again was a word Logan wasn't familiar with. He wondered suddenly if he'd made an error in judging these as fancy women. What sort of whore traveled with her madam, her mother, and a dog?

He was aware that every man within hearing distance was listening avidly to the conversation. It was past time to break up the crowd. The distraction was interfering with the profits in his saloon.

Logan held up a hand to help Elvira and Daisy down from the wagon, noting that the two older women also wore outlandish trousers.

"If you ladies will come with me, I'll show you to your room." He caught sight of one of his employees in the crowd. "Angus, unload the women's baggage and then take the horse and wagon along to Mundorf's stable."

"Yessir, boss." Angus shambled off to do Logan's bidding, and after a moment's hesitation, Elvira placed her hand in Logan's and stepped down from the wagon and into the ankle-deep dust of the street. He assisted Daisy, and in the process got nipped in the arm by the evil-tempered little dog.

He was aware that Hannah had ignored at least twenty-five male offers of assistance and leapt down easily by herself.

She also grabbed two of the traveling bags, again ignoring countless offers of help from the crowd. He noted that she had a sort of dignity that kept the men from being too forward despite her revealing clothing. The fact that she was an exceptionally tall, strong woman didn't hurt either.

Logan picked up the remaining three of the strange, shiny carpet bags and led the way up the steps to the boardwalk and along to the side entrance of the Nugget so they wouldn't have to go through the saloon. He was aware that Hannah was directly behind him.

He felt a surge of pride as he stood back to allow the women to enter his establishment. He'd won the Nugget in a card game shortly after his arrival in Barkerville three months before, and in the short time he'd owned it, he'd made substantial improvements to the run-down establishment.

He hadn't come here to be a hotel keeper, or to relieve careless miners of their gold, although he'd done both since his arrival.

He'd come here to kill a man, but he'd arrived two weeks late. Bart Flannery had reportedly gone to Germany to bring a shipment of fresh girls back to Barkerville. He and his cargo were expected back sometime in August. His woman, Carmen Hall, was running his establishment, Frenchie's brothel, in his absence.

Logan had been on Flannery's trail for almost a year. He'd been bitterly disappointed and impatient at this delay, and he'd considered leaving and waylaying Flannery somewhere else, but his cash was running low and there was gold to be won at the numerous gaming tables.

Winning the Nugget had given him even more reason to stay. It had provided a welcome distraction from his dark thoughts, an opportunity to work hard physically, using the carpentry skills he'd learned as a boy.

He'd cleaned and limed the blackened, smoky walls in the hallway. He'd sanded the scarred but sturdy oak flooring and in the saloon covered it with sawdust, making certain it was changed early every morning so the place smelled fresh and clean. He'd trained Angus to scour the tables each day, and signs on the walls forbade spitting except in the numerous spittoons located strategically around the large, low-ceilinged room.

His saloon was the cleanest in town, not that most of the patrons noticed or cared. Miners were a thirsty, careless lot, generally interested only in a good supply of liquor.

Logan cared, however. It pleased him to have orderly surroundings.

The saloon had emptied with the news of the women's arrival, and now throngs of men were grouped at the wide double doors that opened from the saloon into the hallway. They were elbowing one another so they could get a closer look at the women.

Logan led the way past the saloon. There was a short hallway from which another set of doors opened to a room intended for dining, which Logan used as a private gambling area. It was empty now. Tonight's game had abruptly ended with the women's arrival, and cards and glasses lay abandoned on the tables.

Logan stood aside so they could precede him up the narrow stairwell that led to the second floor.

Here, too, he'd made improvements. He'd brought in a roll of carpeting for the stairs, and put coal-oil lamps in holders at strategic locations so the stairwell was softly lit.

In the lamplight, Hannah's hind view drew his fascinated gaze as she climbed the stairs directly ahead of him.

He couldn't help but appreciate her curves. Those obscenely tight denim pants outlined her body in a manner expressly designed to arouse a man. It was both a disappointment and a relief to reach the top of the winding staircase.

He opened his bedroom and lit the lamp he kept by the door, relieved that the room was tidy. "I'll bring you up fresh bedding, and Angus will come directly with a pallet and some clean towels."

Here, Logan had laid a patterned Turkey carpet on the rough boards beside the bed and installed a small wood stove in the corner for chilly mornings. He'd built a bookshelf and mounted it above the bed for his small, well-used collection of books; he went over to it now and took down the daguerreotype of Nellie that he kept there. He slid it into his pocket and checked to make sure the china pitcher on the washstand was filled with fresh water, glad that he'd scoured the basin and emptied the commode that morning. Even his shaving mirror was wiped free of whiskers and spatter.

He went over to the wardrobe and removed a fresh shirt and several other items of clothing, careful to give Klaus a wide berth. Daisy had set the dog on the floor.

"I hope you'll be comfortable. The saloon will be quieting down in an hour or so. Wake-Up Jake's, a restaurant just down the road, serves breakfast."

"And is the bathroom down the hall?" Elvira sank wearily down on the bed.

Logan grinned, appreciating her humor. "The privy is out in the back yard, in the right-hand corner, directly behind the saloon. Down the stairs, turn left, go through the door to the kitchen and out the back door. There's a supply of candles on the dresser here. And the commode is under the washstand, of course."

"Commode?" Elvira humphed and looked under the washstand. "A pot! Now that takes the cake, that does. I thought I was past emptying bedpans, but looks like I was wrong. So how do we go about having a hot bath or shower?"

"The stove's been out most of the day. I'm afraid a hot bath tonight isn't possible. By tomorrow noon there ought to be enough hot water for bathing. I'll send Angus up in the morning with a kettle."

He should have considered the complications of housing women before he got himself into this, Logan thought with disgust. Men were a lot easier when it came to such matters as hot baths. Most of the miners settled for one a week, and they took that at the bathhouse down the street.

Hannah had dumped the bags on the floor and was now staring at the calendar he'd pinned to the wall.

"July seventh, 1868?" She shook her head. "Where on earth did you ever find an antique calendar like that in such good condition? It looks almost new."

"It is new. It's this year's calendar." He pointed a finger at the inscription. "Occidental Hotel, Quesnellemouth. I stayed there on my journey in to the gold fields this spring, and the proprietor kindly gave it to me."

She looked from the calendar to him. She'd turned pale, and he saw her swallow hard. The lump on her forehead was angry-looking, raised and turning blue. "Please, Mr. McGraw, don't tease me. It's been a long and difficult day, and I'm tired. You know as well as I do that's not the date." Her voice quivered.

"Call me Logan, please." He frowned at her, touched by her sudden vulnerability, but totally at a loss as to how to help her. Why should the exact date be such a matter of concern to her? Finally he pulled out his pocket watch and looked at it. "You're quite right, it's past midnight, so the date is actually July eighth." With a flourish, he tore the page off the calendar and crumpled it.

"Stop being a total idiot." Her husky voice throbbed with passion. It was a relief to have her angry again. He raised an eyebrow and waited for the rest of the tirade.

"You know darned well I mean the year, not the day. You're about a hundred and thirty years out, aren't you? When we left Victoria this morning, it was nearly the end of the nineteen-hundreds. We didn't exactly go through any . . . any time warp. We just drove along the highway until we had that darned accident on that wooden bridge, didn't we, Elvira? Mother?" There was a definite note of panic in her voice.

The two women looked at one another uncomfortably. They nodded and murmured agreement.

"So, Mr. McGraw, don't stand there and lie to me about the date. I don't find it the least amusing."

Logan studied her. He realized she meant every word she said, and the other two women were looking at him in a questioning manner, as if they, too, expected an explanation or an apology.

They were all addled. Maybe the accident they spoke of had been more serious than he'd supposed. Maybe they'd all banged their heads. "You are confused. I assure you all, it *is* 1868," he said at last, quietly and firmly. "I suggest you have a good night's rest, and perhaps by morning you'll feel better." He strode to the door and then a new thought struck him and he turned.

"Would you like me to send Doc Carroll up?" He gestured at Hannah's forehead. "Perhaps that bump on your head was more serious than you realize—"

The words seemed to be the final straw. Hannah lost her temper completely. Her hands balled into fists, and her entire body trembled with rage. Logan wondered uneasily if she was capable of throwing something at him.

"We don't need a doctor, for heaven's sake!" she shouted. "We're perfectly fine, it's—it's the rest of you that need psychiatric help, if you ask me."

Logan decided that the wisest course was to let himself out the door. He closed it softly behind him and shook his head.

He'd just given over his precious bedroom to total lunatics. And he'd noticed that Hannah was wearing a diamond on her engagement finger.

Was it just an ornament, or was she affianced to someone? He scowled and trotted down the stairs, wondering why the hell he was even curious.

The door closed behind Logan, and the anger that had fired Hannah fizzled out, leaving her as flat as two-day-old soda. With a sound somewhere between a moan and a sigh, she sank down on the straight-backed wooden chair beside the wardrobe, stretching out her aching legs and kicking off her sandals. Klaus came trotting over and sniffed her dirty toes, then ran back to Daisy, whimpering piteously.

"He has to go out," Daisy sighed. "And I have to, too. There's no way in the world I'm using any pot."

"I'll come with you. I don't know how I've

lasted this long," Elvira declared. "Good thing I had the foresight to bring my flashlight along. Imagine him suggesting we use candles. It's a wonder someone hasn't burned the place down. You coming, Hannah?"

She shook her head, and then burst out, "How can the two of you stay so calm? You heard what he said. You can see that calendar—" She threw out a hand and pointed at it. "What he's saying is impossible. But there's no electricity, no telephone, no bathroom, no nothing." She realized she was beginning to sound hysterical.

"It's either a misunderstanding or a joke," Elvira said firmly. "Maybe they're making a movie up here, and having a bit of fun with us, like you said before."

Her words made sense, and Hannah calmed down. "Of course. I bet that's it." Certainly Logan McGraw was handsome enough to be a movie actor.

"Whatever it is, we'll find out in the morning. But right now, I have to find a bathroom, and fast," Elvira said.

"I'll wait here for the sheets and the—the pallet, whatever that is," Hannah said.

Daisy rummaged through her luggage and found a leash, which she clipped on Klaus. She came over to her daughter and put her hand on Hannah's arm.

"Don't worry about all this, dear. Things always look brighter in the morning. Just like Elvira says, I'm sure there's a perfectly reasonable explanation."

Hannah summoned up a facsimile of a smile, wondering why Daisy wasn't hysterical. "I sure hope so."

When they were gone, Hannah heaved an immense sigh and flung herself down on her back on the bed. Privacy, even ten minutes worth, would go a long way towards restoring her sanity.

Logan McGraw had upset her with his insistence on the date. She frowned and turned her head towards the calendar again. If this was a movie set, where were the cameras? The crew?

The strangeness sent her brain skittering off in a panic. She forced herself to safer territory and focused on Logan McGraw instead of the date.

He was an imposing man, that was certain. He topped her by at least four inches, which made him six foot two, and his shoulders and muscular development were impressive. His dark brown hair was shoulder-length and worn loose. It had a touch of curl, and it shone under the lamplight.

He had a luxurious mustache, but he wasn't bearded, although many of the other men were.

There was a steely determination in his deep-set eyes and the set of his square jaw that suggested he wasn't a man to challenge too much or too far.

What color were his eyes? She folded her hands behind her head and closed her own, and the moment she did his face was there before her, like a photograph.

Very deep blue eyes. His skin was deeply tanned, his mouth generous. And she'd noticed his hands, too. They were the hands of a man who was used to physical labor, veined and scarred and very strong.

The rigors of the day had taken their toll, and weariness swept over her like a soft, welcoming blanket. Her forehead throbbed and she drifted somewhere between waking and sleep. She thought of Brad, but it was the visual image of Logan McGraw that was more powerful, like an anchor, steadying her.

Chapter Six

A knock at the door startled her, and she bolted up to a sitting position and tugged down her sweater.

"Come in."

A young man with black curly hair, hardly more than a boy, fumbled the door open and stepped into the room. His arms were loaded with sheets and towels and a folded quilt. He ducked his head shyly and looked at Hannah from under thick eyelashes any female would envy. "Boss said bring these here. I'll go get the pallet. I left it at the bottom of the stairs. I couldn't carry it all at once." He dumped the armload on the bed and bolted out the door again.

Hannah gathered up the towels and hung

them on the railing at the back of the antique washstand in the corner.

"Here ya go, lady. Where ya want I should put it?"

Hannah had already decided that whatever a pallet was, she much preferred it to the idea of sleeping with anyone.

"Here, under the window."

He arranged it where she indicated. It was a primitive futon, a mattress with thick striped ticking that seemed to be filled with straw instead of cotton.

"Ya need me fer somethin' more?" It was obvious he was very eager to please her, and Hannah smiled at him.

"That's just fine, thank you very much, Mr—?"

He turned scarlet and rubbed a hand through his curls.

"I ain't no mister. Just Angus, lady. Angus Percival." He was an exceptionally good-looking boy, short and slender, with beautiful clear blue eyes, but now that Hannah really looked at him, there was something in his manner and his speech that clearly indicated he was mentally challenged. Compassion washed over her, and she thought of Stephen, the young boy at the hospital who'd attempted suicide.

"You've been a tremendous help to me, Angus. Thank you so much." She'd tossed her purse on the bed, and she opened it now and took out her wallet, extracting a five-dollar bill and offering it to him as a tip.

It was a long moment before he reached out and took the bill from her. He held it close to his eyes, peering at it curiously, turning it over and studying the engraving on it as if he'd never seen money before.

"It's real purty. But it ain't money."

Hannah felt a stab of pity. He must have some particular disability when it came to numbers.

"Of course it's money. It's five dollars, to thank you for your trouble, Angus."

He turned towards the door just as Daisy and Elvira came in, and his whole face lit up when he spied Klaus.

"Ahhh, you gotta little pooch." Angus was entranced by the dog. He dropped to one knee and stroked Klaus's ears, murmuring to him and putting his nose close to the dog's muzzle.

"Watch him, Angus, he bites." Hannah was alarmed, because Klaus was anything but a friendly dog, but to her amazement, the temperamental animal licked the boy's hands and face and generally acted delighted to meet him.

"He's a good doggie. Ya think I could maybe take him fer a walk sometime?"

Daisy shook her head. "Oh, I doubt he'd go with you, dear. He's very attached to me."

With a final caress for the dog, Angus left, and in silence the three women quickly stripped the bed and remade it. They were all too tired for conversation.

Hannah spread the rough cotton sheet and heavy quilt over the lumpy pallet, and each of the women washed at the handbasin and got into her nightclothes. Klaus had sullenly settled on the carpet beside the bed when Daisy insisted, but Hannah suspected it was only a matter of time before he'd be sleeping where he always did, on the bed at Daisy's feet.

"Oooo, I'm beat. And I hope that dog realizes he's not sleeping on the bed." Elvira turned the lamp wick down, and darkness was total and complete once the soft light was extinguished.

Hannah had opened the tiny window, and a cool breeze blew over her and freshened the air, punctuated with the rushing sound of the nearby creek and the splashing and creaking of waterwheels. There were muted men's voices from the saloon downstairs, the sound of a man singing. *Why weren't there any cars? Televisions? Radios?*

"Night, Mom. Night, Elvira."

They murmured sleepy responses, and within moments Hannah heard their breathing change to the rhythms of sleep. Elvira snorted and rolled over, then settled into a steady, deep-throated snore.

Hannah had to smile when she heard Klaus leap up on the bed and, with a protracted groan of pure pleasure, settle himself at Daisy's feet.

Hannah drew the quilt up to her neck and curled herself into a ball. She pondered the events of the day and worried like Klaus with a bone over the things she couldn't make sense of, like this town that everyone insisted was Barkerville, and the calendar on the wall with its incongruous date, and Logan McGraw. Was he an actor, as Elvira thought?

Hannah doubted it. He was too authentic, too *real* to be anything but what he seemed.

1868. Her brain struggled for explanations and came up empty. At last, weariness overcame her, and she gave up trying to figure anything out. Tomorrow would bring answers, she promised herself.

She heard doors open and close along the hall, but there was surprisingly little noise from the other rooms.

At last she slept. . . .

And woke what seemed only moments later to the sound of birds chirping, dogs barking, the low, faraway rumble of men's voices, and the seemingly constant sound of the water wheels she'd heard in her dreams all night long.

The other two women were already up. Daisy was in her bra and panties, washing in the basin, and Elvira, still in her long pink flannel nightgown, was making the bed.

"Morning," Hannah mumbled, sitting up and yawning. "What time is it?"

"Past eight." Elvira plumped the pillows and

smoothed the quilt with more force than seemed necessary. "There's dog hairs all over this bed. And Hannah, I do envy someone who can sleep in the morning . . . I'm awake at the crack of dawn myself. But I always maintain you get more done that way. Not that I got much sleep last night on this lumpy mattress. And with my bladder, climbing up and down those stairs to use the toilet is just ridiculous."

It wasn't the cheeriest of morning greetings. Hannah thought of poor Gordon, faced with this sort of grumping first thing every day. She looked from Elvira to her mother, wondering if Daisy, too, was out of sorts.

"Morning, dear." Daisy sounded all right. She was drying her face and arms and using deodorant and then spritzing on cologne from her travel case. "This slop bucket is getting full. Where do you suppose we're supposed to empty it?" She might sound more cheerful than Elvira, but Hannah noted the nervous tremor in her voice.

"You aren't meant to fill the basin to the brim that way, Daisy," Elvira snapped. "You have to conserve water when it doesn't come out of a tap. Leave the bucket. Surely there's some sort of maid service in this joint."

Daisy turned to Hannah. "We tried not to wake you, dear. Are you stiff from sleeping on that pallet?" She bent over her suitcase to get her clothes, and Hannah felt shock ripple through her. In the bright morning light, Daisy's body was skeletal, little more than skin stretched over delicate bone. The sight was disturbing. Daisy seemed so very fragile.

Hannah suddenly felt panicky. What if her mother should get sick on this trip? Wherever they were, it felt a long way from modern-day Victoria and medical services.

"Hannah?" Daisy turned and looked at her. "Did you hear me, dear? I asked you how you slept."

"Not too bad." Hannah yawned and untangled her sleep shirt. She struggled to her feet, peering out the window. It was a glorious day, sunny with blue skies. She found she was looking down into the small, tidy backyard of the Nugget. There was a patch of grass and a collection of rough log sheds. Beyond the yard was the swiftly flowing creek.

As she watched, Angus came through a back gate carrying two large buckets of water. To Hannah's surprise, Klaus was trotting along at his side. They disappeared into the lower part of the building.

"Klaus is out there with Angus?" Hannah had never known the dog to take to a stranger.

"He had to pee, your mother wasn't dressed, and there were any number of men clattering up and down the stairs," Elvira snapped. "So the dog went out with Angus. That boy brought us up a single pitcher of warmish water. He says the men in the other rooms only get a pitcher morning and night, and that it'll be noon before there's enough hot water for a bath, if you can believe that." She went on, "I must say, this is really roughing it, which is why I never went camping with Gordon. And I'd kill for a cup of good hot coffee right this moment. I can't be expected to start the day without coffee. I asked Angus to bring some up, but he's slow-witted. I'm not sure he even understood. Shall I wash next, or will you, Hannah?"

"Go ahead. I'm not really awake yet." Elvira's bad temper was depressing first thing in the morning. Hannah found her duffel bag and extracted her hairbrush. She dragged it through her hair, wondering how long it would take Elvira to give her a headache.

Daisy was putting on blue slacks and a button-front blouse, and now she sounded out of sorts too.

"That's unkind of you, Elvira, talking that way about Angus. Klaus has certainly taken to him, and Klaus is an excellent judge of character."

Elvira snorted. "The day I'd rely on an animal to make my judgments for me, I'd have to be soft in the head."

Daisy's head came up and her lips trembled. Hannah felt like lying down on her thin pallet, pulling the quilt over her head, and howling with frustration. She *hated* wrangling first thing in the morning. She *hated* being here with these two. She wanted to be home, in her own little apartment, with her radio playing soft FM music, unlimited hot water pouring over her from her shower, and the pleasing prospect ahead of her of a challenging day spent at her job.

And good strong coffee dripping through her machine. She had to admit that Elvira had a point about the lack of coffee.

"I'm done. You'd better use what little's left of this water, Hannah, before it gets any colder." Elvira dried herself briskly and shoved her legs into black slacks, pulling on an oversized white shirt as if it was a mortal enemy.

"Why don't you two go on down and locate the restaurant Mr. McGraw mentioned?" Hannah suggested. "I'll come as soon as I'm ready."

"Logan. He distinctly said his name was Logan, and that's what I intend to call him. But you can suit yourself, of course." Elvira shouldered her huge handbag and stalked to the door. With her hand on the doorknob, she turned. "Daisy, are you coming or not?"

It seemed pure luxury to have them finally shut the door behind them. With a sigh of relief, Hannah shucked off her cotton sleepshirt and refilled the basin with an inch of warm water and an icy dipperful from the bucket, scrubbing sleep from her eyes and shivering as she sponged the rest of herself with the rough washcloth. It was a laborious way to have a minibath, but when she was done, she felt much better. A glance in the mirror told her that the lump on her forehead had gone down a little overnight.

She formed her long, heavy hair into a single braid and put on fresh underwear, clean jeans, and a thin, loose black cotton T-shirt. If it got really hot later, she decided, she'd change to shorts; she'd brought two pair along. She used a dash of mascara and some lip gloss and shoved her bare feet into her sandals, still damp from the river.

She'd have to pay a necessary visit to the outhouse and then find Wake-Up Jake's and get some coffee. She'd studiously avoided even looking at the calendar, and she refused to glance at it now as she grabbed her handbag and made her way out the door. Even so, the year was emblazoned on her mind's eye in indelible ink, and she had to quell a spurt of panic.

The air in the corridor smelled bad, of cigar smoke, stale beer, and male sweat. The doors to the other rooms were all closed. She wrinkled her nose, trotted down the stairs, turned left, and found a door that led to a large, deserted, and dilapidated kitchen. It, too, was empty. It was long and narrow, with two windows, a back door, and another that she discovered led to a lean-to shed.

The outhouse was clean enough, but it left a great deal to be desired as far as toilets went, and tissue consisted of old torn-up newspapers. She studiously avoided looking at the date on any of them before she hurried back into the house and scrubbed her hands at the basin by the door. Then she made her way to the front of the building, glancing into the pub as she passed.

Logan McGraw was there, hair tied back in a clump on his neck, white shirt rolled to the elbows and open at the throat. His bare forearms were corded with muscle and covered in a dark mat of hair. All the chairs were up on the tables, and with wide, graceful sweeps of his arms, he was spreading fresh sawdust from a bucket onto the clean-swept wooden floor. He was whistling a cheerful tune, and for a moment Hannah stood and frankly admired him. The man was even better looking than she remembered.

He turned and caught sight of her. "Morning, Miss Gilmore."

It didn't seem necessary to be quite so formal, Hannah decided. He had come to their rescue last night, and she was grateful.

"My name's Hannah. Good morning—ummm, Logan."

His white teeth flashed behind his mustache. "I trust you slept well, Hannah?"

His deep voice seemed to linger over the syllables of her name, turning what had always seemed to her ordinary and unattractive into something exotic. She returned his smile.

After Elvira, it was a pleasure to meet someone who wasn't cranky. "I slept really well, thanks. In fact, I slept late, Mom and Elvira have already gone to that cafe you suggested for breakfast. Can you tell me how to get there?"

"I'd be pleased to escort you." He rolled down his shirtsleeves, fastened the buttons at his neck, and lifted a dark suit jacket from the coat-tree near the door. He slipped his arms into it, settling it on his broad shoulders and donning a Stetson.

"I'll be at Wake-Up Jake's if you need me, Sam," he called to a man stacking glasses behind the bar.

Hannah stopped at the door for a moment, her heart beginning to hammer as she looked apprehensively up and down the street. Her eyes were dazzled at first by the bright sunlight, and she was hoping against hope that this morning all the confusion of the night before would disappear, that it would be obvious that the town was a clever tourist trap or the movie set Elvira had thought it to be.

But as she walked along the crooked boardwalk, she knew it wasn't so, and her heart sank. Everywhere she looked were indications that the twentieth century had somehow bypassed this town . . . or hadn't yet arrived?

She walked along beside Logan, trying frantically to find an explanation for what was patently impossible.

What she was looking at was quite simply a bustling mining center straight out of the last century. There were men everywhere, just as there'd been the evening before. The narrow roadway in front of the Nugget was dusty, busy, and smelly. There seemed to be animal droppings of one sort or another every few feet.

Logan moved in front of her to shield her from the worst of the dust as a team of horses passed, pulling a wagon loaded with lumber.

Several rough-looking men openly stared at her as they hurried along the street pushing some sort of barrow with an assortment of buckets and spades piled on it.

A man ambling past on horseback gave her a half bow and swept his western hat off in a courtly gesture. Across the street, in the open doorway of a building whose hand-lettered sign read BLACKSMITH, a heavily muscled man in a leather apron fanned an open fire and then thrust a piece of iron into the blaze.

From the door of a bakery came the enticing odor of fresh bread, but it seemed that every second establishment was a saloon, and even at this early hour, men were gathered inside, their voices loud and boisterous.

And then a short, round woman stepped out from the doorway of the Post Office, coming towards them, a handbag tucked under her arm.

She wore a dark green dress that reached her ankles and covered her wrists. Her hair was swept up and a hat was perched on top of its intricate rolls.

After so many men, Hannah wanted to run over and embrace her. Instead, she waved a hand and smiled. "Hi. Good morning."

The woman's shocked gaze raked over Hannah, head to foot and back again, and then, with a lift of her chin she turned away. She hurried down the steps, picked up her skirts, and crossed the street.

Hannah stood and stared after her, shocked and hurt at the blatant snub. "Who . . . who is that?"

"Mrs. Heatherington." Logan's voice was carefully noncommittal. "The bootmaker's wife."

For some reason, the woman's dress and her unfriendly manner held a harsh reality that broke down the last shred of denial Hannah could muster.

She no longer had any doubts that she was in Barkerville. Against all reason, she also knew now that the date Logan had supplied the night before was accurate.

It was July 8th, 1868.

She had to stop and lean against the side of the nearest wooden building, because she felt nauseated and very, very dizzy.

Chapter Seven

"Hannah? Are you feeling ill?" Logan took her arm, his forehead creased in a frown.

She couldn't answer, because for the first time in her life, she thought she was going to faint. She forced herself to draw in deep breaths, and slowly the sick sensation in her middle disappeared, but her mind went over and over the situation like a mouse in a maze.

How could this have happened? Time travel was a fantasy, a device used by science-fiction writers and moviemakers, but certainly not something that happened to ordinary people like her, or her mother, or Elvira.

"Are you all right?" He'd slid an arm around her waist and was supporting her.

"Yes. That is, I . . . I think so." She drew in a

shaky, shallow breath that hurt her chest. "Yes, I'm—I'll be fine in a moment. It's—it's just—"

But she couldn't tell him. She couldn't explain, because she didn't understand any of it herself. No wonder he'd looked at her last night as if she belonged in an institution.

Had she suddenly gone mad? Was this whole thing happening only in her mind, while her body was in a locked ward?

The strong male arm at her waist didn't feel like an illusion. Shaky but no longer dizzy, she thanked him and drew away.

"Wake-Up Jake's is not far, just along here." His eyes stayed on her, and he walked close beside her. Together they climbed up and down the series of uneven platforms that constituted a sidewalk. All the buildings were built on log posts three or four feet above the ground, but each building was a different height from its neighbor, and so was the boardwalk in front of it.

Stunned and bewildered, Hannah stumbled twice, and Logan caught her, steadying her when she might have fallen. She was conscious of him close beside her and grateful for his support.

"Careful, you can break an ankle on this infernal boardwalk," he cautioned. "It's most treacherous at night. There's been more than one broken leg." He grinned, obviously trying to cheer her. "However, the accidents were related more to whiskey than the sidewalk."

Maybe she could get through this if she concentrated only on the present moment.

"Why . . . why is it so uneven?" She didn't care, but it was something to focus on.

"Each merchant is responsible for the portion in front of his establishment."

"And why are the buildings all above the street this way?"

"To protect them from the spring flooding of William's Creek. Freshet was nearly over when I arrived this spring, but I'm told the water runs like a small river down this street during runoff."

Hannah could feel the glances she attracted from every pair of male eyes in the vicinity.

"Why are there so many men and so few women?"

Logan gave her a curious glance. "Barkerville is a gold rush town. Until the Cariboo Road was built three years ago, the trail in here was too strenuous for all but the hardiest women. Even now, females are few, and in great demand. Any unattached woman can pick and choose among suitors."

"Is that why everyone's staring at me this way? And why did that woman act the way she did?"

He hesitated. "I do believe it has something to do with the manner in which you're dressed." He seemed to be trying to choose his words carefully. "It's your—uh, britches that are attracting all the attention, Hannah."

"My jeans?" She thought of the way Mrs. Heatherington was dressed and realized he was probably right. Women in this time and place didn't wear jeans. Had she packed any dresses? She couldn't remember. On the verge of hysteria, she thought that she really should have brought along the book of etiquette Brad's mother had given her. It probably explained exactly what to do in predicaments like this.

The whole thing must have its funny side, but she couldn't even smile. In fact, she felt a lot like crying.

"Here we are." He led the way up a final wooden stairway to double-fronted glass doors with WAKE-UP JAKE'S lettered on them.

Logan held the door open for her and, still in a daze, Hannah walked in.

The smell of frying bacon and the welcome aroma of hot coffee were at least familiar. The large dining room had a long table down the center with numerous smaller tables scattered here and there.

Here, too, the customers were all male, and when Hannah entered, every head in the place turned her way. She did her best to ignore them, walking past without making eye contact, focusing her attention on her mother and Elvira, but horribly conscious now of her tight-fitting jeans.

They were seated in front of a window at the far end of the room. As Hannah drew closer, she saw that they had heaping plates in front of them, but they didn't seem to be eating. They, too, were attracting a great deal of attention from the men in the room.

When they were close, Hannah realized that Daisy was on the verge of tears. Elvira looked stern behind her glasses, but when she turned to gaze up at Hannah, her chin wobbled.

"Good morning, Miss Elvira, Miss Daisy." Logan removed his hat and gave them each a polite bow as he drew out a chair and held it for Hannah.

"Good morning, Logan. You will stay and have breakfast with us?" There was a note of desperation in Elvira's tone.

"We insist. We'd like to repay you for your hospitality." Daisy gestured to a chair, and her hand was trembling.

Hannah silently willed him to refuse. In light of what she now knew, she and Daisy and Elvira had urgent things to talk over.

Logan hesitated, but after a glance around the room, he sat down. "That's most kind of you. I've eaten, but I'd enjoy a cup of coffee."

There was a rustling and an audible sigh from the nearby tables of men, and it dawned on Hannah that Logan was acting as a sort of bodyguard, buffering them from any unwanted attention from the other men in the room.

He waved a hand at the young male waiter. "There's not a lot of choice as far as the menu goes, I'm afraid," he apologized to Hannah. "Breakfast here is porridge, bacon, beans, toast, and coffee."

"Just some toast and coffee," Hannah told the waiter. She wasn't hungry at all. Her stomach felt as if she'd been punched.

The moment the young man moved away, Daisy reached out and gripped Hannah's hand hard. "I'm so glad you're finally here, Hannah." The words tumbled out in a panicked flood, and Daisy's face crumpled as tears began trickling down her cheeks. "I don't understand what's going on and neither does Elvira, but something's not right about this. All these men, staring and staring at us—"

She indicated the other patrons with a surreptitious little wave of her hand. "They began coming over to our table the moment we sat down, one after another, asking us the most personal questions, about whether we're married, and what our plans are. Hannah, one even *proposed* to me, if you can believe it, not five minutes ago. I'd never laid eyes on him in my life, and I really think he meant it."

Daisy sniffled and Elvira handed her a tissue. "And outside . . . it's so primitive. Did you see all those horses? And men *spitting* everywhere." Panic was beginning to make her voice quaver. "And there's no telephone. I asked the waiter, but he didn't seem to know what I was talking about. And Elvira insisted I leave Klaus with that boy, Angus, because of all the horses, and now I'm worried about that, too. What if he steals Klaus?" Her face crumpled and she mopped at it with the tissue.

Daisy's tears were a reminder to Hannah that her mother wasn't going to be very much help in this mess, and she felt a familiar surge of annoyance.

"Klaus is the least of our worries, Mom. I'm sure he's absolutely safe with Angus."

Logan nodded. "You have my word on that. The boy's wonderful with animals."

Daisy was reassured. She blew her nose and took a sip of her coffee.

Hannah summoned up strength she wasn't sure was going to be adequate for the situation.

"I think we've somehow gone through a time warp," she announced. "We've ended up in Barkerville, during the gold rush." Preposterous as her theory was, just stating it aloud made Hannah feel a little better, although she was terribly conscious of Logan sitting at her side, listening and undoubtedly thinking she was nuts.

Daisy didn't scream or faint, as Hannah thought she might. It was Elvira who grew agitated, her face reddening.

"That's simply not possible," she said, emphasizing the words by banging on the table with her hand. "We drove through Quesnel, the modern town, not half an hour before we went off that bridge. If it was there yesterday, it must be there today. And the van—it's certainly not going anywhere, stuck down in that river. We just need to go back to that bridge, that's all. There must be police in this town. We can ask them to help."

Hannah understood how Elvira felt, and what she was proposing was pretty logical. If the van and the town of Quesnel had existed yesterday afternoon, then surely they must still be there today.

The waiter brought thick slices of burned toast and set them in front of her, along with a large earthenware mug filled with coffee, and Hannah took a grateful sip. It was hot, strong, and every bit as good as the coffee she brewed herself. It was reassuring to find even one small familiar thing here, and a faint ray of hope began to blossom as she took another sip and thought over Elvira's suggestion.

It made sense. If they'd come through some kind of time gate yesterday, surely they could go back through it today. And Elvira was right about reporting their predicament to the police. At least it was a place to start.

"Where is the police station, Logan?" She turned to find him studying her, an unreadable expression in his deep blue eyes.

"Barkerville has no police barracks. Despite the occasional theft of gold such as you witnessed yesterday, there's not a lot of crime here. There is a jail, down the street a ways. The postmaster here in Barkerville, John Bowran, is also the constable, but I doubt he could be much help to you. It's Judge Baillie Begbie who is in charge of law and order in the Cariboo."

"Well, then, we'll pay him a visit as soon as we're finished here." Feeling better for having made the decision, Hannah realized she was hungry after all. She took a bite of the toast, trying to find portions that weren't charred.

"Judge Begbie is a circuit judge," Logan explained in a patient tone that Hannah found annoying. He sounded as if he were humoring them. "He has a residence in Richfield, but he's off dispensing justice somewhere else at the moment. He's not expected back until August."

Hannah shoved the toast away. "Well, then, we'll just have to find some way to get back to that bridge on our own. C'mon, Mom, Elvira. Let's go."

"Wait just a moment, Hannah." Logan put a restraining hand on her arm. "You arrived late last night, and you're determined to travel back along the Cariboo Road today?"

"Absolutely." She gave him a challenging look. "What sort of transportation is there between here and Quesnel?"

"The stagecoach makes the journey once a week, but you've missed it. It left yesterday morning."

"So what else is there?" A sense of desperation was growing in her. "Can't we hire something?"

He gave her a considering look. "I'll arrange for a buggy if you'll explain to me exactly why you need to make this journey today. I'm not certain I understand."

She looked directly into his eyes, and her tone conveyed her anxiety as she searched for words.

"Something happened to us on the road from Quesnel last night. We're from a different time, a time far in the future—1997. We have to get back there, Logan. It's just not possible for us to stay here. We were driving along the road in my van—" She saw the puzzled look on his face and struggled to find a word that he'd understand. "My . . . vehicle. The . . . the . . . thing we were riding in to get here. I was driving. We came to a wooden bridge, and it was foggy."

She shivered, remembering the thick mist, the way the horse had balked at going through it. Now she wished they'd paid attention to the poor animal's reaction and headed back the way they'd come.

"It was scary. Anyhow, right in the middle of this long bridge, I ran into Billy Renton's wagon. His horse, actually. My . . . vehicle went off the bridge into the water." It was the best she could do at explaining. She leaned forward and put a hand on his arm, squeezing it to emphasize her urgency.

"Logan, we need to go back to that place, right away. We *have* to find a way back to where we belong. I'm certain the location wasn't more than ten miles from here. Do you understand?" She could see that he didn't, but then, neither did she, not really.

He considered for a long moment, studying her face, and at last seemed to come to some conclusion.

"I'm trying to understand, although it's a far-fetched tale at best. The only bridge I know of is little more than a few logs across William's creek."

"That must be it." All three women nodded emphatically.

Logan looked into Hannah's eyes. "I'll take you there. I'll go now and arrange for a buggy. Sam can keep an eye on the saloon for me."

Hannah stood up. Instantly she felt the barrage of dozens of pairs of eyes, focused on her in a way that was unnerving.

Elvira and Daisy also got to their feet.

Obviously feeling better now that they had a plan, Elvira glared at the nearest table of men. "I'll pay the bill," she announced, marching across the room to the cash register.

Daisy put one hand on Logan's arm and the other on Hannah's as they made their way towards the door. In spite of herself, Hannah was relieved to have Logan there. The sheer number of men and their avid interest was somehow threatening.

Logan responded to a chorus of eager greetings, calling numerous men by name, courteous but not pausing to make introductions. Again there was a subtle but definite indication that they were under his protection.

He held the door open for Daisy and Hannah and they hurried through, relieved to be outside.

"Mornin', Logan." A black man wearing a gray suit tipped his bowler hat, smiled a friendly greeting at them all, and stood waiting expectantly. Hannah noted that he didn't so much as glance at her jeans.

"Morning." Logan smiled a greeting this time. "Moses, I'd like you to meet Mrs. Daisy Gilmore and her daughter, Miss Hannah. Ladies, may I present Wellington Moses, who has the barbershop just down the street."

"Pleased to make your acquaintance." Moses swept his hat off and gave them a courtly bow. "And where are you ladies from, if I may ask?"

Hannah and Daisy looked at one another. The question wasn't easy to answer.

"Victoria," Hannah finally said, and she noticed that Logan looked relieved at her simple answer. He probably didn't want people to think he'd befriended lunatics, Hannah concluded.

"Victoria? Why, I came from there myself.

Pleasant town, Victoria. Well, it's a pleasure to make your acquaintance." The dapper little man strolled off down the street.

"I'll just make certain Elvira is managing all right." Logan turned back into the restaurant, and through the glass in the door, Hannah saw Elvira obviously having an argument with the heavyset man behind the till.

As Hannah watched, Logan reached in his pocket and handed the man a small canvas sack. He shook something into a scale as a scarlet-faced Elvira came bursting out the door.

"That—that just takes the cake," Elvira sputtered. She was clutching a twenty-dollar bill in her fist, and she waved it at Daisy and Hannah, her nostrils flaring, brown eyes flashing fire. "That—that imbecile in there wouldn't accept my money. He insisted it wasn't proper currency."

"May I see that?" Logan was beside her, and he reached out and took the bill from Elvira, smoothing it out and studying it. He handed it back without comment, but his eyes caught and held Hannah's, and she saw puzzlement and a sort of wariness there.

By this time, Hannah didn't need any further reminders of where they were or what horrendous complications their time travel could cause. She hadn't given any thought to the fact that money would certainly be different in 1868, but it made sense when she thought about it, as much sense as anything was making this morning.

So now they were marooned in another century without a usable penny to their names, and it was a foregone conclusion that no one took Visa.

They couldn't expect Logan to feed them as well as give them lodging. And she'd planned to pay him for taking them back to the bridge.

She frowned, looking up and down the street, and a sign caught her eye. PAINLESS TOOTH EXTRACTION, it read. OFFICE FEE, $5.00, OR EQUIVALENT IN GOLD.

She suddenly remembered reaching out a hand the night before at Logan's urging, and having the man called Dutch Charlie place what seemed to be heavy pebbles in her palm. She'd dumped them in her purse without a second glance, believing the whole situation to be some sort of hoax, but now she dug in the bottom of her bag.

Her fingers closed over several heavy shapes and she pulled them out.

They were warm and living, and they glinted in the sunlight. Gold—the very reason for this town's existence.

In spite of everything that had happened, Hannah felt a powerful thrill shoot through her. For the first time in her life, she was holding nuggets of gold.

It was an intoxicating feeling. She looked

around, at the miners milling about, at the crude buildings, and again she felt the excitement in the air, the sense of aliveness that she'd felt hovering over this town the night before.

She was actually here, at the time of the Cariboo Gold Rush. Men were coming here from the ends of the earth to find this precious metal. For the first time, the enormity of what had occurred overwhelmed her, and instead of being terrifying, it was exciting.

She held her palm out to Logan. "We can't have you paying our expenses. I don't have a clue how this gold thing works, but will this cover our breakfast?"

"It was my pleasure," he said. "I don't want to be repaid."

"But I insist." Hannah kept her hand extended. "We're not your responsibility, and you must let me pay for our food at least. Is this enough?"

He glanced down and for the first time she heard him laugh aloud.

"Gold is selling at twenty dollars an ounce. You have enough there to pay for three meals a day for at least a month, even at the inflated prices here in Barkerville."

Astounded, she stared down at the nuggets. "I do?"

"Absolutely. I take gold in payment in the saloon. Everyone uses it here as currency. I believe Dutch Charlie gave you several thousand dollars' worth of nuggets last night."

Hannah's mouth dropped open. For heaven's sake!

She hadn't been here twenty-four hours, and already she was well on the way to getting rich.

For just one mad instant, she wondered if maybe they ought to stick around instead of rushing back to the next century.

Chapter Eight

"Did you come to Barkerville to find gold, Logan?"

They were bouncing through town in a buggy that felt as though it had no springs, and Hannah's bottom was bruised before they'd even left the town behind.

"No, I didn't." The answer was abrupt, and he didn't elaborate. Hannah stared at the horse's rump and wondered what to say next. Logan wasn't being very talkative.

The buggy had a small back seat and barely enough room up front for the driver and a passenger. Daisy and Elvira had climbed in the back with Klaus and all the luggage, and Hannah had found herself seated directly behind the horse, very close to Logan.

Hannah slid a glance at him. At close range, his profile was rugged, his nose a bit crooked, as if it had been broken at some point. His hair was tied back at the nape with a leather thong, and his mustache emphasized his square jaw. He didn't resemble the hard-bitten miners in Barkerville. He was just as strong, just as tanned and brawny, but there was something different about him, something dark and faintly dangerous. She was curious about him.

"Where are you from, Logan? Where did you grow up?"

"California. A town called San Jose." Again the answer was curt.

"San Jose? I've heard of it, of course, although I've never been there," Hannah said. "One of my friends at the hospital has a sister who lives near there. She flies down all the time to see her. Isn't San Jose the center of Silicon Valley?"

Logan turned and gave her one of the narrow-eyed looks she'd come to recognize. Once again, she realized she'd said something that didn't fit in the century she was in. Darn, conversation here was like navigating through a verbal minefield.

Fortunately, Daisy and Elvira started asking questions just then about gold mining, and Logan became an excellent tour guide. He pointed out spots all along the creek where men had staked gold claims and were working them.

"What are those noisy waterwheels for?" Elvira leaned forward and pointed as they passed one.

"They're called Cornish wheels. I'm told they date back to the Roman occupation of Britain," he explained. "They power pumps that drain underground shafts, and they power winches that raise buckets of gravel to the surface."

As they left the sounds of the town behind, the hills echoed with the thud of axes and the cracking and crashing of falling trees. Miners were building mine shafts and cabins, and now and then they could be heard shouting to one another down the shafts as they lowered buckets to workers below.

"There are different types of mining taking place all over the region," Logan explained as the buggy navigated the narrow trail Hannah remembered from the night before.

"Some men are digging tunnels into the hills above us because they think that the gold originally found in William's Creek might have washed down from there." The buggy rounded a corner, and now there was a clear view of the creek below them and some of the activity going on.

"Those men are sluicing," Logan said, pointing out a long wooden trough where workers at one end were throwing in sand and gravel they'd dug from the nearby hillside.

"They're using a stream of water from the hillside. It runs down the sluice to wash gold from the dirt."

"It looks crowded along the creek," Hannah said, peering at what looked like hundreds of miners, all working along the banks.

Logan nodded agreement. "It is. There's no room to stake more claims near Barkerville. Newcomers can try their luck on other creeks, or they can work someone else's mining claim for wages. Or, if they have enough money, they can pay to join an existing mining company."

"Do any women file claims?" Hannah was curious.

"Very rarely. A few have applied for mining certificates, but mostly that's just a way for the husband to hold an extra share or work a claim in his wife's name."

"Doesn't sound very fair."

He shot her an amused glance. "Barkerville's a man's town," he commented. "Besides, mining's hard work."

"Women can do the same work men can," she insisted. "Where we come from, some women are miners."

He grinned. "Is that what you do, Hannah? Are you a miner?" His tone was teasing.

"Nope. I work in a hospital. I'm a social worker."

His frown relayed total incomprehension, and again she struggled for words that would explain her job in terms he'd recognize. "I work with people who have problems, maybe with their families or with the hospital staff, or maybe adjusting to illness or accident, something that has happened to them physically."

"How do you do this social work?"

"A lot of it is just talking. When people are upset, it often helps them when you listen or ask questions. If you ask the right ones, eventually they figure out themselves what they should do."

"You're paid a wage for this?" There was an incredulous tone to his voice, and Hannah bristled.

"Of course. Very good money," she emphasized. She was tempted to tell him how much, but she realized that there was probably no fair comparison between wages in this time and in hers.

"And who pays you for all this talking?"

"The hospital. My job is considered valuable and necessary." She'd had enough of his skepticism. "What about you, Logan? Did you grow up running a saloon back in San Jose?" There was sarcasm in her voice, and she didn't care. He'd scoffed at her job, hadn't he?

A sardonic grin tilted his mouth for an instant. "Hardly. My father is a clergyman there."

Again, he obviously wasn't going to volunteer anything more, and Hannah told herself it was rude to pry, even though she was madly curious.

"Oh, look there," Elvira cried out from behind them. Just ahead of the buggy, a deer stepped out on the road for a moment, and then leaped gracefully into the trees.

Daisy and Elvira oohed and ahhed, and Logan began telling them a story about a black bear that had wandered into Barkerville and broken into the supply cellar of Wake-Up Jake's, and again the conversation became general.

The noonday sun grew warmer in the blue sky above them, and the miles passed slowly beneath the wheels of the buggy and the hooves of the horse.

Hannah began watching anxiously for anything familiar from the previous night, but so far nothing registered.

"Elvira, do you remember any landmarks that were near that bridge?" It seemed to Hannah that they must be close to the area by now. According to her watch, several hours had passed since they'd left Barkerville, and she had a feeling the buggy was going along somewhat faster than the wagon had.

Elvira couldn't remember anything special, and neither could Daisy. All three women now became quiet and tense, watching the road ahead expectantly. The small river wound along, but everything looked different in the daylight.

"This is the bridge I spoke of," Logan announced after a time, and Hannah's heart sank.

It was a small log affair, nothing like the long one she remembered, even though the steep bank down to the creek might have been the same.

It couldn't be, though, because there was no sign of her van.

"Can we go a bit farther?"

Obligingly, Logan drove the horse across the logs.

They bumped along the trail for another half hour, but there was no sign of that other bridge. There was only the stream, the woods, and the rough track that passed for a road. When they began to pass through a narrow rocky canyon, Hannah knew for certain they'd come too far.

Her voice strained, she told Logan so, adding, "There must be another road. We must have somehow turned off onto another road last night. Are you sure there isn't a fork somewhere?" But she'd been watching closely, and she knew there wasn't.

Logan turned the horse and buggy. "I assure you, this is the only road of any sort between Quesnellemouth and Barkerville."

His words confirmed Hannah's worst fears. The bridge, the van, the route back to their own time, were gone. It was a terrible disappointment, and behind her, Hannah heard Elvira start crying.

Hannah didn't feel like crying; instead, she wanted to punch something, rage, scream out her frustration at whatever quirk of fate had landed her where she was.

Her frustration and anger burst from her in a torrent of words. "I'm supposed to be getting married in less than two weeks. The wedding's all planned. Worse yet, it's all paid for, the cake's ordered, the dress is being altered, gifts have arrived already. Brad didn't want me to go on this trip in the first place. Now he's going to be furious when it dawns on him I'm not coming back. And I can't even let him know why."

"Brad is your fiancé?"

Hannah nodded.

"Then I should think he'd be worried rather than angry," Logan commented in a dry tone.

Hannah's anger found a target. "Of course he'll be worried," she snapped. "How would you feel if your bride-to-be drove off on a Friday for a simple little weekend trip, and disappeared? He'll have the R.C.M.P. alerted, and there'll be a province-wide alarm." A horrible thought struck her. "When . . . if they find the van where we left it in that creek, they'll think we're all dead."

Elvira was sniffling into a tissue, and she wailed, "Gordon will never know what really happened to me. I never thought the day would come when I'd miss him, but I do."

It slowly dawned on Hannah that Daisy was the calmest of the three women.

"You okay, Mom?" Hannah turned to look at

her. Daisy looked back at her with a composed expression.

"I guess we'll just have to make the best of this," she said. For someone who'd spent most of the past year crying, her mother was being amazingly optimistic, Hannah thought.

Daisy even managed a small smile. "We're all in this together, dear, and that's a comfort, isn't it? It would be so awful if it were only one of us."

Hannah turned around again and stared at the rutted, empty road with the trees overhanging it, and it seemed symbolic. There was no wide, modern road to take her back to where she'd been. There was only this winding dirt trail through thick woods, leading to a place she didn't want to go, a place filled with hundreds of wild men whose hungry eyes made her feel like a thing instead of a person.

It was impossible to absorb the implications of what had happened all at once. Hannah felt she could only break off tiny pieces and examine them one at a time, because looking at the entire scenario would send her into full-fledged panic.

She was panicking anyway. If there was no way back, then this pointless journey through time was permanent. She'd live the rest of her life in an era devoid of everything she was accustomed to—cars, microwaves, computers, probably even tampons.

It was a concept so overwhelming that it made her insides tremble. There were so many issues to think about. She tried to calm herself by sorting them out in order of importance.

There were the immediate ones, like money. Elvira might be able to get work at the hospital, but Hannah knew she was going to have to be financially responsible for Daisy. Her mother had never worked outside her home, and it didn't seem likely she'd start now.

Thank goodness they had the gold Dutch Charlie had given her. It would be an enormous help, but they had to think of it as an emergency fund, she decided.

She'd have to find work, and Logan's reaction when she'd tried to describe what a social worker did was proof that there wouldn't be any openings for someone with her specialty in Barkerville. She'd have to get some other sort of job. The idea was both frightening and depressing, and she wasn't even aware at first that Logan had stopped the buggy beneath some trees, close to the stream.

"Hannah?" His large, warm hand on her forearm startled her. He was looking at her with kindness and concern, and she realized that she was on the verge of hysteria and that somehow he knew it.

His strong shoulder was very close to hers, and the temptation to just plop her head there and sob out her fear and anxiety was almost overwhelming.

You don't know him well enough to cry all over him, the rational, stern part of her brain warned. And there were Elvira and Daisy to consider, too. Elvira was still gulping and sobbing behind her. It wouldn't do any good for her to collapse as well, Hannah lectured herself.

"This is a good spot to have our lunch, don't you think?" Logan's voice was casual, and the simple question was calming. "Some food would make you all feel better."

When they were walking home from the restaurant that morning, Daisy had gone into the bakery in Barkerville and, with one of the gold nuggets, bought what was available for a picnic.

Logan gave Hannah's arm a reassuring squeeze and in a single lithe movement leaped down from the buggy's seat to the grass, holding out a hand for her. She took it, jumping down beside him. Elvira gave one last fierce honk into a tissue, and then she and Daisy and Klaus also climbed down with Logan's assistance.

Soon they were all busy spreading the lunch on towels on the grass, and Logan was right. After Hannah had eaten a meat pie and a scone, which proved delicious, she felt much better. They drank water from the stream, the coldest, sweetest water Hannah had ever tasted.

They packed up the food that was left, and Daisy and Elvira wandered off after Klaus, talking to each other in low, worried tones.

Klaus was chasing butterflies through the deep grass, barking and growling as if engaged in mortal combat. Logan laughed at him and even Hannah had to smile.

Logan began stacking the women's travel bags more efficiently in the back of the buggy, and Hannah went over to help. She pushed her nylon bag firmly into a corner, and it struck her that the few toiletries and changes of clothing in the bag were now all the possessions she owned in the world. Again, she struggled to hold back the tears that threatened.

Logan was watching her. "I understand that this trip was a severe disappointment for you, Hannah. Will you be staying on in Barkerville now?"

"I don't know." She hadn't given it any thought. "For the time being we will be. I guess it would be the same year no matter where we went?"

His smile flashed, but it was sympathetic. "I believe it would, yes."

"Then I can't see that it matters where we're living right now. We don't have enough money to travel very far anyhow. So Barkerville's as good as anywhere, I guess."

Her voice betrayed how despondent she felt. She stared down at her sandals, shoulders slumped, arms crossed on her breasts. "Eventually I think I'd like to go back to Victoria."

But would she be able to stand it, seeing the city where she was born with none of the familiar places she loved? Her mother's home, her apartment, the hospital . . . none of them would be there. Tears of self-pity and fear filled her eyes and trickled down her cheeks.

He came close to her and gently tipped her chin up with a forefinger, stroking away the tears. "This man Brad you're pledged to marry." His voice was thoughtful. "Is it he you mourn, Hannah? Is he the reason you're so distressed?"

Hannah sniffed and didn't answer for a moment, searching for an honest response. She did miss Brad, of course, but there were many other things she missed as well.

Logan fished a clean white handkerchief out of a pocket and handed it to her.

"I do miss Brad. We were about to be married," she slowly admitted, using the handkerchief to dab at her eyes and nose. "But I also miss my friends, my job, my . . . my apartment, my clothes, my furniture, my mother's house. I miss the city where I grew up. And it's not as if I can go back and visit, because they're gone now, aren't they? They're lost to me. I can't go back, not unless a miracle comes along. It scares me. It makes me feel like a homeless person."

He stood quietly looking down at her. "I don't understand exactly where it is you come from. I don't understand this talk of a future time, but

I know you're not from anywhere I'm familiar with. Your clothing, your manner, the things you speak of, are all foreign to me."

"Yeah. Well, it's the same for me with you. For all of us. Everything's weird, like falling into the pages of some history book. It's really scary."

He nodded. "I can see that it would be." His half-smile was sardonic. "If it's any consolation, Barkerville wasn't at all familiar to me either when I arrived."

"You never did tell me why you came."

He shook his head and looked past her, to the stream and the woods beyond it. His expression hardened for a moment. "I'm a gambler by profession. Barkerville is a good place to win gold."

His words shocked Hannah. "But I thought . . . I mean, you own the saloon. I thought you were a businessman."

"I *won* the saloon," he clarified. "In a poker game, the first week I arrived. I'd never run a business before, but I could see that there was great potential in it. Miners need a place to spend their gold, and they spend it lavishly. The man who'd owned the Nugget didn't put much effort into making his business successful. That's a great waste."

His expression hardened again, and his voice was harsh. "I despise waste of any kind."

Hannah despised gambling. She thought of her father and the money he'd lost over the years, on the stock market, in get-rich quick schemes that never panned out, in businesses that lost more money than they ever made.

There hadn't been money for her education. She'd scraped by on student loans and summer jobs. The money Michael had lost had been Daisy's, some of it originally from the great-grandfather who'd mined for gold right here in Barkerville.

The way her father and Logan went about it might be different, but in the end all gambling was the same.

She stepped back, putting distance between Logan and herself. She realized he was all the things her father had been—handsome, charming. A gambler, her shocked mind realized.

He was the last man she wanted to have anything to do with.

Chapter Nine

"We should be on our way." Her tone was curt, and she didn't look at him again. "I'll go get Mom and Elvira."

Hannah hurried off across the meadow, angry with herself for the keen disappointment she'd felt when Logan told her what he did. Why should it matter what or who he was?

On the bumpy ride back to Barkerville, Hannah insisted that Daisy ride up front with Logan. They chatted, mostly about Klaus. In the back, shoulder to shoulder with Elvira, Hannah was lost in her own thoughts, barely listening to what was being said.

"Why did you ladies decide to come to Barkerville?"

Logan was asking Daisy the very question

Hannah had asked him, and she heard her mother explaining about her great-grandfather, Ezekial Shaw, and how he'd come here and staked a claim.

"I've met Zeke," Logan said calmly, and Elvira and Hannah gaped at each other.

"He comes in the saloon now and again. He has a claim north of Richfield—I've heard it's a good one."

"I'd love to meet him." Daisy's voice was filled with excitement.

Hannah wasn't sure she wanted to. The thought of meeting her great-great-grandfather was too much right now. In fact, it made her feel queasy. There was something unnatural about it.

"I'll send word for him to come by, next time he's in town," Logan promised. "He was in last week, so it'll likely be two, three weeks before he comes again. He and his partner are shaft mining. They sink a hole forty to fifty feet deep until they reach bedrock and then take the gravel out and wash it for gold. In this good weather, they work sixteen or eighteen hours a day for weeks at a time."

Hannah tried to imagine what such a life would be like. Did they have a cabin, or were they, like so many other miners, making do with a tent?

Cabins, tents. Hannah realized she hadn't yet given any thought to where *they* were going to live. Logan had generously offered his room for one night, but now it looked as if they were going to need permanent accommodation.

Depression washed over her. It was one more problem in a pile that felt as high as the surrounding mountains, and it was going to have to be addressed right away.

"Do you know of a house we could rent, Logan?"

He turned, shaking his head. "There aren't any houses to rent, or cabins, or even rooms. That's why so many people are living in tents, and why all the trees are cut down around town. The mill can't keep up with the demand for lumber, partly because so much is needed for the mines and the flues."

"Where can we buy a tent?" She heard Elvira groan in protest.

"There's no need. You'll stay on at the Nugget until something decent comes available." His tone was definite, but Hannah wanted to refuse. She no longer wanted any part of his generosity. But there were Daisy and Elvira to consider, so she swallowed her pride and just said thank you, determined to turn the town upside down the first chance she got. She'd find them another place to live, she vowed, and soon.

Tired out from the emotional ups and downs of the day, Hannah fell into a half doze, and the sun was nearing the horizon when they again entered the noisy, dusty main street of Barkerville.

Back in Logan's room, all Hannah could think of was a bath. Hot, sweaty, and filthy from the trip, she couldn't bear the thought of still another meager sponging off in the washbasin.

"I'm going down to find us a tub and some hot water," she declared.

The noise from the saloon was deafening, but there was no one in the hallway that led to the back of the building. Hannah made her way into the deserted kitchen.

The wood range was lit, sending off dizzying waves of heat, and six buckets were sitting on the stove, filled to the brim. The water was steaming hot.

Now for a tub. Hannah opened the door to the lean-to shed at one end of the kitchen, finding neatly stacked kindling and, off in a corner, a round galvanized iron tub.

With some effort and several pauses to get her breath, she carried it up the stairs and returned for a bucket of the hot water. Outside the back door were two barrels filled with cold water, and with Elvira and Daisy helping, they carried up enough to make the water bearable.

They drew straws for the first bath, and Elvira won. They'd draped sheets over chairs to provide a modicum of privacy, and Elvira's groans of pure pleasure made Hannah's anticipation of her turn that much keener.

Of course, each batch of dirty bathwater had to be hauled down and dumped in the back yard between baths, and another pail of hot water carried up.

Hannah was carrying the buckets for her own bath up the steps just as one of Logan's boarders was coming down.

She set the buckets on the stair and pressed herself to the wall to allow him to pass. He was a burly, red-faced man, and he stopped just above her, his small, piggy eyes going from her breasts to her hips and back again before he ever looked at her face.

"Now what's a pretty little lady like you doin' carryin' water up here?" He grinned, revealing a mouthful of bad teeth. "I'm Jeb Slater, at yer service." He reached for the buckets and, before Hannah could protest, sloshed them the rest of the way up the steps and stopped at the door of Logan's room.

"Thank you, Mr. Slater." Hannah reached for the buckets, but Slater hung on.

"I'll take 'em in fer ya. Havin' a nice hot bath, huh?" He was leering at her, and the suggestive note in his voice made her skin crawl.

"Elvira, open up," Hannah called, and as she'd hoped he would, Slater set the pails down and backed away. By the time Elvira opened the door, he was sauntering down the steps. Hannah watched him for a moment, and he turned and winked at her suggestively. He gave her the creeps, and she hated the thought of him sleeping just down the hall.

But Hannah forgot about him as she slumped in the tub at last, her long legs dangling over the edge, wondering if the baths she'd had in her own time had ever felt as good.

She washed her hair, wondering how long the small bottle of apple shampoo she'd brought along would last. Daisy rinsed for her by filling the pitcher from the stand and pouring it over Hannah's head.

When she was done, she rummaged through her luggage and found that she'd packed a dress after all, a long, loose, calf-length blue one. She slipped it on, feeling better than she had since she'd left Victoria.

Daisy bathed Klaus and then they all used the last of the hot water to wash out their underwear. Elvira strung a makeshift line across the corner of the room, using a length of the rope they found hanging on a nail on one side of the wardrobe. Elvira said it was a lariat, but it made a fine clothesline.

Hannah was relieved to find Jeb Slater nowhere around when she spilled the last of the dirty water in the yard and returned the tub to its place in the shed.

She slumped into one of the wooden chairs at the kitchen table, feeling deliciously clean but totally worn out. Did she have enough energy to make it back up the stairs one last time?

Her stomach growled, reminding her that she hadn't eaten since the picnic on the road, and suddenly she wished with all her being for a telephone and a nearby pizza spot that delivered.

The kitchen door banged and Angus shambled in. He smiled and swept his wide-brimmed hat off when he saw Hannah. "Hiya, miss. Sorry I'm late."

She gestured at the empty tub. "We used all that hot water on the stove, Angus. I hope it was meant for baths."

He nodded emphatically. "Yes'm. Boss tole me before you went ta fill up the buckets so's all you ladies could have baths. I was s'posed ta carry it up fer ya, but I was over at the stables with the horses, an' I forgot." He looked crestfallen. "I always forget stuff. Sorry, miss."

"Everybody forgets things, Angus." Her mind registered the fact that Logan had assumed all along they'd be coming back here with him tonight. He'd just been humoring them, taking them on that trip.

Her stomach growled again.

"Angus, do any of the restaurants around here do take-out food?"

Angus looked blank and scratched his head.

Hannah rephrased the question. "Is there anywhere that would make supper for us women and let you bring it back here?"

Now he nodded vigorously. "Shore. Wake-Up

Jake's sends food alla time to the Hotel de France fer the whores what lives upstairs."

Hannah wondered if Angus knew what whores did for a living, and decided he probably did. She'd noticed several brothels on their way through town.

"Would you bring us three orders of dinner? I'll get you some gold, just wait here a minute."

She dashed up and retrieved the canvas sack of gold dust Daisy had received in change for a nugget at the bakery, and Angus hurried off.

There was a tin of coffee beans, a grinder, and a blue enamel pot in a cupboard, and Daisy made coffee while they waited.

Half an hour later, Angus was back with steaming containers of greasy stew, thick slices of bread, and an entire apple pie that Daisy invited Angus to share.

Although the women were too hungry to be critical, the food left a lot to be desired. The stew was poorly seasoned, with a layer of oily fat floating on its surface, and the crust on the pie was too tough to chew.

Angus was anything but fussy, however; he devoured half the pie himself, forking in one huge bite after the next.

Logan came in just as they were finishing what they could eat of the pie. Hannah had settled for scraping off the crust and eating the apples.

"I hope you don't mind our taking over your

kitchen this way. Would you like pie and coffee, Logan?" Daisy was playing hostess, gesturing to the good-sized piece of pie that Angus hadn't been able to devour.

"I'll skip the pie, but I'd enjoy coffee. Angus, you're needed in the saloon." Logan poured himself coffee from the pot and sat down in the chair Angus had hastily vacated, right beside Hannah.

Logan had obviously bathed and changed his clothing, just as the women had, and Hannah wondered how he'd managed it without carting water up and down a flight of stairs.

He was wearing a black suit, beautifully tailored to his tall frame, with a sparkling white shirt and a narrow black bow tie. His luxuriant hair was tied neatly back in its familiar tail at the nape of his neck. He smelled of cigars and some sort of aftershave.

"Evening, Hannah." He gave her a long look, and Hannah was suddenly aware that she'd left her own hair loose to dry. It was probably curling like crazy all around her head. She reached a hand up to smooth it, reminding herself sternly that she had no reason to notice how he looked, care what he thought of her, or even to be anything but polite to him.

"Hello, Logan." She stared down at her coffee cup, but it was impossible to ignore him. He was right at her elbow, and in spite of her best intentions, his presence seemed to charge the room with an excitement it hadn't had before.

Logan tried not to stare at the glorious mass of curly flaxen hair that flared around Hannah's head like a nimbus.

The saloon was overflowing with customers; he knew he shouldn't linger. He'd only come through to the kitchen to find Angus and put the boy to work clearing glasses from tables. Patrons were lined up three-deep at the bar, and every table was filled. Sam was run off his feet.

The reason for the Nugget's sudden popularity was evident to Logan. Word had gone out about the women's arrival in town, and every eager single male in the entire vicinity had turned up tonight hoping to catch a glimpse of the three females.

Their presence was good for business, but if those crowds of men got one good look at Hannah the way she appeared at this moment, he was liable to have a riot on his hands.

He hadn't seen her in anything but those britches, with her hair braided. Now she was wearing a dress that resembled a nightgown, and the feminine garment suited her wonderfully. Her glorious mass of curly golden hair framed her strong, straight features. The loose blue gown had a shocking neckline that barely came up to her collarbone, and it was sleeveless, baring her rounded shoulders and her tanned arms.

He'd already noted, as had most of the rest of

the male population, that none of these women wore a corset. Hannah's soft, full breasts and slender hips were tantalizingly hinted at under the thin cotton. Her bare ankles showed beneath the hem of the dress, and her feet were naked in their strange leather loops.

The smell of her was intoxicating, like apples warmed by the sun. He drew in a deep breath and slowly let it out again, wondering if she had any idea how damnably desirable she looked.

He hadn't been with a woman for months. His sister's death, the knowledge that Flannery had planned to use Nellie as a prostitute, had made it impossible for Logan to find ease with women in the trade, as he'd done in the past. Now each of the fallen angels had Nellie's face, and Logan felt only compassion and sorrow for them, instead of desire.

A sudden overpowering surge of raw sexual need made it unwise to get up from the table. Silently cursing his lack of control, he did his best to focus on whatever Daisy was saying in hopes that it would distract his attention enough to allow his erection to subside.

"Elvira and I were wondering why you don't serve food here, Logan? You have people renting rooms upstairs, and there's that great big dining room out there."

"I can't cook, and it's most difficult to find someone who can," he responded, trying not to even glance at Hannah.

He added, "Unfortunately, most of the cooks in town have a tendency to drink too much, and their cooking suffers."

Elvira stabbed a fork at the pie crust she'd left on her plate and wrinkled her nose. "Is that what's wrong with this? It's as tough as an old boot. Does the cook at Wake-Up Jake's drink?"

"He does, but Harry's not too good at pastry even when he's sober." Logan knew him well. "He's presently in the saloon, and I'm afraid breakfast at Jake's will suffer in direct proportion to how long he stays at the Nugget tonight."

Elvira humphed. "Well, why don't you simply send him on his way before he gets plastered?"

Logan had to grin. Elvira had a cut-and-dried way of speaking that amused him. "How much a man drinks is his own affair," he said, adding ruefully, "even when my breakfast suffers for it the next morning."

"Well, I could make you breakfast here," Daisy offered timidly. "All we'd need are some supplies."

It was something Logan hadn't considered. "What would you need?"

Daisy got up and began poking in cupboards and drawers. She found a pencil and a scrap of paper and before long had scribbled a list. "Are any of the stores still open?"

"Two of the proprietors are in the saloon. They'll be glad to accommodate me." Logan reached for the list, and Hannah spoke for the first time.

"There's not much point in stocking up on a lot of stuff, Logan, because we'll be looking for another place to stay starting tomorrow." She shot him a cool look. "I'm sure you'd like your bedroom back. We're very grateful to you, but we know we're imposing." She got up and sloshed water from the kettle into the dishbasin. She dumped the dirty dishes in and began washing them with more energy than Logan felt the job required.

"Actually, I was going to speak to you about accommodation." He hadn't been going to do anything of the kind, but seeing her standing there in that flimsy blue dress with the last of the evening light spilling down on her through the window addled his brain, and he became reckless.

"There's a small room at the back of the building coming vacant in two days." There was going to be mayhem when he evicted the four miners currently taking turns with the two cots, but everything had a price.

"You're welcome to rent it if you like." Inspiration struck. "And Daisy, if you'd truly enjoy doing some cooking, we can try opening the dining room, and of course we'll come to a fair understanding as to wages."

Daisy blinked. Then she clasped her hands in front of her chest and her eyes widened. "Oh, gracious. Are you offering me a job cooking, Logan?"

He smiled at her. He really liked the timid little woman and her cranky dog. "I guess I am." He was too much a gambler not to hedge his bets, however. It wasn't likely she could possibly be a worse cook than Harry, but a person never knew.

"You can practice on Angus and me at breakfast, and if that works out, then why don't we try serving meals for, oh, say a week, and see how it goes?"

It shouldn't be a problem to get the dishes cleared off the tables early enough so that the regular gambling games could still go on. He told himself it would be a welcome change not to have to rely on the restaurants for every meal, but honesty made him admit that the only real reason he was considering serving food was to provide a way for Hannah to stay on at the Nugget.

He was a fool. He ought to be out building her a cabin to live in on the opposite side of town, because there was no room in his life for a woman, however much she intrigued him.

It was finally safe to stand up.

"I have to get back to the saloon. Thank you for coffee." He held up the shopping list. "I'll have these supplies here by morning. And Hannah?" He knew what he was about to say might cause fireworks, but it needed to be said. The pants were bad enough, but the dress was incendiary.

"It's not wise to go out on the street dressed as you are. Drunken miners are a rough lot, and you could well be in danger."

Her eyes widened in surprise and then narrowed, shooting fire at him. Her cheeks turned pink and her jaw tightened. She glared at him and then deliberately looked down at herself, raising her head slowly to give him a contemptuous look.

"For heaven's sake, you were the one who went on and on about my jeans. Now you make it sound as if I'm parading around in a bikini. This dress covers me from my neck almost to my ankles. What more do you want?"

Actually, he very much wanted to know what a bikini might be, but now wasn't the time to ask.

Chapter Ten

"It has nothing to do with me, Hannah," Logan assured her. "And I don't mean to insult you. I personally consider what you're wearing most . . . attractive." He cleared his throat. "I assure you, miners who've been drinking whiskey are seldom chivalrous, and unless a woman dresses the way other women do, assumptions are made."

Her chin shot up. "Well, you nasty-minded men can make all the assumptions you like. I assure *you,* I can take care of myself."

"I'm glad of that." He doubted it. She obviously had no idea how outrageously shocking and sexually appealing she looked in her skimpy costume, or how rough a mining town could be.

"I wasn't exactly planning on walking the streets looking for excitement tonight anyhow," she snapped. "I'm beat. I'm probably going to go straight to bed. Hauling water up and down those steps is enough aerobic exercise for one day. I don't need to wrestle randy miners into the bargain." She gave him an assessing glance. "Exactly how do you take baths, Logan? Do you have to haul water up and down stairs, or is there an easier arrangement for men?"

He smothered his amusement. She went from wrestling miners to bathing without a hitch. "Ming Wo has a bathhouse over near the creek. I usually use that."

"Humph," Elvira snorted. "And I suppose women aren't allowed in?"

This time Logan couldn't subdue his smile. "I know for a fact the men wouldn't mind, but you women might not be comfortable with the facilities. Ming has a large one-room cabin with four tubs and not much privacy. You could always rent all four."

He was joking. Women didn't use the bathhouse.

Hannah took him seriously. "What would it cost for an hour or two? Anything's gotta be better than hauling that water up and down."

"Ming charges a dollar a bath. I'll inquire if he has an hourly rate if you like." Once again, she'd surprised him. He still couldn't fully accept the preposterous story these women told of where they were from, but there was no doubt they were interesting. Hannah was more than interesting. Right now she made it difficult to concentrate on anything except his anatomy.

"What time would you like breakfast?" Daisy was nervously examining the wood cook stove. "I've never actually used one of these. Do you think Angus could help me get it going in the morning?"

"I'll make certain he lights it for you, and there's a good supply of wood in the shed. I usually eat about seven." He nodded his head politely. "Good night, ladies."

It was anything but a good night in Hannah's opinion.

After the lamp had been extinguished, Elvira began sobbing into her pillow, and Hannah's heart ached for the older woman, and for herself and her mother as well. What had happened to them all was frightening. More than once today, Hannah had felt like crying herself.

"There, there." Hannah could hear Daisy patting Elvira's back. "Don't cry, dear friend. Things always look worse at night."

Elvira's sobs were terrible to hear. She blew her nose and wailed, "But I m-might never see Gordon again. It's awful, because I know he's out there s-somewhere, but there's no way to get to him, or even tell him where I am."

She sniffled and blew her nose again, and her

voce was stuffy from tears. "You know we've had our ups and downs, Gordon and I, but I do care for him. I do."

Lying in the darkness, listening because she had no choice, Hannah doubted Gordon had any inkling of that. Elvira's tongue was sharp enough to slice through steel, and all Hannah had ever heard her do was criticize her husband.

Elvira started to cry again and Hannah felt mean. Elvira was hurting, and Hannah could sympathize with her feelings; there was no way to contact Brad, either, and the frustration of that alone was terrible. It was hard to imagine never seeing him again.

"It's a little like death, I suppose," Daisy was remarking in a wistful tone. "When Michael died, all I could think of were all the things I should have said when I had the chance."

"I'm sure you said most of them, Daisy." Elvira's voice regained some of its tartness. "I never heard you utter a mean word to Michael. I certainly never understood how you could stick by that man in spite of everything."

Elvira was sounding more like herself already, Hannah decided with a wry grin.

"Oh, there were lots of times when I felt like leaving him."

Hannah could hardly believe her ears. She'd never once heard her mother confess any misgivings about her marriage. What had always driven Hannah nuts was the way her mother defended her father, no matter what he did.

"And why didn't you?" Elvira sounded as curious as Hannah felt. "Goodness knows he gave you reason, losing your money the way he did."

"Because I was always madly in love with him, right up to the day he died," Daisy confessed with a sad little laugh. "And he with me. He went through money, and goodness knows he drank more than he should have, but there was never another woman for him, Elvira. And I knew there never would be." Her voice grew soft and secretive in the darkness. "We had such fun together, when times were good."

Hannah's face flamed in the darkness. Something in her mother's tone made it plain she was talking about sex, and no matter how old she was, it was shocking for Hannah to think of her parents as passionate lovers.

"And even when they were bad," Daisy was saying, "he adored me. It's hard to explain that kind of love to someone who's never experienced it." Instantly, Daisy realized what she'd insinuated, and she added hastily, "Oh, Elvira, I don't for one second mean that you and Gordon—"

"It's all right, Daisy. Ours was never a love match." Elvira was silent for a long moment, and then she said in a sad tone, "To be honest with you, I've envied you at times."

"Me?" Daisy sounded as astonished as Hannah felt.

"Gordon's a good man. He's been a good provider. We both wanted financial security and we've got it. He never drank. But it was my sister he had eyes for, and when she married someone else, he turned to me. I always knew I was second choice, and I guess I never forgave him for it."

There was such pain in her words that Hannah wanted to cry. "And then he wanted children, and I couldn't have any. I felt such a failure. And I wanted to adopt, but then *he* wouldn't." She sighed. "We spent our lives at cross purposes." She fell silent, and Daisy didn't reply. There wasn't much a person could say, Hannah thought.

"Well, it's all water under the bridge now," Elvira said after a while. "We should try to get some sleep, I suppose, if you're serious about getting up at the crack of dawn just to make breakfast, Daisy."

The other two women were soon snoring softly, but Hannah lay wide awake, thinking over what she'd heard.

It almost sounded as if Daisy had had the better marriage, after all, which went against everything Hannah had ever suspected. How could a marriage based solely on sexual attraction be better than one where finances and goals were the important thing? Sexually, she and Brad were . . . she fished around for a word. Compatible came close.

Comfortable? She supposed so. But whatever they had, it sure didn't sound anything like what her mother was talking about.

Logan was suddenly there in her mind, and she spent a long, guilty time trying not to think of him in that way.

Then it seemed Hannah had just dozed off when Klaus decided he wanted to go out. Daisy continued to snore softly, so the dog finally jumped down from the bed and nudged at Hannah with his wet nose.

Cursing the animal, Hannah staggered to her feet, pulled on her sandals and a sweat shirt, and grabbed the flashlight. She made her way down the stairs, eerily aware of the sound of male snoring from the rooms along the corridor. The saloon was closed for the night, which meant it had to be long after midnight.

She wondered where Logan was sleeping, and whether or not he snored, and that led to other things, like whether or not he wore pajamas. Somehow she doubted it.

When she made her way back up the stairs, Klaus stopped suddenly at the top and growled, peering down the dark corridor with the hair on his back standing erect.

Heart hammering, Hannah shone the light along the dark hall, and a certain door suddenly clicked shut. Klaus growled again and then made his way to the door of their bedroom.

Hannah hurried after him, wondering if someone had been watching her. She thought of Jeb Slater and shivered.

Back in bed, she was not able to fall asleep again, for some time, and she was restless for the remainder of the night. They had no alarm clock, and Daisy fumbled with the flashlight several times, turning it on to peer at her watch and waking Hannah in the process.

Then Daisy insisted they all get up at five-fifteen, a prospect so awful that even Klaus objected. He whined and tried to snuggle back into the cozy nest he'd made at the foot of the bed, but Daisy put him firmly on the floor and gave Elvira a shake.

"Wake up. You, too, Hannah. I can't do this by myself. I don't know why I ever got into it. What'll I do if that boy hasn't lit the stove? I've been worried sick all night. I don't know how to cook on that antiquated thing," she moaned.

Elvira grunted and sat up, rubbing her face with her hands. "For heaven's sakes, Daisy, shut up," she commanded. "It's only breakfast. How far wrong can a person go with some bacon and eggs?" In spite of the tears and the confidences of the night before, Elvira sounded just like her old cranky self again.

From her pallet on the floor, Hannah figured that Gordon was probably going to adjust rather quickly and happily to Elvira's disappearance. She certainly would if she were in his shoes, she decided as Elvira went on complaining about the cold water.

Hannah snuggled further under the quilt and wished her mother had kept her mouth shut about this cooking production. She, too, felt cranky and depressed this morning, and she wanted to sleep longer. Outside, dawn was barely beginning to turn the sky gray, and the muscles in her arms and legs hurt, probably from carrying all the bath water up and down.

Hannah suppressed a groan as she rolled out of her blankets and got to her feet. She staggered over to the washstand, pouring water into the basin and sloshing her face and arms. Just as Elvira had warned, the water was icy cold, and although it woke her up with a jolt, it didn't improve Hannah's mood.

God, she wanted hot water from a tap, coffee from an electric perk, a toilet that flushed. She wanted a room of her own. She wanted to go home.

Everything in this era seemed to require twice the patience and triple the effort it did in her own time. When she contemplated staying in Barkerville for an indefinite period, Hannah wished she could just lie back down on her pallet and pull the blankets over her head and sleep for a very long time . . . namely, until someone found out how to transport the three of them and Klaus back to their proper place in history.

Urged on by Daisy and trailed by a snappy Klaus, they went down to the dark kitchen.

Angus was shaving slivers from a block of wood with his pocket knife and laying them carefully in the firebox of the stove.

Elvira lit the coal-oil lamp, and Hannah went to the outhouse, shivering in the cold mountain dawn. By the time she came back, the stove was going and Angus was giving Daisy a careful lesson on keeping it at a steady temperature.

"You gotta remember to put wood on *all the time,"* he instructed. "This is the damper. You gotta move it this way as the stove hots up if'n you wanta cook in the oven or keep the wood from burnin' up too fast." It was obvious that the care and maintenance of a fire was something Angus took very seriously.

Daisy was paying close attention to Angus's instructions. "How did you learn to start fires in stoves like this one?"

"Yeah, how did you? You're good at this, Angus," Hannah said, standing as close to the stove as she could get in hopes that it would warm her. "It would take me all morning to figure out how to get this thing going," she told him.

Angus wasn't used to compliments. He looked at her as if he thought she was teasing him, and then a wide, pleased smile broke over the boy's face. "Jeannie showed me how. She shows me lotsa things."

"And who's Jeannie?" Elvira, too, was hovering near the welcome warmth beginning to radiate from the stove.

"My sister. We always took care of each other." A shadow flickered across his face and his smile disappeared. "Then Jeannie got married, to Oscar. I don't like Oscar." There was fear in his dark eyes. "He hurts me when he's mad, and he hurts Jeannie, too." He began to wring his hands anxiously, and shift from one foot to the other.

Hannah felt a stab of pity for him. "Does your sister live here in Barkerville, Angus?"

He shook his head. "Nope. Down the trail 'bout three miles, and then inta the bush."

"Does she come into town? I'd like to meet her."

Angus was pulling his fingers and making the knuckles crack. "She don't get ta come inta town much. Oscar don't like it. And I can't go see her neither."

It sounded to Hannah as if Jeannie's marriage left a lot to be desired. She wondered exactly what this Oscar character had done to Angus. Compassion for the boy filled her, and she tried to set his mind at ease. "I'd like to meet your sister, but only when it doesn't cause any problems."

"Okay, miss. Not now, though. I gotta get water now to heat up. Can Klaus come?"

Daisy assented, and Angus took the buckets

and headed out the door with Klaus bounding along at his heels as if he were a puppy again.

"Sounds as if his sister has herself a real prize in this Oscar," Elvira commented, and Hannah had to agree.

Daisy wasn't listening. "Look, everyone, Logan kept his word about the groceries."

The table was heaped with supplies: dried beans, molasses, a tin of butter, a cloth bag of sugar, eggs in a basket, a bag of flour, a package of baking soda, and a tin of salt.

"Hannah, could you put some of this stuff away? Just leave me out the bacon and eggs. And Elvira, maybe you could set the table. Oh, dear, there doesn't seem to be any bread, does there?" Daisy was measuring coffee into the pot and adding water. "I wonder if I should try making biscuits? How do you tell if the oven's at the right temperature?"

Hannah sighed. Her mother was never going to make it through this—she just knew it. Daisy might be a good cook at home with all the conveniences, but here?

When were cornflakes invented, anyhow?

Chapter Eleven

But Hannah's mother surprised her.

By quarter to seven, there were biscuits in the oven, although Daisy kept saying she didn't hold out much hope that they'd be edible when they emerged. Hash browns made from potatoes Hannah had peeled and sliced sizzled in the black iron frypan the bacon had cooked in. There were eggs ready to slide onto a griddle, and the coffee smelled wonderful, although Hannah had only managed one quick cup.

It was unbelievable how much there was to do. The stove was a constant challenge; damped down too much, it smoked. Add too much wood, and everything was in danger of burning. Too little, and nothing cooked. The food needed watching every minute; finding necessary utensils involved a major search; and everything needed scouring before they could use it.

Hannah wondered if this cooking thing would get any easier as time went on. She doubted it; without a microwave, electric kettle, toaster, griddle, or blender, a cook needed eight arms and four sets of eyes, as far as Hannah could see. And there wasn't even a sink; dirty dishes had to be washed in the dishpan and dried by hand.

Hannah's mood hadn't improved. Now she was uncomfortably hot, and she was hungry as well. The kitchen was no longer cool. The wood stove had heated it to what must be eighty degrees, and the morning sun was glaring in the window. Elvira opened the door wide and complained bitterly.

Hannah kept trying to find a moment to run upstairs and put on something cooler than the warm sweatshirt she'd pulled on at dawn, but an increasingly frantic Daisy kept her busy every second, bringing more wood from the storeroom, locating suitable platters to hold the food, filling kettles with water to heat for washing up, checking on the infernal biscuits every two seconds.

If it took all three women this much work just to make breakfast for Logan, Angus, and themselves, exactly how did Daisy think she was going to be able to cook for half-a-dozen men?

And she'd have to do it without Hannah's

help. Hannah had decided that the instant this breakfast extravaganza was over, she was going to wash the sweat off, put on something cool, and march out and find a job that didn't involve burning her fingers from shoving wood into the maw of a vicious cookstove, or getting her hands swollen and her nails wrecked from washing stacks of dishes.

She had a university education, she reminded herself, slamming the oven door shut for the umpteenth time. She was a career woman, not a domestic servant. She'd disliked cooking and cleaning in her own time. She certainly wasn't going to make a career out of it now just to please her mother. Or was it Logan McGraw she was pleasing?

At five past seven he appeared, rested and well groomed in his usual dark suit and white shirt, boots polished to a high sheen. The very sight of him made Hannah's blood boil.

"It smells wonderful in here, ladies," he greeted them cheerfully, pouring a cup of coffee from the pot on the stove and leisurely taking a seat at the table. "I trust you all slept well?"

Hannah blew hair out of her eyes and gave him a stony look. Didn't he have the slightest idea what it was like to sleep in one small room with two women who snored all night and a dog with a weak bladder?

Didn't he realize that making it smell wonderful in the kitchen had involved an hour and a half of ridiculously hard physical work? Didn't he realize it was hotter than an inferno in here?

She was trying to come up with a suitably scathing remark that would indicate exactly how she felt when a trail of smoke and the smell of burning alerted her to the biscuits, which she'd forgotten for all of two minutes. She snatched the oven door open and grabbed at them, but it was too late. They were burned beyond recognition.

Hannah shot an apprehensive look at her mother, fully expecting Daisy to dissolve in tears and run upstairs, leaving her and Elvira to cope with the rest of this ludicrous performance.

But Daisy just looked at the incinerated biscuits and shook her head sorrowfully. "Throw them out the back door, Hannah, the little birds might like them," she said in a remarkably calm tone. "Take those hash browns out of the frying pan and put them on a plate. I'll need the frying pan washed and oiled and heated up again while I mix up some pancake batter."

Hannah gaped at her mother, then hurried to do what she'd asked. What on earth had come over Daisy? At home in Victoria, in their proper place and time, the slightest mishap had reduced her to floods of tears. Pressure of any kind brought on a migraine, which necessitated bed rest and quantities of pills and a great deal of pampering.

Here, in a situation that made Hannah consider hysterics, Daisy was coping wonderfully well.

What was going on? Hannah scrubbed diligently at the stubborn potatoes stuck to the bottom of the iron pan, wondering whether Daisy had brought extra-strength tranquilizers with her. If she had, Hannah figured she'd ask her mother to share them.

In spite of the burned biscuits, breakfast was an enormous success. The pancakes Daisy whipped up were light and fluffy, and even though there was no maple syrup to smother them in, they tasted wonderful.

Even Hannah's bad temper had almost disappeared by the time she'd finished eating. The kitchen felt cooler, too. Logan had opened the window and propped open the door leading to the hallway, and a breeze was blowing through the room.

"My compliments to the cook," Logan said, raising his coffee cup in a toast to Daisy when he'd finished the meal. "I believe we'll be swamped with customers when word gets out about your cooking, madam. If you agree, I'll spread the news that we'll be serving meals as of dinner tonight. Is that agreeable, Daisy?"

Still pink from standing over the blazing cookstove flipping pancakes, Daisy now turned scarlet with pleasure. "You mean you really want to hire me to cook for you?"

"Absolutely. Is tonight too soon? We can always delay until tomorrow."

"Tonight's fine. I'll make a thick soup. We'll have to order bread from the bakery, though. I need to experiment a bit more with that oven before I try bread."

Hannah couldn't believe that anyone in her right mind would want to do this again, but obviously Daisy did. She was almost wriggling with joy as Logan assured her she was now the cook at the Nugget, but warning bells went off in Hannah's head at her mother's next words.

"I couldn't have made breakfast without Hannah and Elvira to help me. With the three of us, we'll manage dinner just fine."

Hannah looked up, straight into Elvira's horrified eyes. It was obvious the other woman had no more intention of slaving in this kitchen than Hannah did.

"I'll give you a hand with dinner, but I won't be able to help after today, Daisy. I'm—ummm, I'm going to the—the hospital this afternoon to see about getting hired on as a nurse," Elvira blurted out, and the surprised expression on her face told Hannah that she hadn't thought of doing so until that very moment.

"And I'm going to find a job in one of the businesses around town," Hannah said firmly. She didn't even try to be diplomatic. "Cooking drives me nuts, you know that, Mom. Besides, we're all going to have to earn money. Logan certainly can't afford to hire all three of us to work in the kitchen."

Logan was smiling, and Hannah didn't trust that smile at all. "Oh, I don't know about that," he purred. "If Daisy thinks she needs the assistance, I suppose I could—"

Hannah kicked him hard under the table, and he winced and then roared with laughter.

After breakfast, Hannah helped wash up before she headed upstairs with a kettle of hot water. She scrubbed her face and arms and sponged the sweat off the rest of herself.

She carefully chose a calf-length denim skirt to wear on her job hunt, the only skirt she'd brought with her.

One skirt, one dress. She was going to have to buy some clothes. She paired the skirt with an ivory T-shirt, adding a long-sleeved camp shirt in navy blue to cover up her bare arms. She'd swelter, but better that than have people fainting at the sight of bare arms.

How the dickens could arms offend anyone, she wondered as she brushed and rebraided her hair? If Logan thought the blue dress was suggestive, he ought to be exposed to what was stylish in her own time. She suddenly wished she'd brought a mini, just to really scandalize him.

But her cheeks flushed and a different kind of warmth swept through her body when she remembered the hot and lusty glances he'd shot her way the evening before. He wasn't the kind of man to be shocked for long by a short skirt, she admitted. With those looks and his calculated charm, he probably was on intimate terms with half the women in town.

The thought made her uncomfortable, and she hastily dumped her wash water in the slop bucket and wiped out the basin, then grabbed her handbag and hurried downstairs.

She walked past the door of the Nugget and looked in.

There were already at least a dozen men in the place, and as she passed, every single one turned and looked at her.

Hannah felt the impact of those hungry male eyes on every inch of her body, and it made her skin crawl. She forced herself to walk slowly and steadily to the door and open it without another glance into the saloon.

Being a woman in Barkerville was very much like being an exotic animal in some zoo.

Head high, she sailed out into the street, blinking in the sunlight. She fumbled in her bag for her sunglasses and at the same time dredged up a dose of resolution.

If just being female set her apart in this town, then damn it all, she was going to find some way to make it work for her.

* * *

Being female might set her apart, but it wasn't an advantage when it came to getting a job.

By three that afternoon, Hannah felt like a balloon that had lost most of its air as she made her way back to the Nugget. To avoid the stares of the men in the saloon, she scuttled around the side of the building and up the back steps. She fumbled the kitchen door open, dumping the bags she carried on the wooden counter.

It was even hotter in the kitchen than it had been that morning. Daisy and Elvira, their faces flushed and damp, were in the middle of preparing dinner.

Daisy was humming to herself, browning onions over the stove.

Elvira looked as if she were about to have a stroke. Her face was scarlet, her thin blond hair plastered to her skull, her narrow mouth pursed into a knot. She was hunched over the table peeling a mountain of potatoes, and she shot a venomous look at Hannah.

"So, you've finally decided to favor us with your presence." She mopped at her forehead with a tea towel and viciously attacked another potato with a lethal-looking knife. "I hope you realize I've been waiting for you for three hours now. I couldn't very well go over to the hospital when your mother's working herself to death here. That scoundrel of a boy is nowhere to be found. He's not as slow as he seems when it comes to avoiding work. And this kitchen is no place for women in menopause with hot flashes, let me tell you."

Hannah longed to tell Elvira to put a sock in it, but instead she said, "I can take over now if you want to go and see about that job."

Hannah had a half-peeled potato and a knife in her hand before the words were fully spoken, and Elvira was gone.

"*Did* you find a job, dear?" Daisy added some chopped carrots to the onions.

"Yeah, I finally did, but it took me hours." Hannah set the knife down and filled a mug with blessedly cold water from the pail, drinking it down in one long draught before she picked up the knife again.

"It's a jungle out there, Mom. I've got a much better idea than I had this morning of the social status of women in 1868 and, believe me, it's worse than anything I could have imagined."

She'd been confident that finding a job would simply entail presenting herself at any of the businesses along Main Street and explaining that she had an education and was eager to work. All the businesses she visited were run by men who, she soon learned, had no intention of hiring a woman to do a job a man could do.

None of them were the slightest bit interested in whether or not she had an education.

She'd had several slimy offers to "keep house" for men whose rapacious eyes told her more than words just exactly what they expected in the way of services.

"Logan was right about being judged by what you wear, Mom."

Over and over again, men had looked her up and down and snickered, and then told her to go apply to someone called Carmen Hall over at Frenchie's. It didn't take a genius to figure out that Carmen Hall was a madam, and that Hannah was being mistaken for a prostitute.

She didn't tell Daisy all those humiliating details, but she jabbed the knife towards the bundles on the counter.

"I had to use some of our gold to buy us clothes. The only way I got hired at all was by promising to wear what my new boss calls *modest and appropriate attire,* which as far as I can figure doesn't include a stitch that any of us own. I saw a few women today—not many, but I did pay attention to what they were wearing, and we're going to have to wear the same kind of clothes. Wait till you get a load of what *that* consists of." She rolled her eyes and swiped at a potato.

"Straight out of a museum—long skirts, blouses with high necks and long sleeves, ugly long stockings, dresses with snaps and buttons where zippers ought to be. And everything needs to be ironed because wash-and-wear isn't even a gleam in anyone's eye yet. There's no such thing as ladies' ready-to-wear up here, either. Believe it or not, the only place to buy women's stuff is the barbershop."

Daisy laughed. "From that Mr. Moses Logan introduced us to?"

"The very same. He stocks perfume, hats, shawls, and stockings, as well as ladies' wear. He's a nice man. He was the one who sent me over to Pandola's General Store. He'd heard Pandola was looking for a clerk."

"Is that where you'll be working, Hannah?" Daisy dumped the frypan of caramelized onions into the soup pot and added liquid from a stock pot. Her movements were swift and confident, and she looked happier than Hannah had seen her in a long time.

"Yeah. I'll be there from seven in the morning until seven at night, six days a week. The hours are criminal and the pay is ridiculous, but it was the only job I could find. The owner, Joe Pandola, is a little Italian man. He kept saying I was a good, bigga strong girl. He actually had me lift a couple of boxes to prove I could do it. I thought he was going to make me flex my muscles next. And he asked was I absolutely sure I wasn't married, as if I would make a mistake about something like that."

You should *be getting married, in just a few more days,* a small, sad voice nagged. Her wedding seemed to be little more than a dream she'd had in another lifetime.

"I asked him why, and he told me that it's not

considered proper to hire married women as clerks. Can you believe that? And he'd obviously heard about you and Elvira. He grilled me about whether you two were married. The only good thing was he didn't ask how we got here or why we came," she told Daisy with a deep sigh. "He had me add a string of numbers, but then he didn't even check to see if they were right. He really wasn't very concerned whether I had a brain or not."

"Oh, but he'd realize how bright you are just by talking to you, Hannah. It's perfectly obvious you're exceptionally intelligent. I knew when you were just a baby. You were talking in complete sentences almost before you could walk." A reminiscent smile lit Daisy's face. "I was so proud of you, I used to take you to the park, and the other mothers always thought you were much older than you were."

Hannah stopped peeling and gaped at her mother. She couldn't remember Daisy ever telling her that before.

Hannah swallowed, wondering why she suddenly felt like crying.

Chapter Twelve

Daisy moved the big black soup pot to the back of the stove and tilted the stove lid, again checking the fuel supply. She reached into a box and pulled out a small log, expertly shoving it into the stove and replacing the lid.

Hannah watched, impressed at how well her mother seemed able to cope with the monolith of a stove, to say nothing of the drastic changes in her life. She seemed to be doing better than either Elvira or Hannah.

"Did you apply anywhere else?" Daisy filled two cups with coffee, added sugar to her own, and handed the other to Hannah.

"I'll say I did. I must have gone to ten other businesses—the drug store, the post office, even a couple of hotels. One of the hotels was willing to hire me as a chambermaid, for the grand sum of fourteen dollars a week and room and board. I asked to see the room I'd be in, and it was a smelly cubbyhole with no windows. Logan was also right about accommodation up here. Neither of the hotels had a single empty room to rent. Apparently lots of people are living year-round in tents."

"I remember reading that about Barkerville," Daisy remarked. "I wish we hadn't left those guidebooks in the van. They told about what things were like here in the early days. I had a good book at home, too. I read it when I got interested in my great-grandfather. I wish now I'd brought it with me. I've forgotten some of the details, and it would be so helpful. Why, we could predict the future, couldn't we?"

"Yeah, and with the general mentality in this day and age, they'd burn us as witches."

"Speaking of fire, Hannah, do you recall exactly when Barkerville burned to the ground?"

Hannah shook her head. She knew the event had happened, but she had no idea of the date. She hadn't bothered to read the guidebooks. She'd counted on Daisy and Elvira to know all about Barkerville.

"I think it was in the fall of the year, but I can't remember the exact date," Daisy went on. "Elvira will probably know. She's got a better head for things like that than I have. I know the whole town was rebuilt afterwards. They improved those terribly uneven walkways and made the street wider."

"Did the entire town burn?"

Daisy thought about it and then nodded. "I'm pretty sure it did, except for maybe one or two businesses. When you look at the way the buildings almost touch one another and all those stovepipes sticking out every which way, it's pretty obvious there's a fire hazard here."

Hannah thought about the Nugget. "This is one of the few buildings that's set apart from the others. Maybe it won't burn. Anyhow, we should warn Logan."

Hannah thought about all the work he'd done on the Nugget and felt sad at the thought of it going up in flames. Then she remembered that he'd won the entire thing in a gambling game. Maybe he deserved to lose it as easily as he'd gained it. But she couldn't quite make herself believe it.

All day, she'd fought down surges of panic whenever the realization hit her that this primitive town, this impossible place, was going to be her life, at least for an indeterminate time. Those desolate feelings surged up now inside of her, along with all the small humiliations the day had brought, tramping from one business to the next, practically begging for jobs that in her own time she'd never have had to consider, and being insulted just because she was a woman.

She felt the sobs building in her chest, and she didn't have the energy to suppress them any longer. She gulped and set her coffee cup down with a thump. Then she laid her head on the table on her folded arms and began to cry.

"Oh, Hannah. Please don't, dear."

Through her tears, Hannah realized that Daisy was stroking her back, comforting her, and it felt good, although it took several moments to curtail the wrenching sobs that shook her. Finally she raised her head and accepted the tissue her mother offered.

"We . . . we'd better stop crying all the time. We won't even be able to b-buy any more of these," Hannah hiccuped, folding the soggy tissue and carefully using every bit of it. "There are just so many things we'll have to do without, Mom."

"Yes, I do know what you mean." Daisy glanced around the primitive kitchen. "But it's also a bit exciting, isn't it?"

She caught a glimpse of Hannah's incredulous expression and hastily added, "I mean, I miss all the conveniences of home. This is quite different, but . . . but in some ways, it's thrilling. I can't wait to meet Ezekial, and for the first time since your father died, I feel . . . well, I guess I feel *needed* again." She got up and began mixing up flour and soda and sugar in a basin. "Hannah, I actually have a job, one that I know I can do, and that's incredible."

"Well, I'm glad at least one of us feels okay about all this." Hannah tried not to sound grumpy, but it was difficult.

Daisy looked remorseful. "Oh, I do realize it's different for you and Elvira. I don't have anyone to go back to, and I know she's missing Gordon quite badly." She gave Hannah a sidelong glance. "And I suppose you're lonely for Brad. There's your wedding, too. I'm sure you're worrying about missing your wedding."

"Yeah, I really am." Feeling disconsolate and annoyed at her mother for, of all things, her optimism, Hannah blurted, "I keep hoping this is all a bad dream and I'll wake up."

Daisy nodded, her expression thoughtful. "It's funny, but that's the feeling I had every day until we ended up here. Now, I don't seem to feel that way at all."

She glanced at the stove, then down at her floury hands. "I wonder if you could check that stove for wood, dear? I'm going to need it quite hot, because I'm making scones."

For the remainder of the afternoon, Hannah worked, helping prepare what seemed enormous quantities of soup, scones, baked beans, and a vegetable dish Daisy had devised from dried peas, potatoes, and carrots.

She didn't say so to Daisy, but she wondered who on earth was going to eat this much food. The soup alone filled what looked like a small washtub, and Daisy cut out enough scones to feed an army.

But later that afternoon when Hannah finally found a moment to run upstairs to wash her face and hands and armpits and change her sweaty clothes for something fresh and cool, she was alarmed and astounded to see men lining up outside the closed doors of the dining room.

She wished there were at least a few women among the throng, but there weren't. She'd learned enough today to suspect that a fair number of those men were coming more for a glimpse of the new women in town than for the food.

She stomped up the stairs, thinking that being female was anything but a comfortable state in this place. She was fed up with men staring at her and making comments on what she was wearing.

She washed and surveyed the meager wardrobe she'd brought with her, remembering the uncomfortable reactions her clothing had roused earlier today. Well, Logan had warned her.

For a few moments, she actually considered putting on the clothing she'd bought that day, but one look at the long-sleeved shirtwaists and ankle-length skirts cured her of that notion. Serving food was messy work that required practical clothing, and with the heat in that kitchen, she'd die in long sleeves.

If the men were hungry enough, she reasoned, they wouldn't give a hoot what the serving person had on, would they?

So she donned her jeans again and a cool shirt and hurried back down to the kitchen, and for the remaining hour until dinner was to be served, she set tables and worried that maybe Daisy hadn't made enough food. She didn't mention it to Daisy, however. Her mother was now suffering a severe case of stage fright, muttering to herself and moving from one chore to the next with a distracted air.

Angus arrived at four-thirty in a clean but unironed shirt, his hair brushed but standing up in back. "Boss says I'm a waiter now," he announced proudly. "I already washed my hands, see?" He held them out, palms up, for Hannah to inspect, and she had to smile at his innocence.

At five, Logan appeared, impeccable in a starched white shirt and well-tailored dark suit. "Are you all ready, ladies? We've got quite a crowd out there. Word of the new cook has spread like wildfire." He winked at Daisy, smiled at Hannah, brushed dust from Angus's pants, and straightened his shirt. Then he opened the doors to the dining room. Instantly what looked like a horde of men surged in.

Within moments every available seat was

taken, and Logan went back out to assure the overflow crowd that if they wanted to wait, the Nugget would go on serving food as long as supplies lasted, and that while they waited, drinks would be discounted in the saloon.

With clumsy help from Angus, Hannah began distributing soup, plates of food, and mugs of coffee as Daisy filled them. Just as Hannah had feared, there wasn't a woman in the place; the clientele was all male, and Hannah was uncomfortably aware of their eyes on her as she moved from dining room to kitchen and back again.

Many of the men attempted to start a conversation, but she was too busy to do more than smile and nod. With the exception of Jeb Slater, they were all extremely polite.

Hannah had just set a bowl of soup in front of Jeb when he leered up at her and without warning grasped her around the waist with an arm that felt like hardened steel.

"Give us a little kiss, sweetheart," he said with a smirk. "I shore do like these pantaloons yer fond a'wearin'."

He reeked of liquor and sweat, and his touch made Hannah's skin crawl. She tried to pull away, but he was extremely strong.

"Let go of me," she ordered, scowling down at him, but he only laughed and pulled her even closer, his fingers digging into her hip, his foul breath enveloping her in waves of stale whiskey and bad breath.

"I said let *go* of me." Hannah made one more attempt at breaking free and when it didn't work, she reached down, picked up the bowl of hot soup and dumped it over Slater's head.

With a bellow of pain, he jumped to his feet, bits of vegetables and broth dripping off him. His chair overturned, and he staggered a bit, rubbing at his eyes. Hannah stepped away, but the area was crowded and she bumped into a chair.

"You . . . you little whore." He lunged at her and lifted a fist, and for one awful instant, Hannah knew he was going to punch her.

Chapter Thirteen

"That'll do, Slater." Logan materialized at Hannah's side, his tone quiet and lethal.

Now Slater lurched towards Logan, fist still raised, and faster than seemed possible, Logan had hold of him. Somehow Slater's arms were pinioned behind him and Logan was two-stepping him towards the door.

The entire assembly had fallen silent, and everyone heard Slater grunting and swearing as he was propelled along the hall and out the front of the Nugget. A stream of curses and then the slam of a door sounded. A moment later Logan walked back into the dining room and surveyed the rough male faces all turned towards him.

"The women staying at the Nugget are under

my protection," he said in a no-nonsense tone. "Anyone not prepared to conduct himself in a gentlemanly manner will answer to me."

No one moved.

"That's settled, then." Logan nodded and sat down, and after a moment everyone began talking and eating again.

Heart hammering, her entire body trembling, Hannah bolted into the kitchen. Daisy, busily filling plates, was unaware that anything had happened.

"I think it's going well, don't you, Hannah? They all seem to like my food."

Hannah swallowed hard and found her voice. "Yeah, everyone loves it, Mom."

She filled a glass with water and drank it down, and in a few moments she was calmer. Soon she was able to go on serving, but she was aware that the men avoided looking directly at her, and apart from polite thank-you's, there were few attempts at conversation. Now the only eyes that followed her every move belonged to Logan.

Elvira walked in when Hannah and Daisy were washing the dishes, and it was obvious she was in a better mood than she'd been in earlier.

"I'm starting work at the hospital tomorrow morning," she announced briskly. "I'll take my things with me in the morning, since room and board are included. I saw our old friend Billy. He sends his regards. He's no cleaner than he was the other night. I warned him I'm giving him a carbolic bath first thing in the morning. Lordie, that hospital's primitive beyond belief. It's like something out of the Middle Ages."

She grimaced. "I keep forgetting this is almost the Middle Ages," she added. "But Doc Carrol seems easygoing. He did say I ought to wear a uniform, although where one might find such a thing in this town is beyond me."

In chorus, Daisy and Hannah said, "The barber shop."

They giggled at the look on Elvira's face, and Hannah explained about the clothing she'd bought for each of them at Moses's shop, and why she felt it wise to wear what was customary for women of the time.

To her surprise, Elvira agreed.

"Just walking along the street today, I realized pants are not the thing here. Not that we'll be here that long, but it makes sense to fit in if we can," she said firmly.

"I'm sure in a short while we'll find some way to get back home. I've been thinking about it, and it doesn't seem logical that if we came one way, we can't find a way to go the other."

Hannah didn't comment. She no longer felt optimistic about that possibility, but she didn't want to discourage Elvira at the moment because the other woman had cheerfully taken over the task of drying the dishes Hannah was washing.

"Elvira, can you remember the exact date of the Barkerville fire?" Daisy was sitting with her feet propped up on a chair, fanning herself with a tea towel.

"Mid-September," Elvira said. She stopped drying and pursed her mouth in a silent whistle. "September 16th, 1868, if I recall. Just over two months from now." She resumed drying. "We'll be long gone before that. But we'll have to warn people all the same, even though we won't be here." Elvira put the plate down and picked up a bowl, polishing it with the towel. "No one was killed in the fire, but most people lost everything they owned."

"Nobody's going to believe us if we do tell them," Hannah warned, scrubbing at the soup pot. She felt cranky, tired, and out of sorts. "We're better off not talking much about how we know things like that."

Daisy nodded. "We'll tell Logan, though, won't we?"

"Tell me what?" Logan came through the door from the dining room. He added a stack of plates to the dishwater, and Hannah scowled at him.

"That this town's going to burn flat to the ground in two months' time," Elvira said dramatically.

"Oh?" He raised one eyebrow and leaned back against the table. "It's certainly possible. Fire's always a danger when buildings are so close together."

"It's not just possible, Logan, it's an historical fact." Hannah rinsed the last of the plates and slammed it onto the counter. "I know you think we're all nuts when we talk about coming from the future, but it's a matter of history that Barkerville burned on September 16th, 1868."

She dried her hands. "Also, you're going to have to hire somebody else to help my mother, because I'm starting work at Pandola's General Store tomorrow morning, and Elvira will be working at the hospital."

"Yes, ma'am." Logan grinned and pretended to salute. Hannah gave him a scathing look and headed for the back door. "I'm going outside for a while. I need some fresh air and privacy."

She slammed the kitchen door behind her, hoping he'd get the hint. Ever since the incident with Slater, Logan had been like a shadow. He'd done it unobtrusively, acting the part of the perfect host, helping seat people, putting everyone at ease, and even clearing away dishes when it was necessary, but Hannah was conscious of him at her elbow.

She should have been grateful that Logan was watching out for her, but instead she found it unsettling. Having him close bothered her, she admitted now, sitting down on the steps and trying to ease the ache in her shoulders and arms.

Maybe she was just hungry and didn't realize it. Watching dozens of men bolting their dinner was a great appetite suppressant. It was a wonder Richard Simmons hadn't thought of it in her own time.

She was too conscious of Logan, she told herself, too aware of the way he looked at her, of the way her treacherous body reacted when he accidentally brushed against her or touched her arm.

What in heaven's name was wrong with her? She was in love with Brad, but he'd never made her so embarrassingly conscious of her sexual self.

Then again, maybe her response to Logan was simply an emotional reaction to the fright she'd had earlier in the dining room. She shuddered, knowing she'd have to see Slater again. He lived at the Nugget.

Slater aside, at this particular moment there wasn't a single soul she *did* want to see. Being with people every minute made her feel claustrophobic. In the past few days, there'd been someone around day and night, and it was making her crazy. She needed to get away for a while on her own, think things through.

What she needed was a good long walk, she decided. The sun had set hours ago, but Barkerville was so far north, the twilight lingered until well past ten these summer nights.

Hannah got up and trotted down the steps

and across the backyard. After a moment's hesitation, she opened the gate, turning left on a footpath that meandered along beside the creek.

The rush of water was soothing, muffling the sounds of dogs and horses and waterwheels and men hollering to one another. Even this late in the evening, Barkerville was noisy, much noisier than Victoria had ever been. She smiled to herself, thinking how ironic it was that a modern-day city would be quieter than a small town in the 1800s.

For a while she hurried along, but soon her steps slowed and she began to relax. It was wonderful to be alone, to leave the town behind. Soon she was out of the main part of Barkerville, on a narrow path that wound through poplars and pine trees.

It was growing darker, but there was still enough light to see, and she ambled along, allowing the peace and quiet to envelop her.

She rounded a corner, and from behind, rough, powerful hands grabbed her. Before she had time to react, her arms were pinioned to her sides, throwing her off balance so that she tumbled to the ground. Terrified, she screamed, but the sound was cut off by the force of the hard-packed earth coming up at her. The man's body landing heavily on top of her knocked her half-senseless, and the world swam and buckled.

* * *

Logan glanced out the kitchen window just in time to see Slater duck out the back gate and hurry along the path beside the creek. What the hell was he doing skulking around the Nugget after he'd been told in no uncertain terms to pack his things and get out?

Logan went to the back door and glanced around the yard looking for Hannah, and when it was clear that she was nowhere in sight, he hurried into the hall for the leather vest that held his derringer. Tugging it on, he leaped down the back steps and ran across the yard, turning in the direction he'd seen Slater go.

Over the noise of the stream, Logan heard a single scream, high and terrified.

He cursed under his breath and began to run.

"Bitch. Whorin' bitch. Burn me, willya?" Slater straddled her, his body impossibly heavy, his ugly crimson face inches from her own.

Hannah tried to draw in a breath and couldn't. She tried desperately—once, again—with no success. It felt as if her lungs had collapsed. Time seemed suspended. She was aware that Slater was ripping at her blouse, ripping at the fastening at the waist of her jeans, muttering obscenities, but she couldn't move, couldn't fight.

Couldn't breathe . . . She had to breathe. . . .

She was aware of his hand closing painfully

around her breast, fingers digging cruelly into her tender flesh, and still she couldn't move, couldn't begin to get air into her lungs. A roaring began inside her head. A red haze formed in front of her eyes, a welcome barrier between her and her attacker, and Hannah began to slide into unconsciousness.

And then Logan was there. She caught a glimpse of the rage on his face, heard the low growl he gave in the instant before Slater's crushing weight was torn from her.

She was able to draw in a single, shallow, agonizing breath, and then another. She rolled to her side, and then into a sitting position, gasping and wheezing, aware that Logan had dragged Slater to his feet, and that in one smooth motion, his fist had connected solidly with the other man's jaw.

Slater grunted as his legs gave way. He fell to his knees, and his right hand dropped to his waist. Hannah saw then that he wore a gunbelt. He fumbled at his holster, and Hannah tried to call out, to warn Logan, but her voice wouldn't work.

"Don't try it, Slater, or you're a dead man," Logan warned. He, too, had a small gun in his hand, and it was pointed directly at Slater's head. Cautiously, he reached down and removed the other man's weapon from its holster, then threw it as hard as he could into the underbrush.

Slater was still balanced on his knees, and with a muffled oath Logan shoved his derringer back inside his vest, reached down, knotted a handful of Slater's shirt in his fist, and dragged him to his feet.

Logan drew his arm back and swung, connecting solidly with Slater's nose. Slater screamed and blood gushed down his face. Logan hit him again, this time in the midsection, and Slater dropped forward on the ground, arms over his head, alternately vomiting and blubbering.

Logan stood over him, breathing heavily, staring down at the man with a murdererous look on his face.

"You've got two choices, you craven coward." His voice was almost a snarl. "Either we go see the constable and ask him to lock you up until Begbie decides to horsewhip you, or you clear out of town within the hour. Which will it be?"

Slater staggered to his feet, holding his ribs. His voice was thick and indistinct. "Not jail, please," he whined. "I'll leave town. I was goin' anyhow."

Logan's fists were still curled, and Hannah thought for a moment that he was going to hit Slater again. "Get moving," he finally spat. "I'll be looking for you, and if you're not long gone by the time I get back into town, this is only a taste of what will happen to you."

Still holding his ribs, Slater stumbled to his

feet and, crablike, scuttled off down the path.

Logan hurried over to Hannah.

"Are you hurt bad? Can you get up?"

With trembling hands, she pulled her torn blouse together and tried to get to her feet. He bent over her, taking her hands in each of his to lift her, but nausea suddenly washed over her in a sickening wave.

She tried to move away but he wouldn't let her. He supported her as she bent over, retching. She was grateful now that she hadn't eaten dinner, mortified that Logan was watching her vomit.

"Did he hit you?" His voice was quiet, but there was an ominous undertone.

"No. He . . . he knocked me down. Hard." Hannah found that her voice, like her legs, was shaky, but working. "I'm . . . I think I'm . . . okay. I . . . I couldn't breathe."

His lips tightened and he glared down at her. "Breathe, hell. In another two minutes, he would have raped you or worse!"

The harsh tone of his voice and his angry words told Hannah that he was in a rage. He'd slid his hands up to her forearms and now he gave her a shake. "Have you no sense whatsoever, woman, wandering around out here alone in the dark? Didn't I warn you about miners?"

He had, and she knew he had every right to be furious with her. She was grateful to him and mortally ashamed of her own carelessness. But she was also emotionally and physically bankrupt, and she sagged in his grasp.

"I'm sorry," she managed to croak. "I'm really sorry, Logan. Forgive me, please."

The honest contrition in her voice must have registered, because his hands loosened their angry grip. He let go of her, just long enough to loop an arm around her waist. "Let's get out of here. Can you walk?"

She nodded, and Logan marched her down the path, half carrying her at times.

Hannah stumbled along, her brain numb, her body stiff and beginning to register bruises and scrapes. He didn't pause until they were in the backyard of the Nugget.

There was a lamp on in the kitchen, and Hannah could see Daisy through the window.

"Logan, wait. I don't want my mother to see me this way."

"I didn't intend she should." He drew her to the door of one of the outbuildings. "Come in here."

Inside the door was a lantern, and he struck a match and lit it, illuminating a well-ordered workshop with a wood stove and two cots covered in blankets, one in each corner. There was a basin on a wooden table and a pail of water, and he gestured to it.

Hannah washed her face and hands and rinsed out her mouth. She smoothed her hair as well as she could. She became aware of her torn blouse and tried to pull it together. Most of the buttons were gone, and finally she just knotted the ends at her waist. Her lacy bra was partially showing, but there was nothing she could do about it.

He'd hung the lantern on a nail and now, with a hand on her back, he guided her to a chair. "Sit," he ordered, and she did, aware that her entire body was shaking as if she had a fever. She felt icy cold.

He took one of his flannel shirts from a nearby nail and draped it around her shoulders. Then he reached under a shelf and extracted a whiskey bottle, pouring a generous amount into two tin cups, handing her one and taking a long drink from the other. There was a chair nearby, and he reached for it and plunked it down a scant two feet from where she sat. He straddled it, elbows balancing on its back.

"Drink. It'll make you feel better."

Hannah had to hold the cup with both hands to keep it from spilling. She tipped it up and took a mouthful. It tasted smooth and smoky on her tongue, but when she swallowed, flames seemed to lick at her throat. She gasped and choked and coughed, and the whiskey burned its way down to her empty belly. Tears streamed from her eyes, and she raised a hand to wipe them away.

Logan was watching her. He fished a handkerchief from a pocket and reached across the narrow distance separating them, gently wiping her eyes.

"You're not much of a drinker," he commented. He didn't smile, but a gleam of amusement shone in his eyes for a moment, and she was relieved to see he wasn't angry anymore. "Take another swallow. It'll calm your nerves."

She did, and this time the liquor still burned, but she didn't choke. A pleasant warmth began to spread through her, and the shaking gradually diminished.

As her fear subsided, a sense of outrage rose in its place. "He tried to rape me. We should have taken Slater to the police instead of letting him go, Logan. He'll probably do the same thing to some other woman. Men like him usually do."

He looked at her for a while and then nodded. "You're right. We probably should have had him jailed." His voice hardened. "He assaulted you. John Bowran would undoubtedly have thrown him in lockup until Judge Begbie returns in August, but there's a problem with that. See, if Slater goes to jail, Hannah, you're responsible for paying his keep until Begbie returns."

Chapter Fourteen

Hannah thought at first that she'd misunderstood.

"What do you mean, his keep?"

"The expense of housing him in the lockup. His food and lodging."

"*I'd* be responsible for that? But that's . . . that's ridiculous." Hannah couldn't believe she'd heard right.

Logan shrugged and sipped his whiskey. "Ridiculous or not, that's how the law operates here. Billy Renton's in the hospital, but if he wasn't, Dutch Charlie would have to pay to keep him in jail. There are no government funds available to pay for criminals, so the victim pays." He studied her, his eyes hard.

"Slater would also claim you led him on, Hannah. He'd insist your clothing enflamed him, that he couldn't help himself, that you deliberately enticed him, that you knew when you walked that path by yourself that he would follow. I hear that Begbie is a harsh, unpredictable judge. It's impossible to say how he'd rule."

Hannah frowned at him. "But you think I'd lose."

He shrugged. "I can't be certain of that. But assault against females isn't uncommon, and I've heard that very few women are successful bringing charges."

She must have looked skeptical, because he shook his head impatiently and added, "I haven't been here long enough to witness it myself, but the men in the saloon talk, Hannah. Apparently there was a case last summer, a French woman named Sophie Rouillard. She worked for a miner as his housekeeper, and she said he owed her money. When she went after him for it, he punched her in the stomach hard, and two weeks later she died. There were witnesses, a coroner's report of serious injury, a trial, but the official consensus of the all-male jury was that she died of a visitation of God brought on by strong drink."

Hannah was incensed. "That's disgusting. I can't believe the other women in town didn't protest."

He smiled at her naïveté. "There are fifteen hundred men in this town, Hannah, and perhaps a hundred women. Married women are considered the property of their husbands, and the single women are mostly prostitutes, reliant on males for their living. Exactly what would you have them do to protest?"

She thought of marches and bra-burning and petitions to the government, and then realized that women were still years away from even having the right to vote. Frustration and a sense of discrimination brought a scowl to her face.

"It's not fair," she insisted.

"You keep saying that, and I agree, it's not fair," he said, "but it's the way things are. I've heard of other, similar cases to Rouillard's, and in every one, the law unfortunately seems to favor the male." His gaze slid to her torn shirt, and his eyes and mouth hardened. "Slater won't bother you again."

"I don't ever want to see him again," she whispered, shuddering at the memory of Slater pinning her to the ground, of his cruel hands as they grasped her breast.

"You won't have to. But you're going to have to change your mode of dress, because unless you do, there will be others who'll mistake your intentions, Hannah."

His tone was soft and gentle, but there was steel beneath the words. "And I may not be there to rescue you next time. I know it irks you to have me make comments on your clothing, but I don't intend to fight gun battles to defend your honor."

Hannah swallowed the defiant retort that came to her lips, that she had no intention of making him do anything of the kind. The truth was, he *had* almost ended up in a gun battle defending her, and she remembered how he'd looked as he held the gun to Slater's head. He'd seemed a stranger all of a sudden, hard and cold, capable of anything. He carried a pistol inside the leather vest he wore. These were very different times from her own.

"Would you have . . . you wouldn't have just shot Slater tonight, would you, Logan?" Her voice was shaky.

He smiled at her, a lazy smile calculated to reassure, and shook his head. "Slater's not worth hanging for."

"I should think not. And just to put your mind at rest, I bought a couple of sets of what you'd consider suitable clothes today. I'm going to start wearing them tomorrow, for work."

"I'm sure you'll find the sacrifice worthwhile." There was more than a touch of sarcasm in his tone, and she grinned at him, and then glanced around the room, relaxed enough now to be curious.

"So this is where you're sleeping while we're using your room?" The shed was primitive, and she felt guilty. She realized for the first time what a sacrifice he'd made in providing them with accommodation, generously exchanging his comfortable bedroom for this.

"Angus and I sleep here. He's been sleeping out here since he came to live with me. I offered him a room inside, but he wants to be out here. He likes to whittle and carve little animals, and we're making a cradle for his sister's baby."

"Angus reminds me of a boy I know back . . . back home. A patient at the hospital named Stephen." She remembered the child-man who'd had such a crush on her, and whose sweetness touched her heart.

He gave her a look. "So you put people like Angus in hospitals where you come from?"

Hannah shook her head. "No, we don't. Generally we try to help them in any way we can, just as you're doing with Angus. Stephen didn't get the help he needed, though. He tried to commit suicide. That's why he's in the hospital. In the time I live in, a lot of young people commit suicide."

Logan's eyes darkened and when he spoke, the terrible bitterness in his voice shocked and surprised her.

"Young people take their own lives in this world, too, Hannah." He tossed back the last of the whiskey in his cup and got to his feet so abruptly, he knocked over the chair.

Without bothering to right it, he went over to the cot and snatched something from a low stool beside it. When he came back, he thrust it at Hannah.

It was the likeness of a lovely young woman, her dark hair a mass of curls, her huge eyes innocent and trusting.

"My sister Nellie." The harshness in his voice made Hannah wince. "She died two years ago. She'd just turned twenty." He rescued the overturned chair and sat down again, the same way he'd been sitting before, straddling the seat, arms resting on the chair back.

Hannah waited, and when he didn't continue, she said in a hesitant voice, suspecting the answer before she asked.

"What did she die of, Logan?"

There was a long silence. Just when Hannah had decided he wasn't going to answer, he spoke. His voice was uninflected and totally devoid of emotion. "Nellie was expecting a child, and she wasn't wed. She was slow, like Angus. My father is a clergyman with very strict rules. Nellie was scared. My father found out about the baby and he gave her hell. She drowned herself."

"Oh, Logan." Shocked and horrified, Hannah looked at the picture again and then at him. "She's so very beautiful, so young. Logan, I'm terribly sorry."

His strong face was like a mask, but the agony in his eyes tore at her heart. It made her long to comfort him, but she didn't know how. The only thing she could do was encourage him to talk.

"Were there just the two of you?"

He shook his head. "I have two brothers. I'm the eldest—I was already fourteen when Nellie was born."

Again he fell silent, his eyes looking past Hannah at something she couldn't see. She quickly added the years. So Logan was now thirty-four, six years her senior. He seemed older, somehow.

He said in the same quiet voice, "Nellie was a late child, and my mother didn't survive her birth." His lips tilted in a fond, sad smile. "Neighbors helped, but my brothers and I took over most of Nellie's care. We did our clumsy best at diapering and feeding her until at last an aunt arrived from England to take over. But Nellie would have none of Aunt Tillie for the longest time. She would only let us boys feed and dress her."

"It must have been difficult for your father, raising four children on his own."

He made a sound that should have been a laugh but wasn't. "My father knows less than nothing about raising children." There was disdain in his tone. "All he knows how to do is pray and preach and condemn. Joy and laughter are foreign to him."

She watched the powerful emotions come and go on his face. "You must have loved Nellie very much."

His tormented eyes met Hannah's for a moment, and then he looked away again. "I did, but I wasn't there to watch out for her. I ran away when she was only three."

"But you went home again?"

"Only twice. My father and I quarreled. He has always considered me tainted by the devil. My brothers were a little more tractable. They followed his dictates as long as they could. We grew apart."

"Where are they now?"

"They both left home early. David joined the army; Andrew homesteaded in Idaho." He gave her a crooked smile. "I haven't seen them in years. We have little but blood in common any longer, my brothers and I." The haunted expression in his eyes intensified. "When they left home, Nellie was alone with my father. I thought of her often. I intended to go back and make certain she was all right, but of course there was the war."

Hannah frowned. "Which war?"

He gave her a puzzled look. "The War Between the States, of course."

Hannah stared at him as it slowly dawned on her that he was talking about the United States Civil War. Once again she'd forgotten for these few moments where and when she was.

"Logan, you actually fought in the Civil War?" Her voice was filled with awe.

He raised his eyebrows, and this time his smile was genuinely amused. "I didn't fight, no. Soldiering is not usually a profitable occupation, Hannah. I'm not a knight in shining armor."

She thought of the way he'd come to her rescue with Slater, and she wanted to disagree. "But you were there? Close to the fighting?"

A shadow came and went on his lean features. "I was there, yes. I bought and sold equipment, guns, supplies." An ironic smile came and went. "To both armies, actually. There were opportunities, and men like me made the most of them. I had no strong feelings for either North or South. In California many of us felt that way, that it wasn't our cause. It's a sickening business, war. No one wins except the politicians and the profiteers. I hope never to have to witness anything like it again."

A deep sadness overcame her. She could have told him how many times war would happen in the next hundred years, but she didn't. "When did it end, the Civil War?"

"Just three years ago, in 1865. I stayed on in Washington for two years afterwards. It was there that a letter finally reached me about Nellie." His voice hardened. "I should have gone back when the war ended, made certain she was all right. But I delayed, and in the meantime a man came along and seduced her. It wouldn't have taken much. She was a loving child."

Hannah could have wept for him. "You can't blame yourself, Logan. What happened wasn't your fault."

His face grew dark and taut and his eyes glittered. The look he gave her was a warning. "She was my sister. What happened to her shouldn't have been allowed to happen."

The suppressed rage in his voice sent a shiver down her back. "What became of the man?"

He looked away, and now his voice was offhand and cool. "He disappeared. No one knew where."

Hannah wasn't sure she believed him, but she sensed he didn't want to pursue that subject. She looked again at the picture of Nellie, and she reached across and impulsively touched the back of Logan's hand. "She was lucky to have a brother like you. I always wished I had a brother. Or a sister. I'd have loved to have had a sister." Her forefinger caressed the picture, touching the soft line of cheek and jaw, the special innocence in the girl's eyes.

He turned the hand she was touching over, so that their palms met. The contact sent a rippling shock through Hannah, and she jerked her hand away.

He didn't resist or react. He hardly seemed to notice.

"You were an only child, Hannah?"

It was her turn to nod. There was an intimacy here in this rough shed, with the lamplight flickering over them, that inspired confidences, and the powerful attraction she felt for Logan made it seem natural to confide in him.

"I didn't get on well with my father, either," she confessed. "Oh, I adored him when I was really little, but after I grew up and saw what he was doing to my mother, I hated him." Her voice shook. Talking about Michael always upset her.

"What sort of man was he?"

She pretended to misunderstand. "A very big man. That's where I got my height from."

"And what exactly did he do to Daisy?" His entire attention was focused on her now, and too late, Hannah realized that telling him about her father would also reveal a great deal about herself, perhaps more than she wanted him to know right now.

Hannah shrugged, trying for nonchalance. "Oh, he made promises he never kept. He drank too much. And he lost all her money."

"He was a gambler, Hannah?" The question was casual, but they both understood its import.

She met his curious gaze defiantly. "Yes, he was. Not with cards. But he took chances on the stock market, on useless investments and idiotic schemes. His gambling was out of control. Daisy had an inheritance that would have made life easy for her now that she's older, but he lost it all."

Logan nodded thoughtfully. "Some men shouldn't gamble."

"No one should," she burst out angrily. "It's a disease, just like alcoholism. It ruins lives. It all but ruined ours."

"Only because your father allowed the gambling to rule *him*." His voice was gentle. "Poker, all games of chance, they're only games, Hannah, best played by men who have nothing to lose but their gold. No wives, no children."

"Men like you?" She was asking a question, one she'd wondered about.

He recognized it, and his smile was lazy. "Like me, yes."

"But haven't you ever thought of getting married, Logan?" She twisted the ring on her engagement finger and for the first time in hours, thought of Brad. She should feel guilty, having this intimate discussion with another man, but for some reason she didn't.

He shrugged, still smiling. "Everyone thinks of marriage at one time or another. I've just never found good enough reason for it." His gaze went to the ring she was twisting, and he jerked his chin at it. "What is it about *him* that makes you want to marry?"

"About Brad? Oh, I—well, I love him, of course." She did, of course she did. She tried to visualize Brad, to make the question easier to answer, but the exact contours of her fiancé's face eluded her. "He's very reasonable. And reliable. And trustworthy."

Heavens, it sounded as if she were describing a family pet. She wracked her brain. "He wants a family, and I do, too. We value the same things in life—security, enough money to live comfortably. We have the same objectives."

What the heck were they? It was difficult to think, with Logan staring at her like that.

He got to his feet in one smooth, lithe motion, and before she could guess what he intended, he reached out and took her hand, pulling her up and drawing her towards him.

One hard arm came around her waist, cradling her under the flannel shirt, holding her disturbingly close to his body. She raised a hand to his chest, meaning to push away, but instead she flattened her palm against his warmth. His big body seemed to radiate heat, and it mesmerized her. All of a sudden she felt hot too.

He studied her leisurely, his blue eyes almost black in the lamplight. There was challenge in their depths, a trace of humor and more than a trace of challenge in his voice.

"There's only one reason to marry, Hannah. I believe it has everything to do with this." He bent his head and brought his mouth to hers.

Chapter Fifteen

His kiss was both savage and sexual. He tasted of whiskey, and he used his tongue skillfully, urging her response. When she gave it, helpless to deny him, he took full advantage, exploring, probing, demanding, angling his mouth to fit hers ever more closely. His mustache was soft and sensual against her skin.

Every pore seemed to tighten on her body, every nerve ending become alive and needy. Locked against him, she could plainly feel his arousal, hard against her belly.

He kept one arm around her waist, but with his free hand he caressed her, cupping her bottom, drawing her against him and releasing her, mimicking the relentless rhythm of his tongue.

She ought to pull away, but she couldn't do

it. Her breasts ached and exquisite sensation flooded through her, a coil of urgent need that wound tight in her belly, so powerful it left no space for reason.

Hunger was suddenly overwhelming. She wanted him in a way she'd never wanted before. She'd never dreamed she could want in this way, with a ferocious need that threatened to consume her.

". . . been gone for hours, I'm worried about her."

The sound of her mother's worried voice from outside the building slowly penetrated Hannah's awareness, and she stiffened and pulled away from Logan, but he held her steady in his arms, soothing her with a gentle hand on her back.

"Hannah? Hannah, where are you?" It sounded as if Daisy was right outside the door. Klaus was barking frantically, and Elvira said something to him in a peevish tone.

"Logan, let me go. Please, I have to go." Her voice surprised her. It was a gasp, husky with desire.

Reluctantly, he allowed her to slip from his arms. His eyes were heavy-lidded, and he was breathing as hard as she was. He smoothed a rough finger across her swollen lips. "Damn your chaperones," he muttered. "We were only just beginning."

Hannah pulled his shirt closer around herself

and reached up to smooth her hair; he watched her silently, his eyes a caress.

"Hannah?" Daisy's voice held a note of hysteria, and Hannah finally moved to the door and opened it.

"It's okay, Mom. I'm right here. I'm fine." She was relieved to discover that it was very dark outside. At least the other women wouldn't be able to see the telltale flush she knew was in her cheeks. It felt as if her lips were swollen.

"Oh, thank goodness you're here, Hannah. I thought you'd gone for a walk, and I got so worried when it got dark and you hadn't come home."

"I was just about to come in the house." Hannah quickly closed the toolshed door behind her.

"What on earth were you doing in there?" Elvira stalked over and opened the door again and stuck her head in the toolshed. "And why are you wearing Logan's shirt? Oh, hello, Logan, I didn't realize you were in here, too. So this is where you're sleeping these days, is it?"

"Evening, Elvira." Hannah heard the amusement in his voice. She didn't find Elvira at all amusing. She hurried up the back steps and through the kitchen. The woman was a busybody, and as soon as she had the chance, she'd undoubtedly make some remark or other about Hannah being engaged to Brad and in the toolshed with Logan.

Well, Hannah decided, she just wouldn't provide the opportunity. She bolted straight up the stairs to the bedroom, longing more than ever for even a few moments of privacy as she lit the lamp. Her emotions were in a turmoil, and she needed time alone to sort them out, but the other women were already coming up.

She could hear them on the stairs. She hung the lamp on its hook and frantically pulled off Logan's shirt and then her torn blouse, thrusting it in her carryall. She hurriedly put on her sleep shirt.

She was bent over the washbasin scrubbing her face when they came into the room, and from there she went straight to her pallet, pulling the quilt up to her chin while Daisy and Elvira got themselves ready for bed.

"He's a handsome young man, that McGraw." Elvira was pulling on her pink pajamas, studiously not looking at Hannah. "He reminds me of a young Clark Gable, don't you think so, Daisy?"

Daisy was brushing her teeth, and she made a garbled sound.

"He's very charming, too, but we need to keep in mind that we're going to find a way back to our own lives, and that our time here is just like a dream we're going to wake up from," Elvira pronounced. "So we shouldn't get too involved in anything because we'll be leaving before long."

Hannah screwed her eyes shut. Elvira was about as subtle as a freight train, warning her about Logan. Part of her felt like sitting up and telling the older woman to mind her own damned business. But another part recognized that Elvira cared for her in her own way; she'd been Daisy's friend for years, and she'd watched Hannah grow up. What she was really telling Hannah was not to get hurt.

As if she needed to be told, Hannah fumed. As if she didn't know that kissing Logan was playing with fire.

Klaus came over and sniffed at her as if he could smell smoke, and she glared at the little dog from under slitted eyelids. He growled at her and took refuge on the end of the bed, on Daisy's side.

It wasn't until the lamp was out and the other two were sleeping that Hannah allowed herself to really admit what had almost happened in the toolshed.

If Daisy hadn't interrupted, she knew she would have made love with Logan then and there, if that was what he'd wanted. *She* certainly had wanted it. Her body tingled and throbbed, remembering.

He'd wanted it, too, just as much as she.

We're only just beginning, he'd told her.

She'd sensed from the first moment she met him that there was dangerous, dark sexuality in

Logan. What she'd never suspected was that it was also there in her.

Her engagement ring felt as heavy as sin on her finger. She turned it round and round, trying to feel guilty about going so willingly into Logan's arms. After all, there was the matter of loyalty to Brad to consider, she reminded herself.

But Brad was a hundred and thirty years away, and Logan was sleeping just outside.

Logan wasn't sleeping.

Angus was snoring. He was a world-class snorer, too. The sound rose and fell in the darkness of the toolshed, but it wasn't the noise that was keeping Logan awake. He lay on his back, bare arms folded under his head, blood pounding through every vein in his body.

He was angry with himself, too angry to sleep, and along with the anger there was this tearing lust, the vivid memory of Hannah in his arms, her swollen mouth warm and eager for his kisses, her lush body pressed against him, wordlessly begging for what he longed to provide.

He'd been lonely most of his life. He'd dreamed of finding a woman to ease that loneliness, but why had she come at this particular time? There was also the confusing issue of where she'd come *from*. It was madness even to consider that the story the women told was the truth, but what was the alternative? Logan had racked his brain searching for a logical explanation, with no success.

Wherever Hannah had sprung from, he wanted her with an urgency that troubled and surprised him. He'd wanted women before, but never with the overwhelming need he felt for this one.

It went beyond need, too. She constantly challenged and surprised him, both intellectually and emotionally. She made him laugh, and he hadn't laughed much in the past year. He found himself confiding in her in a way he'd never done with anyone, as he had tonight, and at this particular moment in his life, he shouldn't be revealing himself to her or anyone. He couldn't afford to be distracted right now by a woman.

He'd come to Barkerville with one single purpose in mind: to find Bart Flannery and kill him. Flannery had seduced Nellie and made her pregnant, and then he'd deserted her, probably because she wouldn't agree to become one of his prostitutes.

Logan now knew a great deal about Flannery; he'd made it his business to find out everything he could. He knew that Flannery had used a comparable method with numerous other women. Logan had tracked several down and convinced them to tell him their stories.

Each story was different, but there were similarities. Flannery was sophisticated and very clever. He obviously took pleasure in seducing innocent young women, introducing them to sex, and then using their new-found passion as a way of controlling them. Nellie had been slow-witted, but many of the women weren't. Flannery was good at what he did. He often hinted at marriage and instead gradually lured girls into prostitution. If they became pregnant, all the better.

It had happened to three of the women Logan searched out, and in each case Flannery used the child as a powerful tool to control the mother. He was evil, and he was also dangerous.

In the war, Logan had seen innocent young men slaughtered, men who didn't deserve to die. In Logan's opinion, Flannery didn't deserve to live. When the time came, Logan would have no qualms about murder.

Death was no stranger to him, and although he'd never killed anyone deliberately, he knew he was capable of it, but he also knew he needed a clear head to carry it out. It would be tricky, killing Flannery here in Barkerville; there was only one constable, but there was also only one road out.

When he was around Hannah, his head was anything but clear. He'd wanted her from the very first night he'd met her, from the moment he'd seen her standing in that wagon in her outrageous pants, accusing him of being an actor.

But wanting and taking were two different things.

Tonight, holding her in his arms, kissing her, he'd sensed that if he'd carried her here to his cot, she'd have stayed willingly. Her need was every bit as urgent as his own.

It would be wrong of him to take advantage of the desire between them, he argued with himself. There could be no future to it. When he killed Flannery, there was a chance he'd end up in Judge Begbie's courtroom accused of murder. If that happened, he'd hang.

It wasn't fair to involve Hannah in his life. Whoever she was, wherever she came from, she could be hurt in so many different ways from knowing him.

And more than anything, he didn't want to hurt her.

At seven the following morning, Hannah walked through the front door of Joe Pandola's General Store to begin her new job.

She was wearing one of the outfits she'd bought the day before, a long-sleeved, high-necked white shirt with tucks all down the front, and a navy-blue serge skirt that came down to her ankles. Even at this early hour, she felt unbearably hot and weighed down by the yards of fabric.

At least she hadn't put on the corsets and layers of petticoats, the long, hot stockings and high-laced boots other women in this era wore. She had her sandals on, but she'd pulled on a pair of white sports socks to hide the sight of her bare ankles, which apparently were erotic enough to drive every man who glimpsed them into a frenzy.

Men in this era must be a lot easier to arouse than they were in her time.

She felt absolutely ridiculous, as if she were in costume for a play. She had noticed, however, that she didn't attract quite as many bold stares this morning from the men on the street as she walked to work.

"Good morning, Mr. Pandola." She smiled at her employer—a short, dark man with flashing black eyes, a little round pot belly, and a bald head. He eyed her clothing and nodded in evident approval. There was just no accounting for taste, she thought. "What would you like me to do first?"

"Sweepa the floor." He pointed at a broom in the corner. "Then washa this basket of eggs. Puta that box of cans on the shelf. Cleana the windows. There's so mucha dust nobody cana see in. Then you refill the barrels witha flour and sugar from the storeroom outa the back."

No wonder he'd been concerned about her muscles, Hannah thought morosely as she set to work. She couldn't help thinking nostalgicly of her cozy office at the hospital, of early mornings spent in professional meetings with colleagues, where coffee and fresh fruit and muffins were laid out for everyone's enjoyment and an invisible cleaning crew had mopped the floors and dusted during the night.

Maybe she hadn't appreciated it all enough, she thought as she mopped sweat from her forehead and traded the broom for a wet rag.

She began washing straw and manure from a small mountain of eggs and her stomach heaved. She'd never realized that this was the way eggs looked when they first came from chickens. By the time she'd washed three dozen of the disgusting things, she wondered if she'd ever be able to eat one again, and there was still a mountain of them.

The minutes ticked past in slow motion, and the heat in the store increased.

A young man came in. He wore rough miner's clothing, but his face and hands were clean and his carroty hair showed the marks of a recent wet combing.

"Whata can I do for you today, young man?" Pandola's tone was ingratiating.

The customer's eyes rested on Hannah. He moved past Pandola as if he were invisible and made his way over to her.

"Miss—?"

She smiled at him. "Hannah."

He ducked his head in a little bow. "Miss Hannah, I wonder if you could please help me? My name's Sandy Walsh. I've just staked a claim out on Keithley Creek, and I need provisions."

Hannah set the rag and the egg down, relieved to be rescued. "Sure. What do you need, Sandy?"

His gaze was bashful but admiring. "Oh, I guess flour, bacon, beans, salt."

Pandola was hovering. "She'sa new here, she's notta familiar witha my store."

"I bin in before. I can show her." Sandy grinned at Hannah. "I got lots of time. I'd be honored to help. Here's the flour, Miss. Here, let me lift that for you."

His pink face grew even pinker, and he stammered out, "I hear you're new in town, and I wondered—that is, would you do me the honor of taking dinner with me at Wake-Up Jake's tonight?"

Hannah thanked him and declined without hurting his feelings. He bought an enormous amount of supplies, and she added his bill carefully, longing for a calculator. At least there was no sales tax to factor in. Sandy left reluctantly, assuring her he'd be back soon.

After Sandy, there were four more male customers during the next hour. Like him, they doffed their caps and smiled and talked only to her, ignoring Pandola's offers of assistance. Unlike him, none of them left. More came in, slipping in the door as if Pandola were giving groceries away today. Some looked at her directly, some were more furtive, but Hannah soon realized that she was the star attraction.

Pandola ran around like a nit in a fit, and all the men ignored him.

Some were shy, some bold. She had offers of rides in buggies, visits to gold mines, meals at restaurants, and two outright proposals of marriage from men she'd never laid eyes on in her life, both of whom assured her they'd struck the mother lode and she'd never have to work again in her life.

It didn't take long to figure out that she was very good for Joe Pandola's business. It was evident that a lot of these men weren't regulars in the store; unlike Sandy, they had no idea where anything was, and they didn't seem to have a clear idea what they wanted, either, except for her.

They bought chewing tobacco, dried beef jerky, several bags of beans, half the mining equipment in the store, and all the chocolate, which she received as gifts once they'd paid for it.

She refused all offers, but she did so graciously, because the men treated her with such obvious respect.

It was much more pleasant than washing muck off eggs or filling shelves and bins.

Pandola was no fool. By ten o'clock, he was restocking the shelves and cleaning the eggs himself, and Hannah was adding up bills and making change out of the antiquated cash register.

By noon she'd hit him up for a raise and received it.

A plump woman in a green bonnet with cabbage roses on its crown came into the store just after noon, and Hannah tensed. It was Mrs. Heatherington, and Hannah remembered her clearly from the first morning in Barkerville when the woman had crossed the street rather than say hello.

Today was different. After looking her up and down, Mrs. Heatherington smiled and greeted her warmly, asking where she was from and how she liked Barkerville.

"I'm visiting from Victoria," Hannah replied, being sarcastic when she added, "Barkerville seems a friendly town."

Apart from would-be rapists and snobby women.

"Oh, what we lack in culture we make up for in congeniality," the woman gushed. "May I introduce myself? I'm Prudence Heatherington, wife of Gordie the bootmaker."

Hannah repeated her own name, and they shook hands.

"I understand your mother and aunt are here with you, Miss Gilmore?" Gossip was obviously alive and well amongst the women in town, and if Elvira had become her aunt, that was fine with Hannah.

"Mother has taken a job as cook at the Nugget, and Elvira is a nurse. She's just started working at the hospital."

"Why, how very enterprising of you all," Prudence gushed. "You must join our reading circle, all three of you. We meet at the library at seven on Sunday evenings. We take turns bringing refreshments. And if an Anglican service suits you, Reverend Reynard holds services each Sunday at ten, in the schoolhouse. We are a small but devoted group, and would welcome three new members to the congregation."

Prudence's new attitude towards her had everything to do with what she was wearing, Hannah realized. It was worth the discomfort if clothing was all it took to be accepted by the female side of Barkerville society.

The afternoon was even hotter than the morning had been, but the heat didn't deter the dozens of men who filed in and out of the store. Hannah smiled and made change and deflected still more invitations and proposals, wondering if she was going to die from heat prostration before the endless day was over.

When seven o'clock finally came, and Pandola locked the door and swung the sign around to Closed, Hannah wearily made her way back to the Nugget, sweating profusely, aching in every limb from the long hours on her feet. She was also aware of the bruises on her hips and back from Slater's attack the night before.

She made her way along the boardwalk, thinking of the previous night and Logan. All day, thoughts of him had come into her head even though she'd tried to keep them away. The memory of his kiss sent ripples of pleasure along her nerve endings, and she felt nervous and decidedly shy about seeing him again.

When she got to the Nugget, she hurried around to the back door, hoping against hope that he'd be busy in the saloon at this time of the evening. Supper would be over; Logan had explained that miners liked to eat early, so as to leave as much time as possible for drinking, and Daisy was pleased to have her job finish early in the day.

"Hi, everyone," Hannah called. The kitchen door was open, and Daisy and Angus were sitting at the table with a fragile girl whose hugely pregnant stomach seemed grotesquely large for her thin body.

"Miss Hannah, my sister's here," Angus announced in an excited tone. "This here's my Jeannie," he boomed, and Hannah was touched by the pride and pure joy in the boy's voice.

Chapter Sixteen

The girl's mass of inky black curls and her huge blue eyes made the physical resemblance between her and her brother startling.

Daisy introduced them. "Hannah, this is Jeannie Chalmers. Jeannie, this is my daughter, Hannah Gilmore."

"Hi, Jeannie." Hannah smiled and extended a hand towards the girl, noting a fading purple bruise on her right cheek. When Jeannie bashfully extended her hand, the thick calluses on her palm spoke of hard physical work. Her hands were terribly chapped and raw-looking. The faded blue gingham dress she wore was clean but threadbare, stretched to its limit across her belly. It was obvious that Jeannie understood hard work and poverty.

Hannah felt compassion swell within her for this child-woman. She wondered how old Jeannie was. She couldn't be more than fourteen or fifteen, and yet she was already married and about to become a mother.

"It's really great to meet you," Hannah said with a smile, wanting to put the girl at ease. "Angus has been such a help to us since we got here."

Jeannie smiled with obvious pleasure, but she didn't say anything. She was visibly shy, and very tense.

"Jean, ya gotta see this little doggie. Klaus, c'mere boy, c'mere." Angus successfully coaxed the dog out from behind the stove, where Daisy had put a blanket down for him. "Ain't he a nice little doggie, Jeannie?"

It was patently clear that Angus worshipped his sister. His love showed in his eyes when he looked at her, and when he sat down again he took her hand and clasped it tightly in his own.

"Angus says you live quite a way out of town," Hannah said. "It's nice that you're able to come and visit."

"I cain't stay long." Her voice was soft and husky, with an undertone of anxiety. "I just wanted ta see Angus fer a minute."

Daisy said, "Oh, you must stay and have something to eat with us, Jeannie. There's lots left over from supper. Hannah hasn't eaten yet and neither have I."

Angus leaned towards his sister. "Stay here, okay, Jeannie?" His tone was urgent, and it seemed he was urging his sister to move in instead of just to stay for some food. "It's real good here. Miss Daisy's a real good cook'; you'd like it lots; boss won't mind."

Jeannie shook her head at him, and reached out to smooth his curls. "You know I cain't stay here, Angus." Her voice was sad and gentle, and she smiled at Daisy.

"Thank you fer the offer, but I gotta go meet my husband soon as he's done at the smithy. We gotta get back home afore it's dark."

"Will you be coming into the hospital to have your baby?" Hannah remembered what Angus had said about Jeannie living out of town in a tent, and she was suddenly anxious for her. "Our friend Elvira is a nurse. She's just started working at the hospital today. She'll take great care of you."

The girl shook her head again. "Oh, no. We cain't afford no hospital. Oscar says he'll help when my time comes."

Hannah tried not to let the dismay she felt show on her face. "If there's anything we can do, we'd be delighted to help." Her heart went out to this girl. She wished there was a way to tell Jeannie that she was offering help with more than just her confinement.

"I thank you." With touching dignity, Jeannie got to her feet. They all stood up, and Jeannie wrapped her arms around her brother, kissing his cheek and hugging him hard.

"Angus, you be a good boy now, hear? You work hard fer Mr. McGraw, so's we can pay him back. I'll come see ya soon as I can manage it."

"I work hard. I like it here." Angus's chin trembled. "But I shore wish you could stay here with me. I'm awful lonesome fer ya, Jeannie."

The door from the dining area opened and Logan walked in. Hannah's heart thumped in her chest, and she was glad the others were present to provide a distraction.

"Evening, everyone." His blue eyes slid across Hannah's face like a caress and then did a quick survey of her long skirt and shirtwaist, but he didn't comment.

Instead, he turned to Angus's sister with a welcoming smile. "How are you, Jeannie? It's good to see you." He strode over and took her hand in both of his.

Jeannie gave him a worshipful look. "Fine, thank you, Mr. McGraw."

"Is Oscar with you, or did you come in alone?"

"He's over at the blacksmith's—the horse threw a shoe. He'll be done soon, so I gotta go."

Logan nodded. "How's the new claim working out?"

"Pretty good." Tension flickered across her face. "We bin workin' it real hard. We hit a couple good veins." She edged her way toward the door. "Bye, all. Thanks fer the coffee, Miss Daisy."

There was tense silence after she left, and then Angus abruptly burst into a storm of tears, weeping like a small child, his mouth wide. "I want Jeannie," he wailed.

Logan started towards him, but Daisy was there first, taking the boy in her arms and patting his back, impervious to the fact that he was almost a foot taller than she.

"There, there, don't cry like that. Look, you're getting Klaus in a state." It was true; the little dog whined and barked at their feet.

"I bet he has to go out, Angus," Daisy said. "Let's you and I take him for a little stroll in the yard."

With Angus clinging to her hand like an overgrown two-year-old, Daisy led the boy and the dog out the door.

Her heart aching with pity for both Angus and his sister, Hannah watched them go. Then she turned to Logan. Her concern for Jeannie overcame her self-consciousness.

"That poor girl, she's hardly more than a child. And did you see that bruise on her cheek? And her hands—she must have to work hard to get calluses like that. Do you know her husband, Logan?"

Logan swore, fierce and low. "Damned right I know him. Everybody in town knows Chalmers. He's a miser and a bully, too damn cheap to hire a man to work his claim with him, so he's using Jeannie, working her like a slave just like he worked Angus."

"How did you come to know Angus?" Hannah knew the boy needed almost constant supervision, and she'd already seen enough of 1868 to know that social attitudes weren't progressive. She realized that Logan could easily have hired someone much more capable to do the chores Angus did.

"Doc Carroll brought him here early last month because he'd run away from Chalmers and refused to go back. The boy was a mass of bruises. Chalmers said he'd fallen down a mine shaft, but Angus said Chalmers beat him, and I believe him. Angus is scared to death of him. Chalmers was in a rage when he found out Angus was gone." Logan's smile was savage. "He thought he could come and just take the boy back, but it didn't turn out that way."

"How the heck did Jeannie end up with him?"

"She was a mail-order bride. From what Angus tells me, their mother was a seamstress in Toronto, and they barely got by. The mother died, and Jeannie got a job in a cotton mill, but the dust made her sick so she couldn't work. She answered an ad for women who were willing to come out here and marry miners. Oscar sent the fare for her and Angus, likely thinking he'd get his money's worth out of the boy. I suspect Jeannie didn't tell him that her brother was simple."

"I'm surprised Chalmers didn't want his money back for Angus's ticket."

"He did."

Understanding came. "You gave Chalmers the money."

Logan shrugged. "It was the only way he'd let the boy go."

"Jeannie ought to leave him, too."

Logan snorted. "She has no money of her own, and she has a baby in her belly. She married Chalmers of her own free will. Under the law, she's his property. If anyone encourages her to leave him, they can be charged under the law for interfering between a man and his possession. Doc's tried to talk to her, but she's scared."

Hannah nodded and her shoulders slumped. "I keep forgetting. In my time, we have women's shelters and there's welfare, and still sometimes women are afraid to leave the men who mistreat them."

"So maybe things in your world are not all that different after all." There was a hint of sarcasm in his tone, and Hannah didn't blame him for it. She'd probably presented the future in the best possible light, and it hadn't been an honest depiction at all.

"No. I guess they're not." She shot him a rueful glance and tried for a smile. "But I get just as furious here as I did there when I meet someone like Jeannie."

His smile was warm and she remembered how his lips had felt on hers, bold, insistent. Her breath came faster, and she felt a flush starting at her collarbone. She knew now exactly how his body felt against hers, hot and hard and needy, and more than anything, she longed to be in his arms again.

His eyes flickered over her and he raised an eyebrow. "I see you're wearing more modern garments today. How was your first day at work?"

She crossed her eyes at his assessment of her clothing, and he laughed. It dispelled the tension. "Work was very, very long, and very, very hot, but I got a raise. Something needs to be done about the labor laws in this century, that's for certain, and I wish I'd paid more attention to exactly how air-conditioning worked." She swiped the back of her hand across her forehead. "Between these heavy clothes, the cookstoves, and no deodorant, it's no wonder most people stink of sweat. I certainly do."

He raised his eyebrows. "You do? I hadn't noticed." His eyes twinkled and he raised his arm and sniffed. "Do I stink, Hannah?"

"No, you smell good. You must bathe more than most," she blurted out, and then blushed crimson.

He laughed. "Ahhh, baths again. I talked to

Ming Wo today. He'll rent you the bathhouse either early morning or late evening if you give him advance warning, two dollars a head, fifty cents extra for doing your laundry. He's doubled his fee, the wily fellow."

"I don't care. That's great—that's wonderful." The thought of submerging her body in a tub of water was intoxicating. "It'll be easier to work all day if I can look forward to a bath in the evening."

"I hear that Pandola's business is much enhanced by your presence, Hannah."

"Who told you that?"

"The best place to hear everything that's happening is in a saloon. Men gossip just as eagerly as women."

"Yeah, well, if the gossips are right, I'm going to wait a day or so and then hit Mr. Pandola up for another hefty raise. If I have to dress this way and suffer the heat in that store, I'll get enough out of him to pay for our baths and laundry. Besides, he has all the makings of a petty tyrant, and I'm not going to let him get away with it."

"Why doesn't that surprise me?" Logan laughed again, and just then Daisy came in without Angus or Klaus.

"The boy's exhausted," she said. "I told him to go lie down for a while. I hope that's okay?" She looked at Logan, and he nodded.

"Of course."

"He asked if he could have Klaus with him for a while. A dog's good company when you're feeling bad. Angus promised he'd bring him in a little later. I've let the stove out, Hannah, but there's sandwiches and the soup's good cold. How about you, Logan? Will you join us?"

"Thank you, I ate earlier, and I have to get back to the saloon. I came to tell you that if it's convenient, you can move into the other bedroom tonight. The men have moved out and Angus went up and cleaned it for you."

After supper, Hannah helped her mother move their few belongings to the new bedroom. Although the new room was smaller than Logan's, it had two single beds, and to Hannah, the thought of sleeping in a bed again instead of the lumpy pallet on the floor was heavenly.

She felt sweaty, and she longed for a bath tonight, but it would have to wait another day. She told Daisy about the bathhouse as they took turns having sponge baths at the nightstand.

The cool water felt wonderful, but the bedroom was still sweltering, and despite the open window, there wasn't a breath of cool air. It was going to be hard to sleep.

By the time they were ready to go to bed, Klaus was still missing, and Daisy grew agitated.

"I know Angus loves him, but I need him here with me for the night," she moaned. "We've never spent a single night apart. I couldn't sleep without him curled up at my feet."

Hannah figured she could nicely do without Klaus wheezing and snorting all night, but she didn't say so.

"You finish getting ready for bed, Mom. I'll go get him." Hannah had brushed her hair, and she was wearing only her cotton sleep shirt. She pulled on her jeans and hurried out.

The moon was bright and she hadn't bothered with the flashlight. She walked slowly across the yard in the direction of the toolshed. It was marginally cooler out here than it was upstairs.

"Hannah." Logan's voice startled her, coming out of the darkness behind her. He was sitting on a chair in the shadow of the Nugget, and she could see the tip of a cigar glowing in the darkness. He got to his feet and strolled over to her, and her heart began to gallop in her chest.

"I'm looking for Klaus. Mom figures she can't live without him."

"I came out to rouse Angus, but he and the dog were sleeping so peacefully I decided not to disturb them. Sam can manage by himself in the saloon for tonight. It's not too busy."

His voice was pitched low, and he was standing very close to her. The moonlight cast mysterious shadows on his rugged face, and she was very aware that they were alone in the darkness.

"It's hot upstairs, too hot to sleep." It was the first thing that came into her head.

There was a long silence, and then he said, "Would you like to come for a ride?"

"A ride? Where to?"

"William's Creek runs into a small lake just west of here. I sometimes go there after the saloon closes, to get away for an hour."

"Could we swim?" The thought of plunging into cool water was irresistible.

"If you like. I often do." There was a seductive huskiness to his tone. "I'll go see if I can rescue Klaus without getting bitten, and then I'll get the buggy from the livery stable."

He was back in a moment with the grumpy little dog. Hannah flew up the stairs and plopped Klaus on Daisy's bed. Then she rummaged in her bag for the swimming suit she'd packed in Victoria so long ago. A half-hour ago, she'd wanted nothing but sleep, and now she was wide awake and brimming with anticipation.

Daisy was creaming her face at the washstand, and she gave Hannah a questioning look.

"I'm going swimming with Logan, Mom." She braced herself for a barrage of questions and cautions and reminders about having to get up for work early in the morning, but Daisy just smiled at her from beneath the coating of face cream

"What a good idea. Have fun, dear."

Hannah waited for the *but* that inevitably would follow, and it didn't come. What was it with her mother these days? Going back in time had changed her. Hannah liked Daisy much better in 1868 than she had in 1997.

Feeling free and young, she raced down the steps and out the door.

The buggy was hitched to the patient horse, and Logan was waiting to help her up into the seat.

The drive out to the lake was like something out of a romantic movie, and Hannah did her best to describe movies to Logan. The moon was full, and it hung above them in the sky like a golden melon. The horse plodded through town and then turned along some invisible path at Logan's urging.

Foliage and tree branches brushed the buggy's sides, and the wheels tilted this way and that on the uneven ground. Hannah had the feeling those same wheels were turning inside of her, tipping her first one way and then the other, slowly but inexorably leading to some unknown destination.

Chapter Seventeen

This buggy was even smaller than the one Logan had taken when they went to look for the bridge. This one had room only for the two of them on its single leather seat.

Hannah tried to keep her thigh from pressing against Logan's leg, but it was impossible. She was sitting so close to him that she was conscious of every breath he drew, and the rocking of the buggy tossed her against his shoulder.

"Do you like to swim, Hannah?"

"I love it. I used to go to the pool at the Rec Center at least a couple times a week."

"Wreck Center?" He turned and gave her a look. "I often feel when I'm with you that you speak what sounds like English, but is actually a foreign language. So many of the words you use are not familiar to me." He shook the reins gently over the horse's back and it increased its pace a little. "That's how I know that as incredible as it sounds, the tale of how you came to be here in Barkerville is the truth. I don't begin to understand how such a thing could happen, but I have no doubt any longer that it did, just the way you described."

So he believed her. She didn't understand why it should mean so much to her, but it did. A rush of emotion washed over her: gratitude and affection and the most enormous sense of relief. It was so validating to know he believed her. She felt warm and incredibly happy and almost breathless.

"Thank you, Logan." There was a tremor in her voice, and he turned and smiled at her. "You're not going to weep, are you?" he asked. "I'm not certain I have another fresh handkerchief."

Bunching the reins in his left hand, he took hers in his right, gave it a comforting little squeeze, and then went on holding it, palm to palm, threading her fingers between his.

"I won't start bawling," she assured him. "It's just that it's been hard to know everyone thinks you're nuts. I've got so much more empathy now for the patients on the Psych ward who believe they're Napoleon or Cleopatra. When I get back—" She caught herself. "*If* I ever get back,

I'll be a lot more open to things that seem impossible."

"Is this *sikeward* the same as a lunatic asylum?"

"Sort of. Except that I think we treat the patients differently than they would now."

For the rest of the journey, she struggled to explain the differences in labeling and in attitudes between his time and her own. It led to a discussion about prejudice, which brought up the subject of the Civil War, and the South's attitude towards people of color.

That led to a discussion of the Chinese who lived in Barkerville, isolated from the rest of the community.

The words Logan used to describe minorities were different from the ones Hannah chose, and in her time his would have been considered insulting, but his convictions were exactly parallel to her own.

The discussion was engrossing. She was startled when Logan pulled the buggy to a standstill and released his clasp on her hand.

"Here we are."

Hannah caught her breath at the unspoiled scene that lay before her. They were on a grassy verge, and just below them was the lake, oblong, hardly bigger than a large pond.

It lay as still as a mirror under the night sky, reflecting the moon on its pewter surface.

Somewhere a loon laughed its crazy song, and as if in response, an owl hooted.

Logan stepped out of the buggy and came around to help her down. She shivered, aware of his hands on her waist, the tickling softness of the grass on her bare ankles. She was conscious as well of the isolation of the setting. For the first time, they were truly alone together.

The air felt like warm bathwater. Hannah gazed at the lake. "Is the water cold?"

Logan's teeth flashed in the moonlight. "I'd say it's refreshing."

"Like ice," she guessed, and he laughed and nodded.

"I'm going in anyway. After the heat today, I'd welcome a shot of ice water." She rescued the scrap of Lycra from the seat of the buggy and then hesitated, suddenly all too aware of the darkness of the surrounding woods.

"Logan, are there bears around here? Or cougars, or, ummm . . ." She tried to think of other threatening wild animals. "Moose, maybe?" she added weakly.

"Yes, all of those." His voice was amused. "And camels; we mustn't forget camels."

"Don't tease. I'm a city woman. I don't know much about the bush, but I do know there aren't any camels."

"Ahh, but there are. A packer named Frank Laumeister decided some years back that carrying supplies in by mules was too slow. He paid three hundred dollars each for twenty-three camels to be sent from Manchuria. At first, it seemed a good idea, but soon he found that the stony ground hurt the animals' feet. Mules and horses couldn't stand the smell of the camels and panicked when they came near. In the end he turned the camels loose to roam as they pleased."

"You know, I vaguely remember that story now, from some history lesson when I was in grade school. Anyhow, it's not camels I'm afraid of as much as bears. I'll just change here behind the buggy." She went to the opposite side and quickly shucked off her jeans and shirt, wriggling into her black swimsuit in record time.

She felt a little self-concious as she moved towards Logan, and she shivered. Her one-piece suit was fashionable and quite respectable by nineteen-nineties standards, but she had some idea now what a woman's swimsuit might look like in 1868—knee length, bulky, and concealing—and this sleek garment wasn't any of those things.

The moon was bright enough so that she could see the look on Logan's face when he caught sight of her, and she knew immediately that the suits he was used to weren't anything like the one she had on.

His expression made her want to giggle. The unflappable Logan McGraw was staring at her with his jaw hanging slack.

* * *

He felt as if he were bareback astride a runaway horse. For a moment he couldn't get his breath.

She was a near-naked vision out of a dream—lush, breathtaking in the silver wash of the moon. The black chemise-like garment she wore left little to the imagination; each rounded curve, each swell and hollow, was traced faithfully by fabric that clung as lovingly as her own skin to the contours of her beautiful body.

He knew then that he hadn't brought her here to swim. At some point during the past twenty-four hours, he'd given up the struggle to be honorable. He no longer cared that it was wrong to want her in his arms. The only thing he was certain of was that he wasn't about to wait any longer. It went even beyond want; she was a craving he could no longer deny.

"Hannah. My god, Hannah, you're beautiful." A powerful shaft of desire speared through him, and he took a step towards her. Running purely on need, he drew her fiercely into his arms, trailing his hands down her shoulders and arms. The feel of her naked skin beneath his palms drove him nearly mad with desire.

She looked up at him, and in the instant it took to lower his mouth to hers, she drew in a shivery breath.

His lips captured her mouth and his hands slid down her body. He felt the muscles beneath the satiny skin contract as his slow, searching palms smoothed across her buttocks and then cupped them, learning the shape and size of her, drawing her sharply into his body, against his erection.

She bucked against him and cried out, a single, wordless song of need.

He reached behind her, to the long single plait of hair hanging down her back, and with nimble fingers he unfastened it, gently loosening the braid, combing the silky mass free with his fingers so he could bury his face in its sweet-smelling glory. "I love your hair. I long to do this every time I'm near you."

An exultant sense of rightness overcame him. They were meant to be together, he and Hannah. Somehow they'd found one another even across the limitless boundaries of time and space. He cursed himself for wasting precious days, but he intended to waste no more.

Worshipping her with his hands, he delved beneath the mantle of hair and brought his palms up the sleekness of her ribs, taking her breasts in his hands through the silky fabric, weighing them, glorying in the way her nipples hardened beneath his stroking fingers. All the while his mouth devoured her, tongue promising, probing, sliding from her mouth to her cheeks, her jaw to her ears and throat, unable to get enough of her taste, of the salt of her sweat and the underlying delicious, subtle tang that was purely Hannah.

There was no resistance, and he expected none. The boundaries they'd drawn in the past were meaningless now. In the space of a few moments, an agreement had been reached, needing no words.

She responded to him fully, pressing against him in reckless abandon, eyes closed, beautiful face intent and yearning, her arms clinging to his back. When his hand slid down her stomach and came to rest between her legs, he cupped the damp mound outlined by the narrow band of fabric, and she arched against his palm and moaned, wet and so ready for him that he had to grit his teeth lest his body betray him before he even got his clothing off.

As if she sensed what he wanted, her hands came round to his chest and unfastened the buttons of his shirt. She pressed her face to his bare chest, touching her lips to his skin, making him shudder.

He slid out of his shirt, and now her skin was against his, tender and satiny against his hair-roughened chest. He could feel her nipples, hard and thrusting, through the fragile fabric of the swimsuit she still wore.

Unable to stand even the slightest barrier between them, he searched in a fever for some fastening, some method of removing the garment, but there were no buttons, no snaps that he could find anywhere. How the hell had she gotten into the thing?

Understanding, smiling up at him, she raised her fingers to her shoulders and tugged, illustrating how the magical fabric gave freely. He put his hands to the straps and stretched them down her arms, and the garment peeled away from her body like the skin from an orange.

"Hannah. Oh, Hannah." He dipped his head and took the tight bud of one nipple into his mouth, suckling gently before he turned to the other. Such magnificent breasts, rounded and full, satin against his cheek and his lips. She gasped and clung to him.

"Hannah, my lovely Hannah." The beauty of her name rolled from his tongue like a love song.

She moaned and he unbuckled his belt, stripping off boots and pants. In the absence of a blanket, he carefully spread his discarded shirt on the grass before he tugged her down beneath him.

The smell of growing things mingled with the intoxicating perfume he associated with her, a faint reminder of apples in springtime.

He could wait no longer. His flesh burned for her. He straddled her naked body, bending to kiss her mouth, a kiss wild and deep. As he did so he slid a hand down, touching her naked wet flesh, exploring the swollen folds and searching out the moist nub that ensured her pleasure, circling it slowly and then more firmly with his finger until she cried out and writhed beneath him.

Only then did he enter her, smooth and slow, burying his tortured flesh to the hilt.

As he thrust into her, Hannah grew blind and deaf to everything except the new rush of pleasure that consumed her. She wrapped her legs around him, reaching up to touch his face with her fingertips as exquisite heat and desperate hunger gathered and slowly grew inside of her.

Their bodies were slick with sweat, and the musky male scent of him filled her nostrils. She could feel him in the very core of her being, rocking in a rhythm that her body recognized and strove to emulate. The intensity built until she thought she would die of it, and now she took desperate handfuls of his long, thick hair in her fists. "Hurry, oh please, Logan, now, please—"

He should have been beyond control, but he wasn't. He was waiting for her. He surged into her, again and yet again, and she hung suspended on an agonizing cusp for what seemed an eternal moment.

Then her body shattered, clamping and convulsing so violently, some faraway part of her was terrified at the intensity.

His climax began an instant after hers, and

with his shout of release she felt his seed spurt hotly into her.

They'd taken no precautions. She understood at that moment that she could become pregnant with his child, and she gloried in the thought.

She understood as well that until now, she'd never understood what passion really meant. She might as well have been a virgin, because what she'd just experienced with Logan was not comparable to anything she'd ever felt before.

The feelings that engulfed her in dizzying waves of intensity had no precedent in her experience. If this was how lovemaking was meant to feel, it was new to her, strange and wonderful.

So this was what her mother and her father had shared. This was at the heart of the love Daisy had had for Michael. For the first time, Hannah understood.

Logan collapsed over her and, careful not to crush her, he rolled to his side, holding her close. For a long while they lay entwined, breath and heartbeats gradually becoming normal once again.

The mare whinnied, and Hannah started in his arms.

Logan laughed softly. "Poor old horse. I forgot to unhitch her and she's righteously angry with me." He kissed Hannah's neck. "Stay here. I'll be back in a moment." He got to his feet, unabashedly naked. He pulled on only his boots, which should have looked ridiculous but instead, Hannah decided, was incredibly sexy, and went to tend to the animal.

Hannah watched him, his tall male body with its powerful muscles splendid in the moonlight. His stomach was flat, his legs long and strong and well formed, his shoulders broad. His strength showed in the effortless way he moved, the easy, offhand way he unhitched the horse and tethered her to a nearby tree so she could graze. He spoke softly to the mare and rubbed her neck, then went to the buggy and retrieved towels. He turned and came walking back towards Hannah.

He was a beautiful man.

She tried to remember what Brad looked like naked, but the image was blurred. He wasn't as muscular as Logan, that was certain, but what had his *face* looked like? She closed her eyes, but the face that sprang to mind was Logan's.

She opened her eyes again, and he was standing over her, reaching down to pull her effortlessly to her feet.

"I thought you wanted to swim, woman, and here you are lying about in the grass instead." His tone was light, but the way he drew her into his arms and held her for a long moment tight against him was an indication that what had happened between them had affected him deeply, just as it had her.

With an arm around her bare shoulders, he

led the way down to the lake. The beach was covered in small, sharp stones, and he swung Hannah up in his arms and carried her down to the water. He set her down to pull off his boots, and hand in hand, they waded in. Just as she'd suspected, the water was icy cold against her skin; she drew in a shocked breath and then splashed his stomach.

"Vixen," she heard him gasp as she dove, and when she surfaced, he was swimming beside her. Like her, he was a strong swimmer, at home in the water.

After the initial shock, her body adjusted to the cold, and it felt wonderful to swim hard, to duck beneath the surface and feel the water close above her head, knowing Logan was only an arm's length away.

They splashed and played like children, shouting and teasing, laughing with abandon. When they'd had enough, they scrambled out, wincing and laughing as they limped together over the sharp stones.

Logan wrapped a towel around her shoulders and spread the other on the grass, drawing Hannah down beside him, his arm around her.

He took her hand and his fingers searched out her engagement ring, twisting it on her finger.

"If you found a way back, would you go?"

It was a question Hannah didn't want to think about. Each hour she spent in Barkerville made her other life seem further and further away, but that didn't mean she liked being in Barkerville. She'd done her best to adjust in every way she could, but she still longed for her old life, her job, her friends, her apartment.

"I don't think we're going to find any way back," she replied, knowing she wasn't really answering his question.

She waited a heartbeat, and then she said in a hesitant voice, "If we did, if it was possible, would you come with me, Logan?"

Chapter Eighteen

He didn't answer for a moment. "I have business I have to attend to here. I couldn't go until it was concluded."

She felt irritated and ridiculously disappointed, considering that the idea of traveling through time again was like expecting lightning to strike twice in the same place. "What business, Logan? The Nugget?"

"No."

The flat denial, with no explanation, irritated her even more. They were lovers. She'd answered all his questions honestly and openly.

"Why did you come to Barkerville?"

She'd asked before, but his answer hadn't satisfied her. Some instinct told her that there was more to know.

"I've told you, I'm a gambler. There's as much gold to be made here at a gaming table as there is sweating in a mine."

"But you have some other business as well? Something secret, that you don't want to discuss with me?"

"It's not a thing I can talk about, Hannah. Not with you or anyone." He drew her closer to his body, but she pulled away, angry now and hurt that he didn't feel he could confide in her.

"Secrets are very bad, Logan," she snapped. "Two people need absolute honesty between them if a relationship is going to work."

His voice was deceptively mild. "You and your affianced, this Brad, you were always totally honest with one another?"

"Yes, we were." She pulled her legs up and circled them with her arms, aware of the hypocrisy of discussing Brad while she sat stark naked under the moon with another man.

"I wouldn't have dreamed of keeping secrets from him, or he from me." She looked at Logan defiantly. He was studying her, and his eyes looked black in the moonlight, the lines of his face harsh.

"You lied, Hannah. To him, to yourself, and now even to me."

"How dare you say that?" Shocked and insulted, she tried to throw his arm off her shoulders, but he held her firmly, his voice still soft but relentless.

"You insist that you love him, but in my arms it isn't him you think of, is it, Hannah? It wasn't his name on your lips when you shuddered and clung to me up there on the grass. So how could you have loved him the way you claim?"

Shame rolled over her in a hot wave. He was taunting her, making a mockery of what had happened between them.

"Let me go. How can you do this? How can you say such things?" She was close to tears, and she struggled to break free of his arms, but he held her easily.

"Listen to me, sweetheart. Listen, and be honest with yourself this once, if you value honesty as you say you do."

She realized that he was angry, just as angry as she.

"Did it feel like this when he kissed you?" He set his mouth on hers and she tried to turn her head, but he held her chin easily, kissing her relentlessly until she stopped struggling and desire mixed sharply with her anger.

He sensed it and eased her back, using her towel to protect her from the earth, and now his mouth found her breasts. The wet heat, the soft tickling of his mustache against her naked skin, inflamed her against her will, and her nipples hardened under the onslaught of his tongue.

"Did you feel this way in his arms, Hannah?"

She was stubbornly silent, willing herself not to respond, but he reached down to inflame her with his fingers and she moaned against his throat and moved with the rhythm he established. She could feel the weight and heat of his erection against her belly, and she reached a greedy hand down to guide him inside her. He gripped her wrist and held her still.

"My name, Hannah. Say my name."

She turned her head away from his kisses, but his skin pressed against hers, rough where she was soft, and the ache between her legs intensified, making her gasp with desire.

He reached for the finger that wore the engagement ring and slowly, gently, pulled it off.

"This is a lie, Hannah. You belong to me. You've always belonged to me."

She could have stopped him, but she didn't.

"You're mine, Hannah. Tell me that you're mine."

She refused to answer. Slowly, so slowly she wanted to scream at him to hurry, he entered her, and with a sob, she moved her hips, her body tensing, striving for fulfillment. Her legs came up and clasped his hips, urging, begging. He moved slowly, thrusting until his entire length filled her.

"Say it, Hannah. Say that you're mine."

She flexed her inner muscles and he groaned. "Damn you, you stubborn woman. Say it, Hannah. Say . . . it."

She couldn't take it any longer. "Logan. Logan, please. I need you, Logan."

He began moving with a powerful rhythm, and she drew in a sobbing breath, understanding with every cell in her body what it was he needed from her. Wild and free, she rode the crest with him, and as it broke she cried out his name, again and again. And as waves of unbearable ecstasy crested and waned, she said what she'd struggled so hard to deny.

"Logan, I love you. I love you, Logan."

He kissed her and smoothed back the tangle of her hair.

"And I you."

He sighed and rested his chin on her forehead, and then he rolled them both so her body rested on him. The sadness in his voice was palpable when he spoke again. "You love me, but if the road is there, you'll go back."

There was no longer room between them for anything but truth. "Yes. I'd have to go." She wrapped her arms around him and held him close, and the words hurt her heart.

"My business will be concluded before winter, but I can't be sure of its outcome, except that if all goes well I'll be leaving Barkerville, and I won't return."

It seemed they had no future, but if she'd learned anything from the bizarre path her life had taken, it was that absolutely nothing was certain, and anything was possible.

"We have right now, Logan."

She bent her head and kissed him.

* * *

It was nearly dawn when Hannah crept into the dark bedroom with the taste and feel of Logan's last kiss on her lips and her engagement ring in the pocket of her jeans.

Klaus growled at her and she shushed him. She slipped out of her clothes and tossed them on the chair, feeling around for her nightshirt.

"Use the flashlight, dear, I'm not asleep. Did you have a good swim?"

Hannah blushed, grateful for the darkness. "Yeah, it was fantastic." She pulled the nightshirt over her head and found the hairbrush, pulling it through the disordered mess of her hair, wishing she could put her life in order with as little effort. Hers, and Logan's as well.

"Mom?"

"Mhmm?

"I'm not going to marry Brad. I mean, even if we find a way back. I wouldn't be able to marry him."

"Oh, Hannah. Oh, that's *wonderful* news." Daisy sounded as if Hannah had just told her she'd won the lottery . . . did they have lotteries yet?

Daisy sat up, her voice filled with excitement. "I never thought you were suited. And I despised that mother of his. But most of all, you didn't act as if you were in love, either of you. It worried me so." Daisy sighed, a deep, contented sigh. "You and Logan are, though, aren't you? I've known since the very beginning that you were right together."

Hannah shook her head and rolled her eyes. Daisy surprised her now on a daily basis, but this next part was going to be difficult.

"We're in love, Mom. And I want to be with him." How could she feel so blissful and so bashful all at the same time? Hannah wondered.

"Of course you do."

"But we're not talking about marriage here." She had to make this absolutely clear to Daisy.

"Well, you can be together without being married," her mother said in a complacent tone. "You young people didn't invent sex, you know. Your father and I were together for three years before we got married. I never wanted to marry, you see. It wasn't until you were on the way that he talked me into going to a justice of the peace."

Hannah couldn't believe her ears. "You lived together? I didn't know that."

Daisy's voice was amused. "We didn't live together, darling. It wasn't done in those days. But we slept together. We were together in every way that mattered."

It dawned on Hannah that her mother was a frankly sensual woman. "You never told me you were pregnant before you got married."

Daisy sighed. "I thought of telling you, but the time never seemed right somehow. You were so smart, darling, so much smarter than me, and even from the time you were little, you were so . . . so *moral,* so certain about what was right and wrong." Daisy gave a sad little laugh. "I used to think I wasn't really fit to be your mother, that you should have had someone much wiser and better than me. I felt so inadequate. I guess I was scared to let you know what I was really like, in case you gave up on me altogether."

Hannah was dumbstruck. *She* had intimidated *Daisy?*

"Oh, Mom. I always thought—I thought it was me, that I wasn't pretty enough for you, that I was too big, too clumsy, that you'd have liked a daughter more like you—"

"Come over here." Daisy's voice was tear-choked, and when her arms closed around Hannah's neck, both their cheeks were wet. "You're so beautiful, my darling. How could you ever think that? What on earth did I do to make you feel that way?"

They cried, and mopped up each other's tears, and something old and hurtful between them was healed by the salt.

The gray morning light began to creep into the little bedroom, and at last they lay down to sleep for an hour, mindful of the work-filled day ahead.

Just before she slept, Hannah heard her

mother say, "Coming here was the best thing we ever did."

Hannah thought it over, and in spite of everything, she decided Daisy was right.

The following Sunday, Hannah and Daisy and Elvira attended church services in the tiny schoolhouse.

Attendance was small and predominantly female; Logan had advised Hannah that miners reserved Sundays for saloons, gambling, relaxation, drinking, and fornication. It was the busiest day of the week at the Nugget, and also at the brothels.

Carefully dressed in their period costumes, which now included bonnets Hannah had bought them, the three women were invited to tea after the service with Prudence Heatherington, Mary Winnard, the blacksmith's wife, and Rebecca Carroll, who was married to Doc Carroll.

Rebecca Carroll was a tall, attractive woman, very religious, with decided views.

"It's appalling to me that Barkerville has twelve saloons and no church building," she stated. "I feel that if women weren't in such a minority in this town, we could prevail upon the men to raise the funds and build one. A church would provide a center where women felt comfortable. There is no suitable meeting place for the respectable women in Barkerville."

Later that week, Hannah thought about Rebecca's remark, and also about the position women held generally in the Barkerville community. Her own experience with Slater, Logan's comments about the courts being sympathetic to men, and the horrifying fact that women were considered the property of their husbands nagged at her.

What was needed in Barkerville, she concluded, wasn't so much a place to meet, but a woman's group who got together and discussed the injustices of the system and used their brains to figure out ways to improve things. The idea was exciting. She'd sponsored numerous groups in her work at the hospital, and she made up her mind to try to form one now.

She decided to bounce the idea off Logan that night, after they'd made love. Although she hadn't formally moved into his bedroom, Hannah now spent most of her nights there.

As if sleeping with him wasn't enough, there was an added bonus; he was usually playing cards or working in the saloon long past midnight, and having his bedroom to herself for hours each evening was sheer luxury. Hannah suspected that Daisy also enjoyed her newfound privacy.

Tonight he'd slid into bed beside her and kissed her awake, and now they lay depleted, her leg still draped over his hip.

She pressed her nose against him, drawing in

the intoxicating scent of his sweat-dampened skin, and she told him about the group she wanted to form, anticipating his support.

She was let down and keenly disappointed when it didn't come.

"If there were more married women in this town and they banded together, you might have some luck getting things changed because those women would prevail on their husbands," he pointed out. "But the greatest majority of the women here are dance-hall girls and prostitutes. They make their money off men and they're not going to support any newfangled ideas that might affect their income."

Hannah moved her nose and her leg and flopped over to her side of the bed. "For heaven's sake, Logan, you're the one who told me how unfairly women are treated by the courts. And the women who end up in court most often are the prostitutes. I'd think they'd be the first to want equal justice."

"If you're going to form a group and encourage the prostitutes to attend, you won't get any of the respectable women," he said reasonably enough.

"Well, I'm going to try it anyway. I'll put notices up in the post office and the stores." Now she hated having to ask what she'd thought would be a given. "Can we meet in the kitchen downstairs?"

He was silent for a long while. Finally, grudgingly, he said, "I suppose you can. But I don't think this is a good idea, Hannah."

For the rest of that night they lay side by side instead of wrapped in each other's arms.

Hannah drew up posters the following night after work. Elvira was in the habit of coming for a visit in the evening, and she was surprisingly helpful.

"There's a real need for basic education amongst the dance-hall girls. I've already seen two botched abortions at the hospital. And Doc says the working girls and also some of the wives get beaten up regularly, but nothing's done about it."

The problem was in knowing what to put on the posters that wouldn't alienate either the married women or the prostitutes. They finally settled on a simple notice that read, "Woman's Meeting, female issues of every sort to be discussed. *All* women welcome. 8 P.M. Wednesday, August 5, kitchen of Nugget Saloon."

The first meeting was a disappointment, because the only other women who turned up besides Hannah, Elvira, and Daisy were Mary Winnard, Rebecca Carroll, Prudence, and a dance-hall girl from Frenchie's who insisted her full name was Gentle Annie.

When she walked in, Mary Winnard and Prudence walked out, but to Hannah's surprise, Rebecca stayed. Hannah outlined what she felt a woman's organization might provide in terms of personal support, education, and eventual change in the community.

Rebecca insisted they should begin by raising money for a church. Elvira said they should do something about the sewage that was being dumped in the creek, not to mention the men spitting on the street, and Gentle Annie said absolutely nothing after stating her name.

Daisy served sweet buns and coffee cake. Hannah suggested they meet every Wednesday, and everyone agreed.

It was a beginning.

Chapter Nineteen

The long August days scorched by with no respite from the heat. Residents said it was the worst dry spell they'd ever seen, and the water level in William's Creek dropped alarmingly.

Daisy served ingenious salads at room temperature and bemoaned the lack of a refrigerator. She bought bread from the bakery so she didn't have to use the stove all day, and Logan hired a crotchety older man called Zeb to help her.

Within a day, it was obvious that Zeb worshipped Daisy, and from then on they worked flawlessly together.

The men she cooked for also worshipped her; they brought her wildflowers, fish they'd caught, venison steaks, and every sort of wild berry, and they laughed uproariously when Klaus, particularly foul-tempered in the heat, singled out someone's ankles as a special target for his sharp teeth. Daisy averaged three proposals a week, and miraculously, she put on weight and lost the transparent fragility that had so worried Hannah.

On August ninth, Daisy learned that her great-grandfather was dead. Ezekial Shaw had fallen down the fifty-foot shaft of his mine and broken his neck. His partner brought his body into Barkerville for burial, and instead of the meeting with Ezekial she'd so anticipated, Daisy attended his funeral.

There were only a handful of mourners. Because there was no church, the coffin was simply carried to the small cemetery up on the hill above Barkerville. It was an open field studded with stumps and crabgrass.

The ceremony was short and poignant, conducted by Reverend Reynard. He spoke of Ezekial's wife and his children, a daughter and a son, left behind in England when Ezekial came to the goldfields to make their fortune.

What shocked Hannah most was learning that Ezekial was only thirty-six years old. She'd somehow had it in her head that he'd be an old man. She and Daisy joined in the hymn and laid wildflowers on his rough wooden coffin.

Afterwards, Hannah walked around the cemetery, reading the inscriptions on the wooden markers. Most of them were young men like Ezekial. The average age was thirty-two.

They'd come from all over the world—Ireland, Scotland, Italy. They'd dreamed of getting rich by finding gold, and some of them probably had; Ezekial must have made a fortune, because the money had passed down through several generations to Daisy.

But they'd paid with their young lives. Had it been worth it? Hannah wondered. Did Ezekial's wife, off in England raising her children alone, think the loss of her husband was fair exchange for gold?

Hannah looked over at Logan, and she knew that all the gold in Barkerville wouldn't make up for one of the nights they spent together.

She paused at a well-tended gravesite surrounded by a little picket fence. There were three small wooden markers, and bouquets of dried wildflowers on each grave.

BABY ELEANOR CARROLL, AGED FIVE DAYS.

BABY FRANCES CARROLL, AGED ONE DAY.

BABY MYLES CARROLL, STILLBORN.

Hannah read the poignant record of Rebecca's heartbreak, and her eyes filled. Three babies, and not one had lived. It gave her a new understanding of Rebecca and her single-minded crusade for a church in Barkerville. Maybe having a place of worship would have been a comfort to her, and to Doc Carroll.

The funeral lingered in Hannah's mind afterwards, and somehow the tragedy of Ezekial's death made the time she and Logan spent together more meaningful.

They made frequent midnight trips out to the lake. He said no more about the women's meetings or the fact that they were still so poorly attended.

She gave up trying to find out about his mysterious business. She developed the knack of living one day at a time, and when the familiar cold terror came over her at the thought of losing him, leaving him, living a life without him, she shoved it into a container in her mind and locked the lid. They had now, and she vowed to make the most of it.

They talked about the world she'd been born into. She described cars, computers, vacuum cleaners, television. He was fascinated by her depictions of airplanes, space travel, UFO's. Her recall of history was sketchy at best, but she filled in the major events of the next hundred years. Logan couldn't believe that the world could possibly be embroiled in so many wars. They talked of events in the very near future, particularly the Barkerville fire, which Logan now believed was inevitable.

He made a point of mentioning the possibility of fire to the businessmen of the town when they gathered for their monthly meeting in the Nugget saloon at lunchtime. He pointed out that there were no fire lanes, no barrels of available water, and no insurance.

They laughed and jibed him for being a worrier, and assured him that the town was built of wood different from other wood and wouldn't burn, a claim so preposterous that he lost his temper and called them windbags and idiots.

Insulted, they moved their monthly meetings to the Eldorado.

One sweltering Friday afternoon in mid-August, Hannah was cleaning the window at the front of Pandola's when a middle-aged man with a Vandyke beard rode slowly past on a beautiful chestnut horse. He looked at Hannah, nodded politely, and tipped his tall hat. There was a regal air about him.

She smiled and waved her cloth, wondering who he was. He looked both handsome and distinguished.

Two miners were just coming out of the store, and they doffed their hats politely to the horseman.

"Judge Begbie's back early this year."

"Things'll quiet down now," the other one replied. "Ain't nobody wants ta stand in front a' Begbie. Don't call him the Hangin' Judge fer nothin'."

Hannah shivered and blamed it on the heat.

An hour later, Pandola said to Hannah, "Miss Gilmore, you watcha the store. I'll be back three, maybe three-thirty."

"Sure, Mr. Pandola." Hannah grinned at her employer, knowing he'd be gone until five. She wondered if the day would ever come when he'd call her by her first name and allow her to do the same with him, but she doubted it.

She'd been working at Pandola's over a month now. During that time, she'd asked on several occasions that he call her Hannah, and he'd reacted as if she'd suggested they fornicate in the back room on top of the flour sacks.

He'd seemingly come to trust and rely on her as an employee, though; for the past two weeks, he'd fallen into the habit of leaving her to run the store by herself while he paid an extended visit to the Nugget saloon each day.

Logan had confided that Pandola was doing his best to court Daisy.

Hannah had asked her mother what was going on, and Daisy blushed and said that Joe was a nice man but not her type.

"Lead him on just a little, okay, Mom? It's so relaxing at the store when he's not there."

Mother and daughter had fallen into a fit of the giggles.

Hannah smiled at the memory. She and Daisy were close in a way they'd never been before, and Hannah loved it. She mopped at her forehead with a cotton handkerchief and unfastened still another button on the high-necked blouse she wore.

The days were unbearably hot, and they

seemed to be getting even hotter. People grumbled about the weather much the way they had back in her own time; the only thing missing was the tendency to blame the searing heat on the greenhouse effect.

It was noon, and the store was empty. She got out her cheese sandwich and the bottle of tea she'd brought for lunch, and drew a high stool up to the counter. The tea was as warm as the air, but at least it was wet; she sipped it while she ate, smothering a yawn between bites. Lordie, she was tired.

She and Logan had gone to the lake the night before, and she'd only managed a few hours' sleep before it was time to get up for work. She wondered if he was as sleepy today as she. He'd been up this morning before her, standing in the kitchen in his shirtsleeves peeling an apple. He fed Hannah bites of the tart fruit and kissed her senseless before she tore herself away and hurried off to work.

She stared down at the wooden counter, imagining Joe Pandola's shock if she used one of the small knives they sold to carve "Hannah loves Logan" into its smooth surface.

It was nothing less than the truth, she mused as she set the rest of the sandwich aside, propped her elbow on the counter, and rested her head on her hand.

She grinned, remembering the title of a

movie she'd watched in what she now thought of as her former life.

Truly, Madly, Deeply. The words had seemed melodramatic to her when she watched the movie, but they made perfect sense now. They described exactly the way she felt about Logan.

A thrill shot through her when she remembered details of the night before. They swam, they talked, but mostly they made love, and Hannah privately wondered if she was turning into a sex junkie.

"Hard night, dearie?"

The raspy, knowing female voice close to her ear made Hannah jump, and she almost toppled off the stool.

The voluptuous black-haired woman on the other side of the counter laughed, but the laughter didn't reach as far as her eyes.

"I'm Carmen Hall." Hannah knew her by sight as the madam of Frenchie's house of prostitution. She'd been in the store before, but Pandola had always served her. He did a good business with the dance-hall girls and prostitutes. They had money to spend, and they spent it lavishly.

She'd heard Pandola talking to one of his cronies about Carmen Hall. Apparently she had a partner, a man named Flannery, who was presently on a trip to Europe to bring back new girls.

Hannah stared at Carmen, fascinated by the

woman's dissipated beauty. She looked about Hannah's age.

Did she love Flannery?

"Where's Joe, dearie?"

Hannah cleared her throat. "He's out for a couple of hours. Can I help you, Miss Hall?"

"He was supposed to order me in a bolt of satin. You know anything about it?"

"I'm afraid I don't. I can have a look in the back, though. What color was it?"

"Don't bother. I'll talk to Joe." She didn't seem in any hurry to leave, however. She wandered over to the corner where Hannah had arranged an assortment of towels and flicked through them with a disdainful air, then ambled over to the counter again and leaned on it, studying Hannah as if she were merchandise.

"I hear you're living at the Nugget."

Hannah nodded.

"Word is you belong to McGraw."

Hannah hadn't realized the whole town knew about her and Logan, and she had to struggle to disguise her shocked reaction. Her cheeks grew hot, but she managed to meet Carmen's eyes straight on. "Where I come from, women don't belong to anyone except themselves," she said in a level voice.

"Ooh, an independent lady," Carmen said with a smirk. "I like that. Hannah—that's your name, right? Hannah Gilmore. Well, I'm independent myself, Hannah. Say, I heard about these meetings of yours from Gentle Annie. She works for me. Sounds like you got some pretty highfalutin ideas. And where would you be from?"

Hannah hesitated. "Victoria."

Carmen's thin eyebrows rose. "Not what I'd call a free-thinking place. Musta changed a lot since I was there."

Hannah nodded. "I suspect so."

Carmen's eyes narrowed. "There was lotsa talk when you three"—she paused, and her voice was sarcastic when she added—"*ladies* rolled into town that night. I saw you the next day. You were wearing some rig even my girls wouldn't be seen in on the street." Her eyes raked down Hannah's modest shirtwaist and skirt, lingering on the sandals on her feet. "That getup you got on now looks ordinary enough. You could use a decent pair of boots, though, dearie. Can't you get McGraw to part with any of that gold he scalps off the miners?"

Hannah looked her straight in the eye, keeping her voice polite but refusing to be intimidated. "I support myself, and actually, I prefer these sandals. They're cooler than boots."

"I bet they are at that." Carmen laughed. "I like you, Hannah Gilmore. Maybe I'll come to one of these meetings of yours. Between you and me we could set some things straight around this town."

To Hannah's immense relief, two miners

came into the store just then. They nodded to Carmen, and she raised a hand in laconic greeting.

" 'Lo, Pete. How's it goin, Virgil?" She moved away from the counter. "Well, dearie, I gotta be getting back. Tell Joe he can deliver that satin."

"I'll do that." Hannah watched the other woman sashay off down the boardwalk.

As she went about measuring out the oats and flour and sugar that the miners wanted, Hannah wondered if Carmen meant what she'd said about attending the meetings. She was still thinking about the encounter when she got off work that evening.

She was almost at the Nugget when Angus came tearing up the boardwalk towards her, the terrified expression on his tearful face signaling that something was wrong. Hannah reached out to steady him as he jerked to a stop beside her.

"I gotta get Doc Carroll quick." He wiped his wrist across his runny nose. "My Jeannie's hurt. Daisy says get Doc Carroll."

Hannah started to run towards the Nugget. There was no one in the kitchen, and no sign of Logan either when she stuck her head into the crowded saloon.

Hannah raced up the steps to the bedroom and tore the door open.

Jeannie lay on her back on one of the narrow beds, her pregnant belly big beneath the sheet.

Daisy had a basin of water on the floor and Jeannie's face was covered with a washcloth.

"Mom? Jeannie?" Hannah approached the bed and the washcloth slipped off. Jeannie was sobbing, a gut-wrenching sound, but it was her face that roused shock, horror, and then outrage.

The delicate girl looked like a prizefighter after a match. Her right eye was blackened and almost shut, her nose was crooked and bleeding, and there was a deep gash on her cheek. Her entire face was bruised and swollen almost beyond recognition.

"Oh, my God." Hannah groped for the girl's work-worn hand and squeezed it. "Oh, my God, what happened?"

"Oscar." The one muffled word was enough.

"I've sent Angus for the doctor. I told him to get Elvira to come back with him, too," Daisy said in a trembling voice. "Hannah, I'd like a word with you." She motioned to the door and Hannah followed her out.

Daisy was on the verge of tears. "Jeannie's pains have started. She's scared to death that brute of a husband is on his way to town after her. She took the horse, but she's certain he'll follow her on foot."

"When did she get here?"

"Twenty minutes ago, no more."

"Where's Logan?"

"He left right after supper. Angus thinks he's

over at Kelly's Boarding House. There's a big poker game there tonight."

"I'm going to get him." Hannah raced down the stairs, skirts gathered high above her knees. Kelly's Boarding House was on the opposite side of the street and a quarter of a mile away, almost into Chinatown.

She ran all the way, using the street instead of the boardwalk, ignoring the ankle deep dust that churned up in stifling clouds around her legs, dodging several startled horses and a wagon.

When she reached the large frame building, she didn't pause to knock on the door. She marched straight in, puffing hard, and found herself in a front parlor. There was a white-haired man sitting in a rocking chair reading a newspaper, and he leaped to his feet when she came in, pipe in hand, eyebrows at his hairline.

"I need Logan McGraw," she burst out. "Get him, quick."

"Oh, I dunno, miss—they said they're not to be disturbed."

Hannah glared. "Get him, or I'll go looking for him myself."

He hurried off, and seconds later, Logan was beside her. Hannah gasped out the story, and Logan's face hardened.

Two minutes later, they were hurrying down the boardwalk towards the Nugget, her hand clamped firmly in his.

"Shouldn't we get the constable?" Hannah was having a hard time keeping up with him, and she was breathless. "Jeannie says Oscar's coming after her."

"Bowran and Judge Begbie are both up at the Lowhee mine investigating a suicide. They won't be back till tomorrow."

"But Oscar's dangerous."

"Damned right he is, and threats about jail won't scare him. Jeannie's his property, and he knows the law doesn't take kindly to women running away from their husbands."

Hannah couldn't believe what she was hearing. "The man's beaten her, for heaven's sake. He belongs in jail. She's in labor—the baby's coming early because of him. He could have killed her."

"I'm not denying that. I'm telling you the way things are. Oscar Chalmers paid good money to bring Jeannie and Angus here. In the eyes of the law, they owe him a debt. The fact that he's a wife beater and a bully and ought to be horsewhipped won't change a jury's mind on the matter one bit."

Hannah was fuming. "But what can Jeannie do? There must be something she can do."

"Technically she can leave him and sign a promissory note to pay back the money he spent on fare. But Oscar's not going to take kindly to that. He's losing a housekeeper, a bed partner, and an unpaid laborer to work his gold mine."

Logan cursed under his breath and increased his stride.

"Chalmers is a mean son of a bitch, and he's cheap as dirt. He'll do his best to drag her back where he figures she belongs."

His words sent an icy chill through Hannah. "What will you do, Logan?"

"Anything I can to keep him from harming Jeannie or her baby." He gave her a stern look. "And Hannah, listen to me. If there's trouble, I want you to stay the hell out of it."

She opened her mouth to argue and closed it again.

He was high-handed, but it was an enormous relief to have him in control.

Chapter Twenty

It was two-thirty in the morning, and even from a distance, Jeannie's awful groans had long ago left Logan's nerves raw.

How did a man bear it when it was his own wife making those agonized sounds? he wondered. And how was Hannah managing, being right beside Jeannie through it all? She was wonderfully brave, his Hannah. All women were, to go through this.

He was sitting alone and watchful in the shadows at the back of the Nugget when suddenly, at two-thirty-four, Jeannie's baby gave its first squawking cry.

Logan heard the sound clearly through the open bedroom window above his head. He shot to his feet and stood staring up at the lighted window, his heart suddenly hammering in his chest. To his amazement, tears filled his eyes and a feeling of wonder came over him as he blinked them away, relieved there was no one nearby to witness them.

He tensed as the crying stopped, concerned for the baby's well-being, but a moment later it began again, stronger and louder than before. He heard Hannah say something in a loud, excited voice, and then Doc Carroll's laugh boomed out.

The tension in Logan eased. Mother and baby must be fine, or Doc wouldn't be laughing that way.

Logan was grinning himself now. A new life had just come into the world, right here under his roof. Babies were a rarity in Barkerville. Would this one's birth be a good omen for the Nugget?

The crying went on and on, and Logan's heart twisted at its urgency. He remembered that particular sound from when he was a young boy, when Nellie was born. It brought back memories of his bungling attempts at feeding her and keeping her warm and dry, and it brought back as well the terrible sense of guilt and remorse that had haunted him since he'd learned of her death.

He clenched his fists and thought of Flannery for the first time in days. There'd been too many times in the past weeks when he'd all but forgotten why he was here in Barkerville.

It had to do with his feelings about Hannah. It was hard to stay focused when she was in his arms and on his mind, but the baby's cry brought back in vivid detail his memories of Nellie, and his resolve to avenge her death.

He crushed his cigar out on the sole of his boot and went over to the toolshed. He'd promised Angus that if he went to bed, Logan would stay on guard in case Oscar turned up. Logan had also promised he'd awaken Angus as soon as the baby was born.

Logan bent over the snoring boy and shook him gently. "Jeannie's had her baby, son, I heard it crying just now. Go on in and find out whether it's a boy or a girl, why don't you?"

Angus startled awake. "Jeannie's okay? She had the baby?"

"I just heard it crying a minute ago."

The boy's sleepy eyes filled with dread. "Oscar ain't come yet?"

Logan shook his head in reassurance. "No sign of him. I'm keeping an eye out like I promised, so don't worry. Now off you go and see your sister and the baby. You're an uncle—how about that?"

"Uncle." Angus scrambled up, pulled on his boots, and took off in a staggering run. Logan slowly walked back outside.

At times during the long night, Logan had asked himself if maybe he was being melodramatic, posting a guard against Oscar. But something in his gut, some sixth sense, told him Oscar Chalmers would come for what he considered his property, and that he'd do it sooner rather than later.

Logan suspected that Chalmers would count on the fact that Jeannie had nowhere to go and no one to protect her. People generally didn't want to involve themselves in marital problems, and everyone knew Oscar's temper and his meanness.

He'd know as well that Jeannie would never leave Barkerville without her brother. He'd guess that she'd have come here to the Nugget.

The lantern wick was turned high in the kitchen, and Logan went up the stairs, hoping that Hannah might have come down, but instead it was Elvira who was poking at the stove, shoving in a stick of wood to revive the dying fire.

The teapot was on a tray, along with sliced bread and butter, a pot of jam, and Daisy's molasses cookies.

Elvira shoved her glasses up her nose and turned to Logan, her plain face beaming. She looked almost pretty in the lamplight. "Jeannie's just fine and the baby's a girl. Prettiest little thing you ever laid eyes on, just over five pounds, but Doc says she's as healthy as can be, which is a miracle considering the circumstances." She was babbling.

Logan had to grin. "That's wonderful news."

Elvira gestured at the loaded tray. "Jeannie needs sustenance. She has to get her strength back if she's going to nurse that child. Doc Carroll could do with a cup of tea and a bite, and I suspect you could too, Logan. I'll get you to set the table down here. It's going to take some time for that kettle to boil again. I've taken all the warm water so I can wash the baby." She lifted the basin and headed for the stairs. "You fill the teapot and then refill that kettle before you bring up Jeannie's tray. And maybe put another stick of wood on that fire and refill the reservoir. I'll want to give Jeannie a sponge bath as soon as everybody clears out."

Elvira was a bossy woman, Logan thought with a grin. She'd have made a good drill sergeant in the army. He gave her a snappy salute, and when she disappeared up the stairs, Logan decided Doc Carroll might like something a little stronger than tea.

He headed into the dark saloon for a bottle of good whiskey, set it and some glasses on the table, and then added plates and cups, bread and cookies. When the kettle finally boiled, he went upstairs with the tray.

The small bedroom was overflowing with people. Hannah looked tired and she was pale, but her eyes were wide and shining when they met his. "Oh, Logan, come and see the baby."

He set the tray down on a stool beside the

bed, noting that Jeannie's face was even more swollen than it had been. In spite of what she'd been through, she looked up at him and tried to smile. "Thank you, Mr. McGraw, fer lettin' us stay here."

"Pleasure's all mine." His voice was suspiciously thick, and he took her hand and gripped it. Then he peered down at the towel-wrapped bundle resting in the crook of her arm.

The baby's head wasn't as big as Logan's closed fist, and it was covered with a shock of bright orange hair. Her black, shoe-button eyes were open, and she seemed to be looking around. One tiny hand waved, and Logan reached out and touched it. The baby's hand closed around his finger and his heart swelled.

"She likes ya," Angus crowed. He was kneeling beside the bed, one hand resting on the baby.

"What's her name going to be?"

"Sophie, after our mother." Jeannie's eyes filled.

"Okay, everyone, clear out now so Jeannie can have her tea and then get some rest," Elvira ordered, and like a flock of schoolchildren, everyone obeyed her.

Back in the kitchen, Logan poured whiskey for himself and Doc, who tipped the glass back gratefully, declining tea and food. "Got to get home. At my age a man needs his sleep."

He left, and as soon as they'd had tea and a

sandwich, Hannah and Daisy went upstairs to bed. They were using Logan's room; he was banished again to the toolshed with Angus. Elvira would sleep on the second bed in Jeannie's room so she could keep an eye on mother and baby.

Logan, alone in the kitchen, yawned and turned the wick down in the lamp until the light was almost extinguished.

Outside, he made a circuit of the building, as he'd done regularly all night, watching for any changes on Barkerville's quiet main street. There were none since the last time he'd looked.

The moon had set, and it was too dark now to travel with any ease, so chances were that Oscar would wait till morning before he made his appearance.

Logan yawned again and slowly made his way around to the back. The lamp in the upstairs bedroom had been turned low, and not a sound came from the open window. Even the baby must have gone to sleep.

He went into the house, thinking he could use an hour's rest himself. He'd stretch out in the upstairs hall, on the straw pallet from the shed. He opened the door to get the pallet out, and a bloodcurdling scream came from upstairs.

Logan wasn't aware of climbing the staircase or even opening the door to the bedroom.

The lamp had been turned low and the shadows in the room were deep and thick. Jeannie was sitting up, clutching the bedcovers to her chest, her bruised, swollen features distorted with terror. Elvira, in pink pajamas, stood beside the other bed, and her face, too, registered horror and fear.

"Well, hullo, McGraw." Oscar Chalmers turned towards Logan and grinned, his thick lips pulled back over yellow teeth. His eyes were bloodshot and he staggered a little.

It was obvious he wasn't sober or rational.

His newborn daughter, swaddled in the white towel, was clamped carelessly under his left arm like a bundle of rags, and in his right hand he held a bowie knife. He was pointing the blade at Elvira, who screamed again, long and shrill.

"Shut up, ya old crow, or I'll cut ya," Oscar roared, waving the blade inches from her nose. Elvira stopped in mid-shriek and clamped a hand over her mouth. She'd been standing, but her knees gave way and she collapsed on the bed, shuddering.

"Put the baby down, Chalmers." Logan tried to keep his voice even and reasonable. He had his derringer in his hand, but he kept it hidden at his side. He didn't dare make a move as long as Chalmers held the child.

"Put her down and we'll talk." He was aware that Hannah had materialized at his side, and he cursed silently, wishing to hell she'd stayed put in her room. At least, after an initial gasp, she was quiet, but now Daisy was there too, just behind Logan.

He heard other voices from the rooms the miners were renting. They'd be out here in another minute as well, and Logan was afraid that the crowd of people might push Chalmers into using the knife.

"C'mon, Oscar," Logan wheedled. "Your wife just had the baby. She's small and she'd not doing so good. Doc said to keep her quiet," Logan lied. "You don't want something to happen to your own little girl, do you, Oscar?"

"Don't bullshit me, McGraw. This kid's fine. I'm takin' it home where it belongs." Chalmers leaned over the bed, the knife now inches from Jeannie's throat. "You wanta take care o'it, ya better get yer sorry ass home soons ya can. And where's the gold ya stole from me, ya thievin' whore?"

The knife waved unsteadily in front of Jeannie's face and Logan held his breath.

"Give me my baby." Jeannie's voice shook uncontrollably. "Please, Oscar, don't hurt her. Ya can take the gold—just don't hurt my baby. Please, Oscar."

"Bullshit." His roar reverberated through the small room, and Jeannie jumped and whimpered. "This kid's mine. She goes with me. That way ye'll be sure to come runnin' home, wontcha? And I want that poke ya stole right now, ya lyin, thieven' little bitch, ya hear me?" He feinted at her with the knife, grazing it across her cheek, and Jeannie shrieked and cowered back against the pillow.

From behind him Logan heard Hannah and Daisy cry out.

Oscar swore at them and the baby started to cry.

"The gold's downstairs in my safe, Oscar," Logan said. "Put the baby down and we'll go get it." Logan's fingers tightened helplessly around the small gun pressed tightly against his leg. His only hope was to try to reason with the other man, because he couldn't get a clear shot.

The baby's cries grew louder and more urgent, and Oscar gave the bundle an impatient shake.

The women all made horrified sounds, and Jeannie's agony was in her voice. "Oscar, don't hurt her. I'll do anything you say, but please don't hurt the baby like that."

"Please don't hurt the baby—" Oscar's taunting voice and sarcastic tone were pure evil.

Icy-cold rage sent adrenaline pumping through Logan's body. His eyes followed Oscar's every move, and his finger rested on the gun's trigger. He only needed one single, clear shot. . . .

Before Logan realized what she was doing, Hannah darted past him. In one smooth motion, she reached out and snatched the baby from under Oscar's arm, whirling away as quickly as she could, her body curled protectively around the child.

Oscar cursed and lunged towards her, the knife raised. Hannah twisted away, shielding the baby as the blade came slashing down.

Both Elvira and Daisy screamed.

Hannah made a choked sound in her throat as the knife grazed her shoulder. Her knees buckled and she fell, but she retained her hold on the baby, curling her body around it in a protective ball, her back to the knife.

Chalmers, thrown off balance by the force of his attack on Hannah, stumbled and caught himself on the iron railing at the foot of the bed. Then he raised the knife again, ready to drive it down into Hannah's back.

For one single moment, no one else was near him.

Logan raised his gun and aimed it at Oscar's chest.

Without hesitation, he fired.

Chapter Twenty-one

The investigation into Oscar Chalmers's death was held in the courthouse, presided over by Judge Begbie.

Hannah, her injured shoulder bandaged and aching, walked into the log building flanked by Logan, Daisy, Elvira, and Doc Carroll. Jeannie had wanted to come, but Doc forbade it. It was only four days since the baby's birth.

The shooting was the talk of the town, and every bench in the small log courthouse was filled, except for the space at the very front reserved for those involved in the proceedings.

Aware that every curious eye in the place was riveted on their little group, Hannah held her head high as she walked along the narrow aisle and sat down in the designated area, Daisy on one side of her and Logan on the other.

She told herself there was absolutely no reason to feel nervous and on edge, but she did anyway. She also felt slightly nauseated. Her shoulder throbbed, and she could smell the pungent ointment that Elvira had smeared on the wound.

Logan, immaculate in his well-pressed black suit and stiffly starched white shirt, reached over and took her fingers in his, giving them a reassuring squeeze, but when she turned to look at him, there was a remoteness about him that had been there ever since Oscar Chalmers crumpled to the floor in a pool of blood.

They'd just gotten settled when Constable Bowran cleared his throat noisily and bellowed, "All rise!"

Everyone stood, and with immense dignity and a fine sense of theater, Judge Begbie emerged from his chambers at the front of the room and sat down on the raised platform.

"Be seated," he boomed in a deep, rich voice that carried to the farthest corner of the building. "Let it be noted that this is an informal inquiry into the shooting death of one Oscar Chalmers which occurred at approximately three-forty-five on the morning of July 30th, in the year of our Lord eighteen-hundred and sixty-eight."

The court clerk was a small man wearing round glasses. He was seated off to one side of the judge, and he scribbled furiously in a large notebook.

Hannah stared up at Judge Begbie, intimidated in spite of herself. The judge was a thin-faced man somewhere beyond fifty, incredibly tall, at least six-four or five, with an upswept mustache and a white Vandyke beard with one distinctive black streak down its center.

Even for this informal inquiry, he wore flowing black robes and a long horsehair wig. He looked stern, and his piercing dark eyes caught and held her own for what could only have been a second but felt much longer.

Hannah shivered. She understood now why everyone seemed afraid of Judge Baillie Begbie, and she pitied anyone who had to stand accused before him. His gaze alone was enough to make one feel guilty, even if one weren't.

He conducted the investigation in a very orderly manner. Doc Carroll was called first, to describe in technical medical terms what the autopsy he'd performed on the body of Oscar Chalmers had revealed.

Hannah listened to the doctor's explanation, concluding that it was a long-winded way of saying that Oscar had died of a bullet that entered his chest, passed through his heart, and lodged in his spine.

She shuddered, unable to forget the agonizing moments she'd spent crouching on the floor with Jeannie's tiny baby wailing in her arms, waiting helplessly for Oscar's knife to stab deep into her back.

When Doc Carroll was done with his statement, Elvira was called. She stood, and Begbie motioned her to come forward so that she was standing directly below him.

Begbie leaned towards her. "Mrs. Taylor, I want to know exactly who you are, where you're from, and how you came to be present on the night in question."

Hannah stiffened. She and Elvira and Daisy had talked over how much of their story might be necessary in court, and they'd agreed that if they were asked, they'd simply give their home address as Victoria, without going into any details about how they came to be in Barkerville.

"I'm Mrs. Elvira Taylor, formerly of Victoria, British Columbia." Elvira's back was ramrod straight, her head high. "I'm a nurse, on an extended visit to Barkerville, and I'm presently employed by Doctor Carroll to assist him at the hospital. On the night in question—"

Hannah felt a surge of pride and had to hide a smile. Elvira had watched enough courtroom scenes on television to know the procedure and the language, and she wasn't about to be intimidated by Begbie. She told what she'd seen in a clear, straightforward manner. Her outrage and horror were evident in her tone when she described Jeannie's injuries and the scene in the bedroom that included Hannah being stabbed, and when she was finished, Begbie gave a satisfied nod.

"Thank you, madam. I wish all those appearing in my courtroom were as vocal and as eloquent." He looked down at his notes. "Mrs. Daisy Gilmore, if you please."

Hannah could feel the tremor that ran through her mother's slight frame, but she got to her feet, walked up to Begbie and told her story. Her voice trembled, and tears ran down her face when she described how Hannah had snatched the baby and been cut by Oscar's knife, but she made it through with real dignity.

Hannah felt enormously proud of her mother.

"Miss Hannah Gilmore." Lordy, it was her turn. Hannah's knees suddenly felt like jelly, and she had to make two attempts to get to her feet. Logan helped her.

"A chair for this witness, if you please," Begbie ordered, and when Hannah sank gratefully into it, he added, "Miss Gilmore, would you like a drink of water?" He held out a glass, filled from the pitcher on his desk.

Hannah took it and gratefully swallowed half of the lukewarm liquid.

Her voice wobbled at first. She said nothing about being a social worker, stating only that she worked at Pandola's store. Once she got through the first few sentences, it became easier to talk to Begbie. When Hannah was finished,

Begbie fixed her with his X-ray eyes.

"I commend your bravery, Miss Gilmore."

Hannah flushed and bit back the denial that sprang to her lips. It infuriated her that everyone considered what she'd done an act of bravery. In actual fact, snatching the baby from that madman hadn't been something she'd thought about or planned; it was as if her body had acted independently of her brain.

Logan was the only one who'd understood. He'd cursed and called her a bloody fool and a total idiot and been utterly furious with her for doing what she had, and she figured he was absolutely right.

He'd also scooped her up in his arms and raced down to his bedroom with her, hollering for Elvira, sending someone running for Doc Carroll, roaring orders and raging at everyone as if she was dying, instead of just bleeding a lot from a cut on the shoulder. Doc had threatened to tie him down and give him a sleeping potion.

The judge called Logan next, and Hannah felt her heart swell with pride as he quietly gave his version of what had happened.

Begbie was in no hurry to conclude the proceedings. When Logan was finished speaking, Begbie leaned back in his chair and stroked his beard, and the rustling from the spectators increased as he simply sat there, staring into the middle distance with a contemplative look on his face.

Hannah's heart was in her throat, and she silently cursed the judge for his need for drama. The hard bench bit into her thighs, and her shoulder had gone from uncomfortable to painful.

Reason told her that Begbie couldn't possibly find Logan guilty of anything, but she'd heard that Begbie made unorthodox judgments at times. She curled her hands into fists and stared at the judge, willing him to end the waiting, to do the only thing possible in this investigation: absolve Logan totally from any wrongdoing, and thank him for what amounted to saving the lives of Jeannie and her baby, and Hannah's as well.

At last the judge cleared his throat and rose to his feet. Like the showman he was, Begbie waited until the excited whispering and shifting of bodies gradually died away. There was hardly a sound in the courtroom when he spoke.

"I have listened most carefully to the witnesses in this matter of the shooting death of Oscar Chalmers, and it is my belief that what occurred is not a matter to be brought before the courts at this time."

Relief swept through Hannah like a cool breeze on a hot afternoon. She could feel tension draining from her body, and she reached over and squeezed Logan's hand, waiting for the judge to commend him.

"Stand up, Mr. McGraw."

Logan did, and Judge Begbie looked at him with a stern expression on his formidable features.

Hannah felt herself grow tense all over again.

"Mr. McGraw, how did you happen to have a gun handy on the night in question?"

"I own a derringer. I was wearing it because I was concerned for the safety of my household and Jeannie Chalmers."

"It is my firm belief that the wearing of firearms leads to tragedy, Mr. McGraw." Begbie's voice rose and he leaned forward, fixing Logan with a formidable stare. "Whatever the circumstances, a man's life has been taken, and that is a deplorable situation. My duty is to keep order and to administer the law, and I am a sworn enemy to the use of the knife and the revolver." He paused again, and the spectators seemed to hold their breath.

"In this case, it would seem you had little choice in the matter. But if there is another shooting in Barkerville, for whatever cause, and you are involved in any fashion, sir—" Again he paused for a long, tense moment, and he dropped his voice to a near whisper. "I assure you, there will be a hanging in Barkerville, Mr. McGraw. Do I make myself plain?"

Hannah couldn't believe her ears. Begbie was

actually *threatening* Logan. Outraged, she started to struggle to her feet, but Elvira beat her to it. The older woman stood ramrod straight and scowled up at Begbie from behind her glasses.

"Your honor, with all due respect, it's contemptible of this court to say such a thing to Mr. McGraw."

"Sit down, madam." Begbie leveled a killing look at Elvira, but she ignored him and went right on talking in her loud voice.

"Logan was the only one who was willing to protect Jeannie Chalmers or her baby. You and the constable weren't around, and Doc Carroll naturally didn't want Oscar coming to the hospital and causing trouble. We have other sick folks there to think about. And I sure didn't see any of the men from the saloon coming forward. They cleared out when they heard Oscar was on the rampage."

"Madam, I said sit down, or I will have you removed from this courtroom." Begbie was on his feet now, his eyes bulging out of his head. "I will not tolerate this kind of behavior—"

Elvira wasn't finished. She raised her voice over Begbie's. "Everyone was quite ready to sit back and let that wife-beating maniac do whatever he wanted to that poor woman and her baby. It just points out the general attitude of this town towards women's rights." She was shouting now. "The fact is, we haven't any!"

"Constable!" Begbie looked apoplectic. "Remove that woman." He leaned forward and pointed a long finger at Elvira. Constable Bowran moved hesitantly forward.

"Don't bother. I wouldn't stick around here if you paid me."

Elvira marched towards the door.

Hannah got up, and Daisy did as well, and both of them followed her. Hannah was surprised and pleased to see Rebecca Carroll also get to her feet, and when she reached the door and glanced back, she saw Rebecca, Mary Winnard, and Prudence Heatherington also walking out of Begbie's courtroom.

A thrill of triumph went through Hannah.

Dear old Elvira had staged Barkerville's first women's protest march.

At eight o'clock the following Wednesday evening, Hannah had to move extra chairs into the kitchen to seat the women who turned up for the regular meeting of the women's group.

Rebecca brought a friend named Louisa Rockwell, whose husband was the new schoolteacher. Mary Winnard was there. Two miner's wives arrived, Ella Purdy and Susan Burtrum.

Gentle Annie was absent.

Jeannie had decided she wanted to come downstairs for the meeting. The women all made a huge fuss over the baby, and each of them registered shock and pity when they first saw Jeannie's battered face.

Rebecca brought Sophie a half-dozen tiny nightgowns with delicate lace at the sleeves and a stack of hand-hemmed flannel diapers, and Hannah knew they were part of the layette she must have sewn during her own pregnancies.

Hannah had already called the meeting to order when Carmen Hall sashayed in.

The room became very quiet, and Hannah held her breath, certain that some of the women would walk out.

She was relieved and surprised when they didn't, although they all studiously avoided looking at Carmen.

Hannah greeted her by name and made her welcome and then stated the purpose of the meeting, to bring women together and discuss issues that affected all of them.

Out of respect for Jeannie's feelings, it seemed no one was about to mention the scene at the courthouse, so Hannah took the initiative, remarking on the power of peaceful protest. There was a buzz of excited conversation, and they all agreed that something needed to be done about the deplorable way women were being treated by the courts.

Elvira suggested writing a letter of protest to Judge Begbie with copies to whoever else was in charge of justice, and everyone enthusiastically agreed. The women were obviously impressed with Elvira.

Rebecca brought up her church campaign, Louisa Rockwell spoke of the need for slates and books at the schoolhouse, and Elvira started a heated argument by proposing that the Chinese children be encouraged to attend school, which horrified Louisa, but which Rebecca supported.

There was a lull, and then Susan Burtrum turned to Jeannie. "Will you be staying on in Barkerville?"

Hannah tensed. It was a question no one at the Nugget had asked, for fear of making Jeannie feel unwelcome.

There'd already been a lot of inquiries about Oscar's claim; it was rumored to be a good one, and Hannah knew that Logan and Angus had gone out there and brought back a small fortune in nuggets from some hiding place Jeannie knew about. She was a wealthy woman now. She'd be able to do whatever she chose, and Hannah was delighted for her.

"Oh, I'll be stayin' on," she said now in her shy voice. "I figger me and Angus, we're gonna work our claim. See, I got my mining certificate. Oscar—" Her voice faltered, but she went on. "Oscar made me get one so's he could hold an extra share." Her bruised mouth tilted into a sad little smile. "And I know all there is ta know about minin'. I worked right beside him alla the time."

There was an excited buzz amongst the women. It was almost unheard of for a woman to actually mine.

"Won't it be too hard on you, with the baby?"

Jeannie shook her head. "I got Angus ta help with heavy stuff, and I can hire another man if we need one."

Elvira stuck her thumb high in the air. *"Yes!"* she exclaimed, and everyone laughed.

Through all of this, Carmen Hall sat utterly silent, her dead gray eyes studying each of the other women and her sullen mouth twisted into a sarcastic little smile.

Although Daisy politely urged her, Carmen didn't stay for the coffee and doughnuts after the meeting, and Hannah could almost hear the collective sigh of relief when the door closed after her, although again none of the women said a word.

Logan did, however. He and Hannah were again using his bedroom; Elvira was back in her room at the hospital, and Jeannie and the baby were sharing with Daisy.

He came in just as she was undressing, and he didn't return her welcoming smile.

"I saw Carmen Hall leaving your meeting tonight, Hannah," he said sharply. "I don't want that woman on my premises."

Hannah had stepped out of her skirt, and she stood in her underpants and blouse, staring at him in amazement.

"For heaven's sake, Logan, we talked about this before I started having the meetings. You knew I was going to make it clear that women like Carmen were welcome."

"Women like Carmen, perhaps, but not Carmen Hall herself," he repeated stubbornly, taking off his vest and unbuttoning his shirt. "I don't want you talking to her. I don't want her near the Nugget."

Hannah's chin came up. "Why her in particular?"

He sat down and tugged off his boots, but he didn't answer, and his silence infuriated Hannah.

"You don't have the right to tell me who I may or may not talk to, Logan. If I choose to—to befriend Carmen Hall, it's entirely my own business."

He glared at her and got to his feet. "Befriend her? Don't talk nonsense. She's a madam. She and her partner are involved in white slavery. She and Flannery are evil, Hannah. You don't know what you're getting into, speaking of befriending Carmen Hall."

"I'm trying to help women help themselves, women like Jeannie. And Gentle Annie. If I have to reach out to them through people like Carmen, then I will." She undid her braid with furious fingers and reached for the hair brush.

"*All* women need support, Logan, not just a chosen few. I can't say one woman is welcome at the meetings and another not."

He jabbed a finger at her. "Carmen Hall is not welcome."

"I don't get you, Logan. I just don't understand you." Hannah brushed her hair with furious strokes. "You ought to be the first one to support what I'm trying to do. You were the only one who stood up for Jeannie. You told me about your sister, that she was pregnant and had nowhere to go, no one to turn to. A group like this one could have supported her." She smacked the brush down on the dresser. "Don't you feel any sense of responsibility for what happened to Nellie?"

He was undoing his pants, and he stopped dead and looked at her. "Responsibility?" His voice was a near whisper. "You dare to speak to me of responsibility?"

She'd gone too far. The sudden absolute rage on his face shocked and frightened her, and she stepped back, away from him.

Chapter Twenty-two

"My sister is dead because of Flannery."

Hannah stared at Logan, confused.

"She was carrying his child. It's a hobby of his, finding innocent girls like Nellie and seducing them, making them pregnant. It's his favorite method of recruiting new girls."

Understanding was beginning to dawn. "You followed him here to Barkerville. Flannery's the reason you're here, isn't he, Logan? You're waiting for him to come back, and then you're going to—"

He didn't confirm or deny it, but she knew it was the truth. She thought of the hidden gun he carried in his leather vest, of the business he'd said he had to conclude, of the fact that he planned to leave Barkerville before winter and never return, and a terrible sickness knotted the pit of her stomach.

"You came here to . . . to kill him?" She wanted him to deny it; she wanted him to laugh at the idea.

Instead, he slowly nodded. "He doesn't deserve to live, Hannah. He's a destroyer of women, beautiful young women like Nellie, but no court would ever convict him."

The awful thing was, she understood. Back in her own time, there were sex offenders, mass murderers, child molesters, whom she'd often thought would have been better off dead. The difference was, she would never have dreamed of murdering them herself.

But these were different times. She shuddered, remembering Begbie's warning.

"If there is another shooting in Barkerville, for whatever cause, and you are involved, in any fashion—there will be a hanging in Barkerville."

"Logan—my God, you can't do this. You can't take the law into your own hands."

"What would you have me do, Hannah?" His voice was sarcastic. "Make a formal complaint to Judge Begbie? Nellie was my sister. You were the one who first spoke of responsibility."

Hannah lost her last shred of composure. "Do you think Nellie would want this? Do you honestly think she'd want you to hang, Logan?" She realized she was shrieking at him when he reached out and placed his palm gently over her mouth.

"Shush, Hannah. You'll wake everyone in the place."

Trembling, she sank down on the bed. There had to be some way to make him see reason, some argument that would change his mind.

"Logan, I love you. Leave Barkerville with me now, let's go to some other place and live our lives together." She gulped and went on. "We could get married, we could have a family—"

He shook his head, and there was no anger in his tone now. He just sounded sad.

"I can't, Hannah. This is something I must finish." He sat down on the bed beside her. "And you can't leave, either. If there's any faint chance of getting back to your own time, it will probably be from here. You have your mother to think of, and Elvira as well. You'd never be content, always wondering if there might have been a chance for you to go back where you belong."

She opened her mouth to deny it and couldn't. He'd taught her about honesty, and no matter how much she wanted to contradict what he was saying, it was the truth.

"Come here, sweetheart." He reached for her, drawing her into his arms. "Nothing has really altered. We have this moment—we have tonight." There was forced humor in his tone. "We might even have tomorrow if we're lucky. Let's make the most of our time together, without quarreling over things we can't change."

His nimble fingers unfastened the buttons on her blouse, and he drew it carefully down her arms, mindful of the healing wound on her shoulder. He lowered his head and pressed his lips against the cut.

"My brave, foolish, beautiful woman."

His lovemaking was excruciatingly slow, as if they had all the time in the world. In the languorous haze of passion, she forgot for a little while, just as he intended she should. But when it was over and he slept, his muscular arms still holding her close against him, Hannah lay awake and remembered, and panic washed over her in a cold tidal wave.

There must be a way—there had to be a way—to stop him.

At four A.M. Carmen Hall and Rosie, one of the best girls, ushered the last drunken customer down the stairs and out of Frenchie's, and Carmen locked the doors.

As usual, the fetid air stank of coal-oil lanterns, stale whiskey, cheap perfume, and cigars, but Carmen didn't notice, and even if she had, she wouldn't have minded. It was a smell that went with the business of making money. Carmen loved only two things: Bart Flannery and gold.

She'd been an old man's mistress in Seattle

when she'd met Flannery five years before. For the first time in her life she'd fallen in love. She'd wanted to run off with him then and there, but Flannery was smart. With his counseling, she'd first made certain she was taken care of in the old man's will, and then Flannery had arranged an accident.

The money she got had bought this building, and she'd become an excellent businesswoman under Flannery's tutelage. She was justifiably proud of the way she'd run Frenchie's in his absence. She'd kept the girls in line and she'd diligently applied the bookkeeping lessons Flannery had taught her before he left.

"Night, Carmen." Rosie yawned and tugged her shiny purple dressing gown up over one lush breast as she headed for the stairs. She wore a variation of the uniform all the working girls at Frenchie's favored, a laced corset cut so low the tops of her nipples showed, a pair of ivory satin bloomers, black stockings with scarlet satin garters, and high-heeled slippers. Her dyed blond topknot was listing to one side and much the worse for wear; it had been a busy night.

In the hall, Carmen turned down the lamps and lifted the heavy wooden drop box that held the night's take. She carried it into her cubby hole of an office. The box had an opening in the top big enough to allow the packets of gold dust and the girl's chits.

Carmen opened the padlocked lid and removed the small canvas pouches the girls had weighed out on the gold scales the house supplied in each of their rooms. The girls were well trained and too scared of Flannery to cheat.

She added up the take and the chits and meticulously entered amounts beside each girl's name in the ledger Flannery kept in the top drawer. The cut was a third for the girls and two thirds for the house. After expenses, she and Flannery split the profits evenly.

When the entries were done, she put the pouches in a bigger canvas sack and opened the combination lock on the large safe in the corner, depositing the gold inside and then relocking the door of the safe.

There hadn't been a lot of profit last winter, but this had been an exceptionally good summer. She and Flannery would soon be millionaires at this rate, and he'd be pleased with her when he finally got back.

She was looking forward to his return; if all had gone as planned, she expected him sometime within the next two weeks. With the new crop of girls, Carmen expected the profits to soar. Miners would be lining up three-deep to sample the new merchandise.

Anticipating the girls' arrival, Carmen had hired a carpenter to turn some of the unused space on the third floor into bedrooms, and just today she'd impulsively decided to have him enlarge the bedroom she shared with Flannery by knocking out a wall and incorporating a small, unused storage room next door.

There'd be space for another wardrobe, and she'd order some new rugs and wallpaper. Maybe she'd line the walls of the addition with mirrors and put a chaise longue in there.

The idea excited her and she wanted it done quickly, so it would be completed by the time Flannery got back. That afternoon the carpenter had already knocked a sizable hole between the two rooms.

She wrinkled her nose when she entered the bedroom. It was in total disarray and there was plaster dust and bits of lathing everywhere.

Holding the lantern aloft, she stepped through the opening, imagining how it would look completed. There was a strip of worn rug on the floor, and suddenly her foot hit a loose floorboard. It gave and she lost her balance, very nearly dropping the lamp.

She grabbed at it and burned her hand, and ended up awkwardly crouching on the floor with her foot twisted beneath her. Cursing, she rubbed her ankle and then got gingerly to her feet, furious with the carpenter for not noticing the board. She leaned down and yanked up the rug and the loose board, and then stood staring open-mouthed into the hole.

There were four canvas sacks lined up beneath the floorboards, identical to the ones she'd just deposited in the safe. Stunned, she reached down and lifted one out, opening the drawstring top. Inside were sacks of gold dust.

Carmen sank to her knees, her brain racing, her heart thumping like a mad thing in her chest.

Flannery. Flannery was the only one who could have hidden these here. She'd believed they were equal partners in Frenchie's; she'd worked like a dog these past months, and while he was gone she'd been meticulous about the books.

He'd claimed they'd had too many expenses last winter to show much profit. And all the while he'd been cheating her.

Her chest heaved, and red spots danced before her eyes. She loved him passionately, but she'd never been fool enough to expect fidelity from him where other women were concerned; it would have been like asking Rosie to turn into a virgin again. Flannery had an insatiable appetite for young girls, and even though it rankled, Carmen had known better than to oppose it.

But in the matter of their business partnership, she'd believed he was absolutely loyal. She'd trusted him in that regard.

She hefted another of the canvas bags, estimating the fortune he'd stolen from her, and deep inside her gut, a volcano of pure rage began to erupt. She cursed and wept and pounded her fists on the floor, and when the storm was over, she removed the sacks of gold dust and hid them in the bottom of her trunk. She replaced the loose floorboard and covered it with the rug.

Tomorrow she'd tell the carpenter she'd changed her mind, and insist he put the wall back up again. A roll of wallpaper would cover any telltale evidence. When he was finished, she'd put the gold back under the floor exactly the way it had been.

She'd been unsure of herself in the beginning, because she'd never run a business before. Now, thanks to Flannery, she knew she could do it alone.

And just as he'd said about the old man, accidents happened every day.

Chapter Twenty-three

As the last days of August approached, everyone in Barkerville longed for an end to the protracted spell of hot weather.

Tempers grew frayed, the water in William's Creek dropped lower than it ever had before, and dysentery raged.

Elvira and Doc Carroll were run off their feet as the hospital overflowed with cases of fever, dehydration, and heat prostration.

Jeannie gathered up Angus and baby Sophie and moved back to the tent on the claim. The Nugget seemed lonely without them, and Hannah woke up at night listening for Sophie's cries.

In the store, she sweltered through the endless days, but it wasn't the heat that bothered her.

Ever since Logan had told her about his plans, things hadn't been the same between them. Discussions became arguments which escalated into heated quarrels as Hannah tried everything she could think of to get him to see reason, but nothing worked.

Sick at heart, she thought of a million far-fetched schemes to prevent Logan from committing murder, but when it came down to it, none were practical.

Two more meetings of the women's group were held, and Hannah was profoundly relieved when Carmen Hall didn't attend either one, although Hannah found herself thinking about the other woman often, wondering if under her tough persona she loved Flannery the way Hannah loved Logan. She was a woman with a woman's heart, wasn't she?

Three more miner's wives turned up at the women's group, and for everyone except Hannah, the evenings seemed both enjoyable and productive. Elvira lectured on sanitation, and the need to boil all drinking water.

Hannah should have felt triumphant about the growing success of the group, but her enthusiasm was gone. Everything seemed pointless compared to her fear for Logan.

With September came the certainty that Flannery would be returning soon. Hannah found herself tensing each time a wagon train came pounding along the street in front of Pandola's. Her work suffered; she was abstracted and short-tempered.

One afternoon when she had a headache from the heat and the smell of animal dung wafting in the open door, she accidentally overturned an entire heaping basket of the eggs she was cleaning. They spattered everywhere, a gluey, stinking mess of shells and slime.

Pandola, who'd given up on his pursuit of Daisy and was in no better a mood than Hannah, threw his arms in the air and hollered a string of what sounded like Italian cuss words.

She couldn't take it any more. She tore off the apron she was wearing, threw it down in the mess, and stamped on it.

"I quit!" she shrieked. "Take your stupid job and shove it up your nose. These damned eggs are better off broken. They're half rotten anyway, and you've got no business even selling them."

Grabbing her handbag from under the counter, she sailed out the door.

Out on the street, the heat struck her like a blow, and the noise of bawling animals and shouting men and waterwheels made her head feel as if it were going to explode.

She turned in the opposite direction to the Nugget, knowing that there'd be no privacy there; Daisy and Zeb would be cooking, and the saloon would be noisy, filled with men trying to cool themselves off with liquor.

She stomped up and down the levels of the boardwalk, not caring where she was going, ignoring the curious stares directed her way.

She hated it here. She hated the noise and the smells and the dirt and the lack of conveniences. She hated the prejudices and narrow attitudes of the times, and the fact that women had no real equality.

She wanted to go home, to her own place, her own time. The single thing that had made Barkerville bearable was Logan, and any day now Flannery would return and Logan would end up either being hanged or disappearing down the Cariboo Road forever, leaving her in this godforsaken place by herself.

She passed the Chinese stores with their exotic-smelling herbs and whiffs of incense, and hurried past the row of windowless one-room cabins occupied by single miners.

A footpath veered away from the ankle-deep dust in the road, and she followed it. It led up the hill, and sweat poured down her forehead as she climbed.

Exhausted and dizzy, her head pounding, she finally found a spot under a tree that provided some shade and plopped down.

She could see the entire town from this vantage point, a confused collection of peaked, two-storied frame buildings, cabins, tents, saloons, warehouses, stovepipes, outhouses, sheds, and flumes. She picked out the Nugget and Pandola's Store. She identified Frenchie's and stared for a long time at the high shingled roof, picturing Carmen Hall and her expressionless eyes and sharp tongue, and suddenly Hannah knew what she was going to do.

Whatever else she might be, Carmen was an intelligent woman, Hannah told herself, and so was she. Maybe the two of them could figure out a way to keep both their men alive.

Before she could change her mind, she got up and started down the hill.

Hannah had never been in a brothel before. The first thing that hit her was the smell, a combination of stale whiskey, male sweat, cigar smoke, and something horrible that reminded her of the eggs at Pandola's. Her stomach lurched.

She was in a sort of parlor, with garish furniture and thick draperies drawn tightly shut against the sun. A piano sat in one corner, and there was a long table laden with bottles of liquor. Above it was a painting of a blowsy naked woman with a suggestive smile, sitting on a stool and pulling one dark stocking up a fleshy leg. Her pubic hair showed and her lavish breasts hung down over her belly. The nipples were elongated and bright red. Hannah frowned at it. Did real women ever have nipples like that?

The sound of women's voices came from the kitchen, and Hannah heard the voice of the blond woman who'd answered the door saying, "There's somebody ta see ya, Carmen."

The tiny dark madam sashayed through the doorway a moment later. Carmen's plucked eyebrows rose when she saw Hannah.

"Well, well, dearie. Come calling, have you? I didn't realize it was my at-home afternoon."

Hannah was having second thoughts about her impetuous decision, but it was too late now to change her mind.

"I'd like to talk to you, Carmen. It's . . . private."

Carmen gave her a long look and then shrugged. "Sure. C'mon in here."

Hannah followed her down a dark hallway, and with a key Carmen opened the door to a small office. She gestured at a chair, then moved behind the oak desk and sat down.

"So, what's this about? You need a donation for the church that group of yours is so keen on building?"

Hannah folded her hands in her lap and then unfolded them again. "No. I want to discuss something, but I need your assurance that what we say in this room is confidential, just between you and me."

Carmen's eyes narrowed and traveled slowly

up and down Hannah's figure. "You got something in your belly you want to get rid of?"

Taken aback, Hannah shook her head. "It's not about me. It's about the man you live with. Flannery."

Carmen's face turned to stone. "Oh, yeah? What about him? You never even met him. He'd already left Barkerville before you got here."

"That's true, but . . . will you give me your word that what I tell you won't go any further? Especially that you won't tell *him?*"

Carmen shrugged indifferently. "Sure." Her grin was cynical. "Some things are best kept just between us girls, right?"

Hannah nodded, wondering how best to explain, and decided to just blurt it out.

"Logan's planning to shoot Flannery, and I want to know if there's any way you and I could prevent it."

Carmen stared at Hannah. "What's McGraw got against him?"

"His sister." Hannah explained about Nellie.

"Well, well." A cruel grin slowly twisted across Carmen's mouth, and then she laughed aloud. When the laughter ended, she leaned towards Hannah. "Why the hell should I care, or you either? They're both big boys—let 'em fight it out. It's not my affair." She pointed a beringed finger at Hannah. "And you been preaching about woman's rights, why should you concern yourself with what men choose to do? McGraw shoots Flannery, he'll hang for it." She lowered her voice to a sarcastic whisper. "Get him to will the Nugget to you, dearie, and between us we could clean up in this town. Wouldn't that teach the men a lesson?"

Hannah got to her feet. Her knees were shaking, and numb horror gripped her. She'd made a terrible mistake.

Carmen was laughing again as Hannah fumbled open the office door and fled down the dark hallway. She yanked open the street door and slammed it behind her.

The sun was still beating down, and she turned blindly and started walking toward the Nugget. Her heart was slamming against her ribs. She'd been a fool. Worse than a fool, she'd been a traitor to the man she loved.

Hannah had no illusions left about Carmen Hall. The other woman would likely tell Flannery exactly what Hannah had said, and Logan's life would be in danger from a bullet instead of a rope.

She'd have to warn him, the sooner the better. And when she did, she knew their relationship would be over. He'd never forgive her for this.

"Yooohoo, Hannah? Hannah, there you are." Elvira hailed her, her voice filled with excitement. She was driving a buggy smack down the middle of the street. Daisy was sitting beside her with Klaus on her lap.

Elvira reigned the horse to a halt and hollered, "Get in here. We've been trying to find you for an hour already. Pandola said he didn't know where you'd gone."

Hannah stared at them, feeling as if the entire day had become some sort of disjointed nightmare. She climbed down the steps to the street and Daisy reached a hand to help her into the buggy. It was a tight squeeze with the three of them on the narrow leather seat.

"What are you two doing? Whose buggy is this?"

"Doc Carrolls. He lent it to me." Elvira shook the reins and the horse started moving again.

"Where are we going?"

"Down the Cariboo Road about ten miles," Elvira said, letting the horse trot along past the business section and through the Chinese settlement. "Daisy's brought us some food, so we can have a picnic later on."

"What about the men's supper at the Nugget?"

"Zeb will manage on his own," Daisy said complacently. "I left soup and pasties."

"Elvira, why are we doing this?"

"Because last night, after I'd finished for the day, a cattle drover brought a man to the hospital. He'd found him wandering along the Cariboo Road. Daniel Conner, his name is. Anyhow, Doc Carroll figured Daniel was either psychotic or drunk, because he thought he'd seen a vision from heaven. Doc checked him over and then gave him a stiff sleeping potion. When I got to work this morning, Daniel was still out of it, but when he woke up just before noon, he told me about watching silver and blue and gold carriages that had no horses pulling them. Daniel said they were traveling along a shiny black road at unheard-of speeds."

Hannah gasped. "It sounds like he saw cars, on a highway."

"Exactly. I quizzed him closely as to the exact location. He was pretty good at explaining where he was when it happened. He'd stopped to water his horse and have a drink by that wooden bridge, Hannah—same place we were. The drover didn't see a blamed thing, so it's probably just some optical illusion or other, but I still figured we should go take another look. I told Doc I needed the afternoon off and asked if we could borrow his buggy to have a picnic, and he agreed. So I picked up your mother, and then we went looking for you." She turned and gave Hannah a look. "Where on earth were you? Old Pandola looked really down at the mouth—said you and he had an argument and to tell you he was sorry and to come back tomorrow."

"He did?" Hannah wondered if she wanted her job back or not. It seemed unimportant after all that had happened. Another thought struck her. "Did you tell Logan where we were going?"

"I told Zeb we were going for a ride in the

buggy. He'll tell Logan," Daisy said. "Logan wasn't home. He took a wagon load of lumber out to Jeannie and Angus this morning. They want that cabin finished before winter. He wasn't back yet when we left."

"Maybe we'll meet him on the road." If they did, Hannah decided with a sinking heart that she'd ride back to town with Logan and tell him what she'd done. It was on her conscience and she felt absolutely sick about it.

They bounced along in silence for a while, all of them sweating copiously. The air was absolutely still. Hannah could smell the horse, and the dust from its hooves sifted over them in a fine cloud.

They reached the spot where Logan would have turned off to get to Jeannie's claim, but there was no sign of him, and Hannah felt shameful relief. At least she had another few hours before she'd have to tell him.

They'd gone another mile when a huge cloud of dust up ahead warned that something was approaching, and soon they could make out two coaches and several men on horseback, riding quickly towards them.

Elvira pulled the horse and their buggy to the side of the road to let the cavalcade past. Clouds of dust billowed over the buggy as the assembly passed by. Hannah saw that the coaches were filled with women. They waved and smiled as they passed.

Hannah's gaze was caught and held by one of the men on horseback. He wore a low-brimmed hat, and from under it his coal-black eyes seemed to caress her face in the moment it took his horse to pass the buggy.

He raised a hand to her and gave a wolfish grin, and a cold shudder spiraled down Hannah's spine.

She was suddenly convinced he was Flannery, returning with his European cargo of women. She thought of Logan, returning to town and learning that the man he'd waited for so long was back, and she envisioned Carmen telling Flannery . . .

"I have to go back," she burst out. "Stop the buggy! I have to get back to town right away."

"Don't be silly, we're nearly there," Elvira declared. "We'd have to follow in the dust of that group that just passed, and I'm not doing it."

Daisy agreed with Elvira. Hannah had no choice except to give in. In abject misery, she sat lost in her own dark imaginings as the buggy jolted its way along the Cariboo Road and the sun dropped in slow motion towards the mountains.

"There's the wooden bridge. This is the place Daniel described," Elvira finally said. They seemed to have been driving for an interminable time, with the usual stops so that either Elvira or Klaus could relieve themselves, and Hannah felt groggy and slightly nauseated from the dust and the heat and her worry over Logan.

"He said he was sitting by that poplar over there, right by the creek."

"Well, I don't see any cars or any highway either." Daisy peered around as Elvira unhitched the horse and led him down to the water for a drink.

"I didn't really expect there would be, but it was worth a try." Elvira sounded disappointed. "Let's have a look around."

Leaving the horse to graze, they walked back and forth along the water. They went across to the woods and up and down the road, but there was absolutely nothing except the cheeping of birds, the chatter of squirrels, the sound of the water, and a deep humming stillness. Klaus trotted glumly at their heels, hot and panting.

"I'm going to wade into the water and get cooled off," Hannah finally decided, and she stripped off her sandals and socks and hiked her cursed long skirts up around her hips.

She waded in. The icy water bit at her skin. Daisy and Elvira followed, and even Klaus minced delicately in and had a drink.

Daisy unpacked the lunch, and they sat on the grass and ate jam sandwiches and raisin muffins, but Hannah had no appetite at all. A black cloud seemed to have settled over her, a despondency that reached to the depths of her soul.

She drew her knees up and rested her chin on

her bunched-up skirt, staring unseeing at the water, trying not to think of anything.

Daisy and Elvira talked quietly, but they, too, had none of their usual energy or exuberance. After a time they gathered up the remnants of the lunch and stowed them in the buggy.

"We might as well get back," Elvira said. It took all three of them to hitch the horse up again, and by the time that was accomplished, Klaus had wandered off.

Daisy called, but he didn't come. They all took turns calling with no success.

Daisy began to get flustered, and Elvira became annoyed. Hannah had no energy left to feel anything.

For the next hour they tramped along the creek, walked up and down the road, and made forays into the woods, shouting themselves hoarse. The sun was dropping towards the mountains. Before long it would be dusk, and now Daisy was frantic.

"We can't go on looking much longer," Elvira warned. "It's going to get dark before too long. We need to start back."

Daisy burst into tears, and Hannah wanted to strangle Klaus with her bare hands. A terrible desperation was growing in her, an overwhelming need to get back to Barkerville, talk to Logan, attempt one last time to reason with him.

"I'll make a trip along the edge of the creek,

just in case Klaus tumbled in and can't get out," she said. Half running, she started off, but she hadn't gone ten steps before she heard the dog, barking frantically from somewhere upstream.

"I hear him," she shouted to the other women, and Daisy gave a joyful cry. There were bushes growing along the bank, and Hannah pushed her way through them. They grew thicker and more difficult to get through as she got farther upstream, and Hannah veered away from the creek into the woods, looking for an easier path, listening all the while to Klaus's high-pitched yapping.

She could hear Daisy and Elvira panting along behind her, and Klaus sounded much closer when she finally fought her way through one last stand of willows, head down to avoid the whipping branches.

She looked up. The water was much wider and deeper than it had been, and Klaus was standing on the edge of it, barking at a group of men.

A truck with a winch was pulling her van out of the water, and behind the men and the truck was a modern highway. A battered station wagon drove by slowly, and a woman in a cowboy hat gawked out the open window.

A white R.C.M.P. patrol car was parked on the shoulder of the highway, its red light flashing, and several uniformed constables stood on the bank, supervising the proceedings.

Behind Hannah, Elvira and Daisy came crashing through the underbrush. She sensed them standing just behind her, as dumbstruck as she at the scene unfolding a hundred yards away.

"No," Hannah whimpered. *"No, no, no—"*

She whirled around and plunged back into the bushes, trying frantically to retrace her path back into the past, back to Logan. But wherever the gateway was, it had now closed behind her.

Chapter Twenty-four

Logan rode slowly back to town, the empty wagon clattering and bouncing along the rutted road behind the horse.

It was late afternoon, the hottest part of the day. He was hot and tired and dirty, but none of those things bothered him at all. For the first time in months, he was at peace. It went beyond happiness, this feeling that had come over him; it was bigger than that.

At some point today, Logan had realized that he wasn't going to kill Flannery after all. Instead, he was going to ask Hannah to marry him, and if by some twist of fate that meant going to live in her future time, then he'd do it. If it didn't happen, they'd make a life in his time—not in Barkerville, perhaps, but somewhere they both chose.

The world was a big place. He had plenty of gold stashed away. They could live well.

It was a quiet revelation, with none of the fire and brimstone that revelations were supposed to bring. He'd been skinning a log with his ax, half listening to the constant stream of innocent chatter from Angus. Jeannie was sitting on a chair by the half-built cabin, her back to them, nursing the baby. Sophie was snorting and making indelicate slurping noises, birds were chattering; the stream gurgled.

He stopped and rested for a moment, leaning on his ax handle, and he'd thought of killing and what it did to people. He'd shot Chalmers, and although it had been a necessary act, it had made him soul-sick all the same, that taking of a human life. Here, in this peaceful place, he realized simply that he didn't want to do it again.

Besides, just as Hannah kept telling him, murdering Flannery wasn't the answer anyway. It wouldn't bring Nellie back; it wouldn't stop other men from taking advantage of girls like her. Hannah said the answer was in education, in providing support in the community, and Logan was inclined to believe her.

It was hard to admit, but the killing rage he'd nursed so long against Flannery was really directed at himself, for not being there for Nellie when she needed him. Maybe in some small way, being there for Angus and Jeannie made up for it.

He was well pleased with the work he and Angus had done today. They'd felled trees and laid the foundation for the simple two-room cabin.

Whether or not Jeannie and Angus would ever grow rich from their claim remained to be seen, but at least they were taking enough gold out of it to live comfortably. Jeannie had the sizable nest egg Chalmers had hoarded away, and little Sophie was thriving.

Logan had to smile whenever he thought of the baby. She was a funny-looking, good-natured little creature, with her shock of bright red hair and her round, shoe-button eyes. From the cradle he and Angus had made her, she'd grinned at him repeatedly, a face-splitting, goofy grin that made her eyes cross and her plump cheeks bunch up.

Logan had looked at her and remembered Nellie, but today the bitterness and anger he usually felt when he thought of his little sister was missing. Tiny Sophie was proof that life went on, that goodness could result from evil; after all, hadn't Oscar Chalmers fathered Sophie?

Logan looked around—at the peaceful landscape, the blue sky, the pine-and spruce-covered mountains—and he knew that life was good, despite the bad things that happened, to individuals, to entire countries and even the world, if the wars Hannah described were inevitable.

She'd made him think about things he'd never considered before. Was the future already written in some massive heavenly book, for instance, waiting for man to enact it? Or could the course of history be changed, if enough people knew what was probable and warned those few who could make a difference?

Probably not. Folks didn't like warnings much. Take the Barkerville fire, for example. He'd tried to convince his fellow townspeople that there was danger, and he'd been ignored. He'd taken precautions himself, because he knew that if Hannah and Daisy and Elvira said fire was coming, it likely was.

He'd filled barrels of water and placed them at strategic places around the Nugget, but if the town went up like tinder, he didn't hold much hope that the Nugget would survive. The only thing in it of real value was his likeness of Nellie and the sizable stash of gold he'd hidden away over these past months.

So he'd taken the daguerrotype and the canvas sacks over to Jeannie's this morning and hidden them in an unused mine shaft; before the fire arrived, he'd take the womenfolk there as well, out of harm's way.

He shook the reins and urged the horse to

hurry, eager to share with Hannah the changes this single day had brought about. He knew he'd caused her heartache and terrible concern, and he wanted to apologize.

When he got to the Nugget, Sam was busy with the early evening crowd at the bar. Logan waved to him and strode past the saloon and into the kitchen.

It was empty, the stove cold, dishes washed and stacked neatly for the next meal. Through the window, Logan spied Zeb sitting in the yard smoking his pipe. Sticking his head out the kitchen door, Logan called, "Zeb, you seen Hannah?"

"Nope." Zeb shook his head. "Ain't seen hide nor hair of Daisy, either. Her and that Elvira took off with Doc Carroll's buggy just past noontime. Ain't come back yet that I know of. They was lookin' fer Hannah, wanted her to go with them."

Logan frowned. "Where were they going?"

"On a picnic, far as I could figger. Daisy said down the Cariboo Road a piece, mebbe ten mile." The old man took a long drag on his pipe. "You missed the big doin's in town here today. The new gals for Frenchie's got here this afternoon. I reckon there won't be much trade in the saloon tonight. All the men'll be over there wantin' to dip their wicks." He guffawed. " 'Cept fer old geezers like me who cain't remember what it's all about."

So Flannery was back. For a moment, Logan felt the old bitterness sweep though him, but by the time he climbed the stairs to his room, it was gone. Everything had changed. He wanted happiness instead of vengeance. He wanted Hannah.

Where the hell was she? He'd planned to drag her up here, apologize for his stubbornness, get down on his knees and ask her to marry him, kiss her senseless, promise to stop gambling if she wanted him to and take up . . . what?

Damn it all, he'd think of something. He unfastened his leather vest and slung it over a chair. He was done wearing it; old Begbie was right, the derringer was an invitation to violence.

Outside, the long summer dusk was thickening, turning into night, and a feeling of anxiety came over him.

Something must have happened to the women. They ought to be back from their picnic by now. He'd head over to the livery stable, saddle a horse, and go look for them.

He was almost out the door when he wheeled around and picked up his vest again.

He was outside, striding down the street, when a young miner hurried up and shoved an envelope into his hand.

"What's this?"

The man shrugged. "I was told to give it to you, Mr. McGraw."

"Private" was scrawled across the envelope in spidery feminine handwriting, along with his name. For an instant, Logan thought it was from Hannah, and he tore it open, his eyes searching for the signature. He frowned. Carmen Hall? What the hell did Carmen Hall want with him?

"Flannery wants to talk about your sister Nellie," the cryptic message read. Stunned, Logan read it, once and then again. His stomach roiled. How had Flannery found out he was Nellie's brother? The only person in Barkerville besides himself who knew that was Hannah, and she'd never . . .

A tiny maggot of doubt twisted inside his chest, and for a moment he could hardly breathe. Hannah had threatened that she'd find a way to stop him, but to go to the enemy . . . she wouldn't do that. She couldn't do that.

Could she?

But Hannah wasn't there to ask, and he had to know.

He turned and started back down the street, towards Frenchie's.

In the hours since Flannery's arrival, Carmen had pampered him, feeding him, bathing him, pleasuring him in all the ways she knew he liked, and through it all she made certain he drank—first wine, then the expensive whiskey from their private stock. In their bedroom, she pointed out the new wallpaper and he admired it. The carpenter had done an excellent job of repairing the wall, and Carmen had carefully replaced the gold.

She knew exactly when Flannery slipped into the storage room to check on it, and the cold fury in her gut threatened to consume her, but she damped it down.

When the moment was right, she told him about McGraw. She was careful how she did it, with just the right amount of bravado and alarm. She told the story of McGraw murdering Chalmers, subtly letting Flannery know that the other man was considered a hero by most of the town, a man no one wanted to challenge.

"His woman told me McGraw considers you a coward," she goaded, knowing that was Flannery's greatest fear, because it was so. "He bragged to her that you wouldn't spend a single night alive when you got back."

When Flannery was just drunk enough to be both mean and careless, she sent the message to McGraw.

Logan shouldered his way through the crowd of half-drunken men and half-dressed women in the parlor at Frenchie's. He recognized most of the men, but some of the women were strangers, part of the new shipment Flannery had imported that day. Several of them were hardened and blowsy, but one was very young, her dazed eyes ringed with kohl and her tender mouth drawn into a grotesque facsimile of a smile. She was perched on the lap of a bearded miner, and he was running his hands up and down her black-stockinged legs.

Sickened, Logan scanned the room, squinting through the haze of cigar smoke.

"Hi, sugar." Rosie stroked a hand down his vest, smiling up at him. "You lookin' for a good time, Logan? You've finally come to the right place. Want a drink first?"

"I'm here to see Flannery."

"Oh, he ain't seein' anybody tonight, sugar."

"It's okay, Rosie." Carmen had materialized beside them. She looked up at Logan, and there was a gleam of excitement in her dead gray gaze. "Hello, McGraw. I was hoping you'd come by."

"What the hell is the meaning of this?" Logan opened his palm, revealing the crumpled note.

"We need to talk private. This way." She led him down a narrow hallway, opened a door to an office, and stood aside. A man was lolling behind a desk, a cigar between his teeth, a glass of whiskey close at hand. His feet were propped on the desk top. He looked up when the door opened.

"Bart Flannery, meet Logan McGraw." Carmen's voice was silky and sly.

Flannery's dark, handsome face registered first shock and then alarm. His boots hit the floor hard, and his hand dropped to an open drawer. He fumbled and withdrew a pistol, waving it in Logan's direction as he staggered to his feet. He was more than a trifle unsteady. He gripped the edge of the desk with his free hand.

Behind Logan, the door closed with a snick.

"So you're the son of a bitch who thinks he's going to shoot me," Flannery snarled. "Where's your gun, hero?"

"Who told you that?" Logan stood, seemingly relaxed but watching Flannery's eyes.

"Why, honey, your fancy lady did," Carmen sneered from behind Logan. "Just this morning, told me all about Nellie, nearly had me crying. She seemed to think that between us we could make you gentlemen sign a peace treaty."

"I've changed my mind, Flannery." Logan's voice was dead calm. "You'll come to a bad end without any help from me. Scum like you always do."

He turned to walk out.

With both hands, Carmen lifted the poker she'd held hidden in her skirts and brought it down hard on his skull.

Logan grunted. His eyes rolled back in his head. He swayed, then crashed to the floor.

"Dammit, Carmen, what the hell you doing—"

Flannery dropped his gun to the desk and started around it, but Carmen had already located Logan's double-barreled derringer, tucked in the special pocket of his leather vest. She knew about derringers; she had one herself.

She cocked it, stood up, and turned towards Flannery. She smiled at him and fired at point-blank range, aiming at a spot right between his ebony eyes. The bullet left a neat dark hole in his forehead, but the back of his head exploded, sending blood and brains flying. His arms flew out to the sides and his body tumbled backward, smashing into the safe and sliding down to the floor.

The air smelled of cordite, hot blood, and urine.

Carmen knelt and curled Logan's fingers around the butt of the small gun. Then she stood up and coolly assessed the scene.

She drew in a deep breath and let out a blood-curdling scream.

Chapter Twenty-five

With trembling fingers, Hannah slid another microfiche into the machine in the Victoria Provincial Archives and scanned the old newspaper headlines, searching for the record of a hanging in long-ago Barkerville, praying desperately she wouldn't find it.

BARKERVILLE BURNS, read the headlines in the Cariboo Sentinel of September 21, 1868. FIRST-HAND ACCOUNT OF CONFLAGRATION.

> Last week, on the 16 September, Barkerville was leveled by a fire that destroyed almost every building in this mining town. Those few structures to elude the deadly flames included Scott's Saloon as well as a

large portion of the celestial community. The Demers Printing Press at the Sentinel was fortuitously recovered after the fire, making it possible to present this first-hand account penned by local photographer Frederick Dally.

So the Nugget burned. Hannah thought of the work Logan had done on the building, of the bedroom where they'd lain in each other's arms, of the workshop where Logan and Angus had fashioned a cradle for Sophie, and sorrow filled her.

She studied the wordy article, searching again for any mention of Logan, but there was none. A half hour ago, she'd found the account of his arrest for the murder of Bart Flannery. She didn't need to look at the microfiche record again, because the words were indelibly imprinted on her brain and in her aching heart.

GRISLY SHOOTING DEATH AT FRENCHIE'S GAMING HOUSE: PROPRIETOR OF NUGGET SALOON AND ROOMS CHARGED WITH MURDER, the September 14th headline had screamed, going on to detail the shooting which the article claimed was witnessed by Miss Carmen Hall, who, fearing for her own life, had hit Logan McGraw on the head with a poker, rendering him senseless immediately after he'd murdered her partner and paramour. Constable Bowran had been called to the scene by an unnamed gentleman.

The Sentinel stated that no immediate motive for the murder was apparent. Mr. McGraw was presently in jail, scheduled to appear in front of Judge Begbie when he returned from Quesnellemouth on September 18th.

Eyes burning from her hours of intense research, heartsick at what she'd learned, Hannah looked up from the machine, staring out the window at the dark, rain-washed street shining in the glow of Victoria's ornate streetlamps.

She'd come here tonight because she knew she had to begin putting what had happened behind her. She had to start getting on with her life, and this had seemed to be a way to begin, to find answers to the questions that plagued her. Instead, she was more confused than ever. How could she know from these old records what had really happened?

It didn't sound logical that Logan would walk into Frenchie's and gun Flannery down that way. It was tantamount to putting his head in a noose. He'd planned to murder Flannery, but he'd also planned to get away afterwards.

Her head was aching, and she had to work tomorrow. It was the end of August, and she'd been home six weeks. She'd gone back to work, she'd tried to pick up the pieces of her existence, but inside her, something vital was missing. Some energy source that had always burned brightly had died down to a bare ember, and most of the time it felt as if it were in danger of going out altogether.

The fact was, she was sick with longing for Logan. Without him, nothing seemed to have meaning. She got through the days, but it took every ounce of energy she could muster. It had taken this long to even work up the courage to come here and try to find out what had become of the man she loved.

Coming back to her own time had been highly traumatic for Hannah. If Daisy and Elvira hadn't been with her that fateful afternoon, she believed she might have gone totally mad. The police officers had spotted them and come running over, puzzled by their long dresses, asking questions that elicited answers no one would believe.

Hannah had been incapable of even trying to explain; the need to return to Barkerville and Logan overpowered every other emotion, and when it became clear there was no way to go back, she'd become hysterical for the first time in her entire life.

She'd been totally disoriented, emotionally distressed, unable to talk with out bursting into tears. She'd looked into a mirror in some bathroom that afternoon and not recognized the woman who stared back at her, white-faced and blank-eyed.

Elvira and Daisy had told the truth, but of course no one believed them.

Hannah's distraught condition prompted an interview by an understandably skeptical doctor in Quesnel. That culminated in all three women spending a terrible night under observation on the medical ward at Quesnel Hospital while the GP who'd treated them conferred by telephone with psychiatric experts in Vancouver.

The media had become involved, and a snide story appeared that night on the television news.

Hannah shuddered, remembering the mob of reporters and TV newspeople who'd surrounded them the next day, shouting questions and shoving microphones in their faces as Brad escorted her and Daisy out of the hospital and into his waiting car.

Gordon, too, had made the trip to Quesnel after he received the news that they were found. Elvira had phoned him from the R.C.M.P. station, and he'd gotten in their car and driven all night to collect her.

Unlike everyone else, Gordon had listened to and believed Elvira's account of what happened to them. When the van was found and there was no sign of them, he'd thought she was dead. He'd hurried into the hospital room that morning and taken Elvira awkwardly in his arms. "I'm so glad to have you back, old girl." His voice was tearful. "It's not often folks get a second chance, is it?"

Elvira had wept and wrapped her long arms around his neck as if she never intended to let go.

"My wife doesn't lie," Gordon had stated in a dignified voice to the reporters who asked him what he made of Elvira's story. "If she says that's what happened, then that's what happened."

It had been very different with Brad. When he arrived in Quesnel after hearing they'd been found, the first thing Hannah blurted out was that she couldn't marry him.

She didn't even have his ring to return to him, she sobbed; it was in Barkerville in a drawer in Logan's room, underneath her underwear. Brad hadn't even asked who Logan was. Instead, he'd given her the look she was still getting used to, the sort of look that Hannah herself might have given . . . before . . . to someone who insisted they'd been abducted by aliens and taken aboard a UFO.

To his credit, Brad had been solicitous and very kind that day, insisting that she was obviously in no shape to make decisions, but it was also plain that he was humiliated and upset at being a part of the media circus that surrounded the three women, and also that, after hearing their story, he honestly believed they were all deranged.

Without too much resistance from him, and to the palpable relief of his family, the marriage was canceled a week before it was to occur.

Hannah smiled sadly, remembering the last conversation she'd had with Brad.

"I thought we were a well-matched couple," he'd said accusingly. "You should have been honest with me, Hannah. If you wanted out of our engagement, you should have just said so. There was no need to concoct this ridiculous story and embarrass me and my entire family after the wedding was all organized."

"I'm sorry." What more could she say? That until she'd known Logan, she hadn't known what loving meant at all?

I think it has everything to do with this, Logan had said as his mouth closed over hers that night in the workshop . . .

"I wish you'd just tell me the truth, Hannah," Brad added in a peevish voice. "Where the hell were you before you wandered out of the bush? I was hounding the authorities to launch a full-scale search—helicopters, volunteers, the works. I don't understand how you could just disappear like that."

She didn't understand herself, but not in the sense Brad meant.

Those relatively few hours were one of the most difficult aspects of the whole situation for Hannah, apart from her shock and dismay at being back at all. The women learned when they burst through the underbrush that they'd only been gone one night and a day; they'd lived two full months in Barkerville, and yet in their own time only hours had passed since their disappearance.

After all that they'd been through, Daisy and Elvira weren't concerned about the time discrepancy; it seemed a minor paradox in an experience that was inconceivable anyway to anyone but the three of them.

But to Hannah, it seemed then and still seemed now to be a repudiation of all that had occurred. It felt as if fate was laughing at her, ignoring the magical time she'd spent with a man she loved with all her heart and soul.

The man she'd betrayed. The familiar accusing voice inside her reminded her how she'd given Flannery the advantage by talking to Carmen Hall.

But if Logan had been hanged, why didn't it say so somewhere in these ancient papers? A hanging in those days, in that place, was surely an event that would have made headlines.

Hannah ignored her aching head and went through the records again.

They'd reported his arrest. The next edition of the Sentinel had been totally devoted to the fire. After that, Logan was never mentioned again. The jail must have burned to the ground, along with the rest of the town. Had he managed to escape, get clean away in the confusion?

With every fiber of her being, she prayed it was so. She was so afraid to hope, and yet a part of her refused to believe he'd died at the end of a rope. The real torture was not knowing.

"The archives are now closing. Please return all research material to the attendants. We will re-open at nine tomorrow morning," a recorded woman's voice announced.

Wearily, Hannah made her way to the exit and out into the dark, wet night. She'd been staying with her mother since their return; after all her yearning for her own apartment, she found she couldn't be alone in it, at least not yet.

Friends at the hospital had tried to be supportive, but Daisy was the only one she could talk to. Her mother listened and understood when she spoke of Logan, and held her when she wept for him. Daisy, too, knew of love and loss.

Since they'd come back, she'd told Hannah more about Michael, intimate little things that allowed Hannah to understand her father in a way she hadn't before and even to forgive him.

Daisy was a changed woman. She'd enrolled in a cordon-bleu cooking class, and she was talking about taking another course in business management so she could someday open her own restaurant.

Elvira, too, was different. She visited often, and even though as the weeks passed the three of them spoke less and less of Barkerville, the experience they'd shared was a bond between them. Elvira was still short-tempered and opinionated, but she didn't complain about Gordon any more, and there was a new softness and contentment to her.

Hannah thought about Daisy and Elvira fondly as she walked home along the rain-washed streets. The summer air was warm and moist, heavy on her skin.

Is it snowing now in Barkerville? Did Pandola rebuild the store and hire someone else to work for him? Are Jeannie and Angus still living in their cabin? Has Sophie learned to crawl?

She stopped suddenly and sat down at a bus stop, oblivious to the city bus that pulled to a stop and opened its doors for her.

In her mind's eye she always saw Barkerville as she remembered it, a dusty, crude mining town, pulsating with energy, alive with gold fever. Until she accepted the fact that it was a ghost town, that nothing of what she remembered was there any longer, she'd stay locked in this terrible inertia.

Maybe there was one way of knowing whether or not Logan had been hanged. His body would have been buried up on the hill, in the little cemetery.

At last she knew what she had to do. She had to go back to Barkerville, see it for what it was, and lay all her ghosts to rest once and for all.

* * *

The thing about jail, Logan mused, was that it gave a man a lot of time to think. He'd been locked up for a day and a half now, and his head had finally stopped aching from the blow Carmen had dealt him. He'd been confused and only partially conscious when he was brought here, his skull feeling as though it had been split in two.

Within an hour Doc Carroll had come and examined him, frowning and asking the question that Logan at first didn't understand.

"Logan, do you remember shooting Flannery before Carmen hit you with the poker?"

Logan had tried to focus despite the red heat of pain that zigzagged through his skull. "I didn't shoot Flannery," he managed to groan. "Where's Hannah? I need to talk to her."

Doc harumphed. "Well, somebody shot Flannery, because he's dead as a doornail. Shot right between the eyes, and with your derringer. Far as Hannah goes, I don't know what the hell's going on. Elvira borrowed my rig and rode out of town with Daisy and Hannah, and none of 'em have been seen since. A drover coming through from Quesnellemouth spied my horse and buggy about ten miles out of town and brought them in this morning. Their handbags and the remains of a lunch were in the buggy. I reported it to Bowran. He's gone out to have a look for them."

A great fear welled up in Logan, fiercer by far

than the pain in his head. He struggled to a sitting position and tried to get to his feet.

"I've got to find her," he gritted out, fighting against Doc's hold on him. "Let go of me."

"Damn it, man, settle down. You're in jail. You couldn't go anywhere even if you were able. I'm doing all I can. I'll let you know the minute there's any news. Now drink this."

Logan had, against his will, and he'd sunk into a fathomless black pit where demons stuck pins in his eyes, his head grew monstrously large, and at last his stomach rebelled.

He groped for the bucket and missed, and when the vomiting was over, he dropped again into a stupor. This time he dreamed that he and Hannah were swimming, but she slipped away from him and disappeared in the dark water and he couldn't find her. He dove until his lungs ached, but she was gone, and in his dream, he wept.

When he came out of that nightmare, Doc was there again. He'd brought a bucket of hot water and clean clothing.

"Hannah?" Logan struggled up, trying to subdue the roiling in his gut.

"No sign of any of them," Doc said as he helped Logan wash and change. "Bowran took a search party out, but there's not a trace."

"Exactly where were they headed?"

"Damned if I know. There was a patient in the hospital. I take it Elvira got all excited when she heard what he had to say, and that's when she borrowed the buggy."

He told Logan about Daniel Connor. "I thought the man was a lunatic, but now I'm not so sure." He shook his head and frowned. "Elvira had some mighty peculiar ideas about medicine, knew things I never heard of. I didn't believe all of them, don't even now, but still . . . maybe Connor did see something out there, something Elvira knew about, too."

Logan listened, and he knew what had happened. The women had found their doorway. They'd gone back to where they'd come from, that future world Hannah had described for him so often. She was gone from him, to a place he couldn't follow. The agony of loss Logan felt stunned him, and he wondered how he'd be able to live with it, to go on.

After Nellie's death, he'd learned to live only in the moment. He forced himself to do that now.

"Guard," Doc was roaring. "This cell is putrid. Get me fresh water and straw."

Gratefully, Logan scrubbed, using the physical action to center his mind on now, only now.

Doc helped as well. He forced Logan to recount every single detail he remembered about the time he'd spent at Frenchie's.

"Sounds to me like Carmen Hall's framed you, Logan," Doc concluded. "With Flannery dead, she's now got Frenchie's all to herself, and with the new girls he brought in, miners are lining up. She'll make a fortune, and that's motive for murder, if you ask me."

Doc leveled a keen gaze on Logan. "Trouble is, she's telling some cock-and-bull story about Flannery seducing your sister, which she says is why you wanted him dead. She says Hannah warned her you were laying for Flannery. Any truth to that?"

Logan told Doc about Nellie. He told him how he'd planned Flannery's death, and how Hannah had begged him not to go through with it.

"She was in love with you."

Logan nodded. "I wouldn't listen, and so as a last resort I guess Hannah went to Carmen Hall, thinking Carmen had a shred of decency left in her and would help to prevent murder. The irony of it is that I'd already changed my mind, but Hannah didn't know that."

He was numb, both in body and in spirit. With Hannah gone, nothing mattered any more. "I guess Carmen saw an opportunity to get rid of Flannery, and I played right into her hands."

Doc nodded and they were silent for a while.

"Trouble is," Doc finally said with a sigh, "no jury's gonna believe you—you know that. And the Judge is a fanatic when it comes to guns and shooting."

In both of their minds was the memory of Begbie, his piercing eyes fixed on Logan, warning that if there was a shooting again in Barkerville, for whatever reason, and Logan was involved, there would be a hanging.

"Begbie's in Quesnellemouth; he'll be back around the seventeenth," Doc said. "Then there'll be a trial. I'll go get hold of Zachary Willings right away, get him sober so he can act as your lawyer. He's the best, long as he stays off the firewater."

Doc was doing his best, but Logan knew his only hope was to escape and run for his life before there was any trial. They both knew that in Begbie's court, once you were convicted, hanging followed immediately.

He didn't want to live without Hannah, but he didn't want to die at the end of a rope, either.

If he was going to escape, it had to be soon.

"You said Begbie would be back around the 17th?"

Doc nodded. "Give or take a few days."

"What's the date today?"

"September 15th." Doc sighed and got to his feet. He banged his fist into Logan's shoulder with a show of false bravado. "Don't worry, lad. I'll dry out Zachary, and we'll get you out of this yet."

Logan gripped Doc's hand, grateful for his friendship, knowing that there was little either Doc or Zachary could do for him.

The only thing that might still save his life was history. Hannah and Elvira had assured him that Barkerville would burn to the ground. The jail was in the middle of town.

The date of the fire, if Elvira's memory was trustworthy, was September 16. Tomorrow.

And if he managed to get loose somehow tomorrow, what then?

He'd try to follow Hannah.

The idea was ludicrous, but it was there in his mind.

"Doc, is this Daniel Connor still in the hospital?"

Doc shook his head. "He's probably in the nearest saloon. From the look of him, he's a drinking man."

"Forget Zachary. Find Connor instead. Send him over here soon as you can. I need to talk to him." Urgency and a sense of purpose were growing in him. "What's become of Billy Renton? I never heard of any trial."

"There wasn't any. Dutch got fed up waiting for Begbie to get back and didn't press charges. Billy's still up at the hospital; his knee's never healed right."

"I need to talk to him, too."

Doc frowned. "Bad Billy Renton? You sure that bang on the head hasn't addled your brain?"

"My brain's working better than it's worked for months. It's my neck I'm concerned about."

Doc gave him a narrow-eyed look. "All I can

say is I hope to hell you know what you're doing."

Logan just smiled. He couldn't tell Doc he was counting on fire and water to set him free.

Chapter Twenty-six

WELCOME TO HISTORIC BARKERVILLE, the sign read, THE TOWN WHERE THE FUN'S PURE GOLD.

Arrows indicated one parking area only for vans and another for cars. A high wooden fence obscured the townsite, and even at this early hour, there were a number of vehicles parked in the lot.

Hannah pulled her red rental car into the designated area and slowly got out, her heart beating hard.

It was a cool September day with just a bit of a breeze, enough to stir the evergreens on the hill above the parking lot, and she stood and allowed the wind to dry her tears before she started walking toward the Visitor Reception Area.

Since leaving Quesnel earlier that morning, she'd cried a lot, unable to control the emotions that driving along the modern highway dredged up in her. She'd recognized the place where the van had been towed from the river, but Hannah hadn't stopped there.

She hadn't recognized many landmarks along the highway, but she hadn't expected to. Her research had told her that the modern highway followed an entirely different route into Barkerville than the old Cariboo Road, and some part of her was glad.

"Welcome to Barkerville." The motherly woman behind the desk smiled and accepted the entrance fee. "Been here before, dear?"

Hannah swallowed hard. "Not for a very long time."

"I expect you'll find lots of changes. Later today we'll have some special ceremonies you might like to attend. This is the anniversary of the day Barkerville burned back in 1868, you know."

Hannah did know. For some obscure reason, it had been symbolic to come here on this day. She was burning her memories.

The woman handed her a paper with a map of the town and a list of the events scheduled. "Judge Begbie will be holding court in the courthouse at 11 A.M."

Hannah gasped, and then realized that of course there were actors who recreated famous characters. All the same, she wouldn't go anywhere near the courthouse.

"Wake-Up Jake's Restaurant is open for lunch, as well as Goldfield's Bakery. Enjoy your visit."

With her heart in her throat, Hannah made her way past the barrier and out the door, down the steps, and into the recreated town.

Breathing as if she'd been running, she stood for a long moment, staring at this place where she'd lived and loved.

It was different from the town she remembered, of course. She'd been here before the fire, and this was how the town must have looked afterward. Many of the businesses were the same, because the very morning after the fire, people began rebuilding their businesses and homes.

The smell was different. There were no steaming piles of manure from horses, no choking clouds of dust from cattle being herded down the main street. There were no men hacking and spitting on the boardwalk, and no Elvira to give them the sharp side of her tongue.

The Cornish waterwheels were silent. No dogs yapped; no men's voices called greetings or insults. It was a ghost town, populated only by tourists and actors.

As if in a dream, Hannah moved along the street, seeing it both as it had been and as it was.

Her heart thumped and her breath caught.

Here, right here, the Nugget had stood. There was no sign of it now. Instead, there was a firehouse.

How ironic that the building Logan had campaigned for would be built on the very site of his saloon.

He'd be pleased. Tears gathered in her eyes and dripped down her cheeks. Here was Wake-Up Jake's, where they'd gone for breakfast that first morning. Here was the livery stable, where Logan had kept his horse.

Pandola's Grocery was gone. Another building stood in its place, called the House Hotel.

The boardwalk was still there, but it was much improved from the one she remembered. She peered through the fenced-off door of Moses Barber Shop and smiled, remembering the gentle black man advising her discreetly on what was suitable to wear under the long skirts she was buying.

She wandered through the town for several hours. She ate a sandwich and had coffee at Wake-Up Jake's, and concluded with a sad smile that the food was much improved.

Finally, with a lump of fear in her chest that made it hard to breathe, she found enough courage to walk up the hillside, along the winding path that led to the cemetery.

There had been increasing numbers of tourists down in the town, but this lonely place was deserted except for her.

When she'd been here at her great-great-grandfather's funeral, the burial spot was only a small clearing in the woods. Now, it seemed there were hundreds of graves.

Hannah's heart twisted at this silent reminder of how many had lived and dreamed their dreams and died in this little mining town.

The old portion was fenced off, its wooden gravemarkers with their simple carved messages standing amidst tall pine trees that hadn't begun to grow when she was there last.

Hannah easily located Ezekial's resting place.

The grave was sunken, but the wooden marker was there, its surface dark and weathered, its message still legible. *Sacred to the memory of Ezekial Shaw, August 8, 1868.*

Blood thundered in her ears as she walked up and down the rows, searching for a marker that said Logan McGraw, praying that she wouldn't find it.

Many of the old wooden tombstones were illegible, and some of the graves had no markers at all. Others, however, were engraved with names she recognized.

Doc Carroll and Rebecca, beside the three small plots that held their babies.

Angus Percival, Beloved Brother and Uncle.

A sob burst from her throat.

He'd died young, only thirty-three. His beautiful, simple face rose in her mind. She couldn't seem to shake the conviction that it was only yesterday when she'd last seen him, holding Sophie in his arms, so proud, so loving.

Rest in peace, dear Angus.

And beside him was his sister.

Jeannie Chalmers, the marker read. *56 years.*

She'd never remarried. But how could she trust again, after Oscar?

The graves of these people she'd known and loved were too much for Hannah to bear. They tore at her heart. She wanted to just walk away, but she reminded herself that she'd come here for a purpose.

Steeling herself against the powerful emotions, she moved on, and on again, and finally, after she'd walked every inch of the quiet graveyard and read every stone that could be read, Hannah admitted to herself that there was no sign of Logan here.

Feeling as if her legs had no strength to carry her, she collapsed on a bench beside the path and looked down on the town that had changed her life forever.

On this day long ago, you burned, Barkerville. Where was my love, that day? Did he escape? Did he leave here, never to return?

Endlessly weary, she walked back down the hill and got into her car.

She sat there for a long while, her whole body trembling. Logan was dead; that at least was certain. Her rational mind told her that he'd died long, long ago, wherever he was buried.

She hadn't found proof here that he'd died at the end of a rope, but she had to accept that time, in whatever fashion, had finally ended his life. She had to release him.

Logan, my dearest one, wherever you are, know that I love you, that I will always love you, but I have to let you go now. It's time to get on with my life.

When she finally managed to control the sobs, she turned the key and started the car, and soon the town of Barkerville was far behind her. Her pilgrimage was over.

She'd planned to stop at the place along the highway where it had all begun and ended, but she knew already there was nothing there. Stopping would revive the agony she'd lived through in the cemetery, the agony she'd experienced that other day when she realized once and for all that Logan was lost to her. It wasn't healthy to keep picking at the fragile scabs on those wounds.

She'd drive on past, she decided, and somehow, sometime, she'd learn to forget.

But a few minutes later, when the road wound around the hillside and she saw the place where the van had gone into the river, her foot stepped on the brake in spite of what her mind told her was sensible. She pulled to the shoulder of the road, cursing herself for a fool. Then she got out of the car and walked slowly down the embankment.

The river gurgled, and birds sang. The sun would soon be gone.

Far downstream, she caught a glimpse of a long-haired man in a Stetson, crouched on his haunches, waiting patiently while his horse drank.

He stood up. He was wearing a white shirt and a leather vest, and something about the way he moved . . .

Lord, was she going to have to go through her whole life seeing Logan in every tall, dark stranger?

She turned to climb back to her car, but from the corner of her eye she saw the man tie his horse to a tree.

He was running towards her.

Terror filled her, awareness that she was in a deserted place on a stretch of empty highway.

"Hannah? Hannah!"

Once before, on her first morning in Barkerville, she'd thought she was going to faint. Now, too, the world spun in dizzy circles an instant before strong, familiar arms closed around her.

"Hannah, my love. My dearest love, thank God I've found you!"

Neither of them could stand. They sank to the grass, clamped in each other's arms, laughing, sobbing, touching.

"How?" With trembling fingers she touched his soot-streaked face. "How?" It seemed the only word she could manage.

He kissed her, frantic kisses that landed on her nose, her eyes, her chin, and at last, at last, her mouth.

He tasted of love and smoke. His mustache tickled. It was a long, breathless time before he answered.

"The water, Hannah." His words were jubilant. His eyes were bloodshot. His hair was singed at the ends. His white shirt was hopelessly torn and stained with dirt and soot. He was wonderfully alive, and he was here.

"It's the water, not the bridge. Billy led his horse down to get a drink; Daniel did the same. You and Daisy and Elvira, you all said your vehicle went into the water."

Hannah turned and stared at the river. He was right, of course. That day, that fateful day she and Elvira and Daisy had bungled their way back, they'd all waded in the stream, even Klaus.

"Do you want to go back, Logan?"

"Back?" He drew away and looked into her eyes. "To Barkerville, you mean?"

She nodded. "I will, if that's what you want." It didn't matter to her anymore where they were. *When* they were. All that mattered was being together. She gestured at the river. "We know how to do it. I'll come with you."

"Never." He shook his head hard. "Barkerville is burning, Hannah. I barely escaped with my life. Doc Carrol forced the guard to unlock my cell—the jail was already burning. And if I hadn't burned, I'd have hanged."

Remorse filled her, and apprehension. "Logan, I did a terrible thing. I talked to Carmen, I told her—"

"Shush." His grimy fingers touched her lips. "It was my own fault, sweetheart, all of it. We'll speak of it later. Be still now, and just let me hold you." A time passed, marked only by their heartbeats.

A car came along, slowed almost to a stop, and picked up speed again in a burst of gravel. The horse Logan had left whinnied in terror and reared, pawing the air with its hooves, jerking the reins that held it to the tree.

"Damn, I forgot the gold." Logan sprang up, pulling Hannah with him. "We can't let that nag get away on us, love." He ran full out, dragging her behind him across the rocky riverbank. "The saddlebags have our entire fortune in them."

Hannah knew he was wrong. She'd tell him so, when she caught her breath again.

Yesterday's gold might buy them the things that only gold could buy, but she knew it was their love that made them truly wealthy.

It was a lesson she'd learned in the past, and one she'd teach their children . . . in the future.